IT HAD TO BE YOU

SUSAN ANDERSEN

Cover art by Grifon Sky, Inc

ISBN: 978-0-9974412-2-2

❀ Created with Vellum

This is dedicated
with affection
and gratitude
to my friends
Mimi and Martha,
who have traveled this
path with me from the beginning.
To
Chery, for another fabulous cover
And to
The ladies of Port Orchard
for our evah-so productive Tuesday breakfasts.
I am so happy to have your friendship and the benefit of your wisdom.
You all added immensely to
Lena & Booker's story

Love to each & every one of you!
~Susie

1

A blonde vision in ice blue satin

BOOKER

September 24th, 1926

"Evening, Mr. Jameson."

Jerking slightly at the unexpected voice at my car window, I look up in the middle of reaching for my folder of club-related papers on the passenger seat. The voice, of course, belongs to Benson, The Twilight Room doorman. I just this instant shut down the Packard 236 in a space he somehow always manages to keep clear for me in front of my club on this busy downtown Seattle street. I don't know how he does it, but half the time he seems to materialize out of thin air. The man is a magician.

Seeing he has my attention, he opens my door. "It is good to have you back, sir,"

"Thanks." I unfold from the car and allow him to close the door as well. But I have to tamp down the twitch it gives me to let someone else perform a task I can easily do for myself. "It's good to be back."

That's a damn understatement. The headache I've been throwing aspirin at all day finally begins to unclench its vicious grip on my temples and forehead. We step beneath the black canopy of my speakeasy, *The Twilight Room* written in a pleasing bold gold arc across its front and along each side. The stylish awning stretches from the curb to the brick siding above the gleaming four-panel fir entry to the lounge. I wave Benson ahead of me—and don't even mind when he wraps his white-gloved hand around the ornate knob and steps back to open the club door for me.

A jazzy rendition of *Manhattan* wafts out of the lounge on a wraith of smoke and its lush sound makes me grin: at Benson as I pass him to enter my club and to myself. Hiring this five-piece band was one of the smarter moves I made this year. They sound better than many a full-sized orchestra.

I'm damn proud of my achievement here and, for the first time since leaving my parents' estate in Walla Walla this morning, my neck and shoulders lose the tension tying them in knots. My visit with Mother went well. She's always supported me in everything I've done. The one with Father? Well, that was about as productive as usual.

Clyde Jameson finds me a major disappointment. He has done so since I skipped college to fight in the Great War—the war to end *all* wars. I left home with a head full of patriotic fervor, but no true knowledge of the realities of warfare. The fact I returned home significantly changed from the malleable boy he remembered merely exacerbates his displeasure.

Despite Father's dissatisfaction, however, he persists in clinging to the belief I'm going to give up my speakeasy any day now and get a "real" job. In other words, join the family bank.

No chance in hell is *that* bushwa ever gonna happen.

Darkness clung like cobwebs to my mood during the interminable drive up from the southwest corner of the state. Shaking it off, I stride through my beloved lounge.

And finally start to feel like myself again.

When I put the Twilight Room together I opted to do it up swank, and it's drawn the money crowd. I had it decorated with women in mind. Most men will show up regardless of the décor, but let their women say *this* is the place to be seen and the fellas will shrug and take them there. So, I gave the ladies plush banquets and small, candlelit tables draped in crisp white linens.

As if to illustrate my thought, I see a dame cupping her hand around her escort's as he flicks the table lighter and holds it out. One of her bejeweled fingers strokes its cool marble surface while he lights her cigarette.

Tonight, as most nights, the club is packed with elegantly dressed men and women, most of whom greet me as I walk past. I smile, nod at everyone and toss off a greeting here and there. But I keep moving.

As I head for my table, the band segues from *Manhattan* into *The Charleston*. The Brasher Sisters, my hoofers Dot and Clara, swan onto the stage, then launch into the hip to the jive dance sensation that's been going strong for the past couple years. They shake their hips in their high-waisted satin shorts and shimmy the fringe on their skimpy tops. Flappers and their Jelly Beans desert the tables to crowd the dance floor fronting the small stage.

"Hi, Mistah Jaaame-es-son!"

The greeting has me searching among the crowded tables to my right, and I locate Sally, the cigarette girl. Not that I needed to see her to know who hailed me. Sally is a New Jersey girl who came to the Twilight Room by way of Los Angeles, where she had acted in several silent films. She'd just begun to make a minor name for herself when the talkies struck a death knell to her career. Sally has a voice that— well, it won't strip paint, exactly. But it sure as hell killed her future in the movies.

Seeing me looking her way, she leans forward to display her ample cleavage, flashes her big, sassy smile and wiggles her fingers in greeting. I return a salute. Then a customer hails her and I continue down to my table, situated where the back edge of the narrow, now jammed dance floor meets its northern counterpart. Before taking a seat, I nod at John behind the long, curved mahogany bar against the wall.

He snags a glass, drops in a couple of ice cubes and pours a generous splash of single malt. Putting the drink on a tray, he hails Millie, who serves this side of the room.

A moment later she dips to set it on a coaster in front of me. Dips equals tips and Millie knows how to keep male customers happy.

"Thanks, doll." I toss a clam on her tray.

Flashing me a smile, she tucks the dollar in some mysterious pocket inside her outfit, one that no doubt snuggles up against her magnificent breasts. I swallow a smile even as I give myself a mental pat on the back for hiring busty women in direct contrast to the current fad for straight silhouettes. It was a deliberate decision on my part, because for all the new emancipation of women, it's the men patronizing my club who still foot nine-tenths of the bills.

"Thank *you*, boss," she coos, interrupting my thoughts. "You're the berries!"

Moments later the band wraps up *The Charleston*. Dot and Clara trot off stage and the flappers and their boys abandon the dance floor, fast-talking as they reclaim their tables.

The band leader carries a large round microphone on a stand to the front of the stage. After arranging it several feet this side of the piano, he bends into it.

"And nooow, ladies and gentlemen, *fresh* from the Tropics Lounge in Spokane, Washington, the songbird you have all been waiting to hear. Please give a *big* round of applause to Miss! LO-la! Baaaaker!"

The audience's applause is polite rather than enthusiastic, but breaths all over the room are sharply inhaled when a blonde vision in ice blue satin rises up through the floor. I watch in satisfaction, my focus more on the mechanics of the lift than my new singer. It's true I made sure to get here in time to hear her, since for the first time since opening the lounge I wasn't involved in the hiring. But we have tested the elevated platform over and over again and had to work out several kinks. This is the first act to actually use it. No one else west of the Mississippi has anything like it, so to say I think it's pretty damn fine...

Well, hugely, ironically understated of me, that is.

A spotlight suddenly picks out my new singer and I stare, forgetting all about the hidden lift.

Damn. The woman is stunning. An honest-to-God tomatah. Leo, my manager, told me as much, but the photos that came with her bio weren't the best quality.

Seeing her in the flesh, I can honestly say they were nowhere close to doing her justice. Her hair is a blond so pale as to be damn near white. The only other person I have ever seen remain a towhead beyond childhood without resorting to bleach was Lena Bjornstad back in high school.

A ghostly rush of a once all-too familiar mixture of lust and anger hits me, and I straighten in my seat. Whoa. Haven't felt *that* in a long, long time. Can't say I'm happy to feel it now. And having learned long ago not to dwell on things I don't have a chance in hell of changing, I shake it off.

Clearly this is not Lena. As my first and—fine, to date *only* —love, she will always have a permanent place in my memory. But she had a totally different body type than the woman onstage. Lena had been boyishly slender and small breasted, with damn little extra flesh on her bones. She had had, in fact, the type of lean body that's all the rage right now.

This Lola dame has breasts and hips and a tiny waist, all lovingly delineated by the blue satin flowing over her curves and clinging faithfully to the dips and hollows.

Which I am still in the midst of admiring when she opens her mouth and draws my attention in a completely different manner.

"Who's sorry now?" she sings in a low, throaty contralto, making me realize my piano player launched an intro while I was obliviously staring. The rest of the band is also playing, but softly, to avoid stepping on that amazing voice. "Who's *sorry now?*"

The vivacious chatter behind me fades away. Lola's version of Isham Jones' popular song is slower, and bluesy in a manner more often heard in the colored clubs. And it is clearly grabbing the lounge's attention.

"Whose *heart is ach...ing, for...breaking each vow?*"

Then there's the way it affects me—like a warm hand stroking down my chest, over the ridges of my abdomen—and down to my—.

I straighten in my seat. I don't even try, however, to bite back my awareness. Because I haven't felt this for quite some time: this let's-buy-the-woman-a-drink-and-see-where-it-leads spark of interest.

Trouble is, though, I have this ironclad rule. I get my sex away from the club and never, but never, mess with the help. I can't say it has ever been a hardship. Then again, I have never been faced with this sort of temptation.

And I shed the rule like a snake its skin and stride over to the bar. As I listen to her finish up the first song and launch into *Careless Love Blues,* I have John refresh my scotch and make me a champagne cocktail for the club's new canary. And smile slightly as I think, *What the hell.* Accepting the drinks a moment later, I turn away.

Some rules are just made to be broken.

I stop at my table to sweep up my folder and tuck it under my arm before making my way backstage. After dropping the paperwork in my office, I head back to wait for my newest hire to finish her set.

She exits the stage a few minutes later, walking in my direction with a slow swivel of her hips that has me hearing a mental *Boom, bumpa boom, bumpa boom* drumbeat. My throat goes dry and I knock back my scotch. Jesus. The woman is even more magnetic at close range. That body—it jiggles subtly with every step she takes. And those eyes—those *lips.*

A niggle of unease itches along my spine when I look at her eyes and lips. Because, I'm reminded again of–

No. I square my shoulders. The thought itching at my brain is just wrong. But there *is* something uncomfortably familiar about the dark-rimmed blue of Lola's eyes and the lush Cupid's bow lips. Not the vibrant red color of the latter, but their shape.

Then my common sense catches up with me and I thrust the

notion aside. I didn't just fall off the turnip truck. Clearly, I'm seeing ghosts where none exist. I step into the singer's path.

"Lola," I say, amused with myself at the way my voice deepens. I offer her the champagne cocktail, abandoning my own glass on a nearby prop table. "My name is Booker Jameson. I own—"

The palm of her hand is a blur as it flashes with lightning speed toward my face. I dodge too slowly and it catches me across the cheek with enough force to turn my head. Stunned, I rear back. "What the—?"

She leans into me, looking fiercer than a mama bear even though the top of her head barely clears my shoulder. She cuts me off with fiery disdain. "I know *exactly* who you are, Mr. Jameson." Snatching the flute I'm still mindlessly holding out to her, she tosses back the champagne in a couple of large gulps, then thrusts the fragile empty back at me. I automatically grab it when she shows every indication of grinding its crystal edge into my chest.

Then she does the impossible and maneuvers her face even closer to mine, a neat trick for a woman half a foot shorter than I. "You're the man who left me to face the consequences of *our*—not mine, Buster, *our*—actions alone. The man who promised he would never forget me, who swore he would write faithfully until he could come back for me."

She takes a step back and her eyes lose their fire, her voice changes from lava-hot to ice cold. "In other words, a damn liar." Then she turns on her heel and struts away.

Leaving me blinking at her departing back. "Fuck," I whisper—a word I once reserved for the trenches, and lately, for conversations with other fellas when no women are present. A second later, as the truth I had instinctively known but convinced myself I did not sinks in, I say with a little more volume, "Fuck!" Then, "*Jeez*-us, hell." I watch the swing of her satin hem disappear around a corner. And feel a wave of something that feels surprisingly like...happiness.

"*Lena?*"

2

SUSAN ANDERSEN

In the Biblical sense, you could say

LENA

"Of all the speakeasies, in all the world," I seethe as I hoof it as fast as I can through the backstage area toward my dressing room, "I had to sign a contract with the one owned by that dirty lowdown *RAT*?"

All right, I kind of yelled that last part. But I'd been so thrilled about moving to Seattle. It was a big step up from Spokane and seemed ab-so-lute perfect at the time. I'd considered it the smart move of an honest-to-God businesswoman along her chosen career path.

I sure hadn't had a clue Booker Jameson owned the joint. And even if I had, it never would have occurred to me he wouldn't even have the first idea who I was!

Rage and a bitter sense of betrayal thunders through my blood. So insulted am I—and so preoccupied with that bounder's ability to make my blood boil with caustic ire—I dismiss the interested looks cast my way by the two-man stage crew. The curious female dancer stretching over her long, shapely leg propped atop a work bench, however, makes a stronger impression. Perhaps because she watches me with such big-eyed, non-judgmental interest. But then her gaze drops along with the forehead she presses against her shin.

And I give my shoulder an impatient hitch. Of *course* I'm more aware of her. I just watched her and her sister on stage before my Twilight Room debut.

I draw in deep, calming breaths, but a fat lot of good they do me. I am so darn livid I can barely see straight.

And I'm *hurt*.

I hate to admit that last part. And in truth, the heart-stomping pain coming back to haunt me is a mere phantom of the agony it once was. So how the heck can I ache over something that's no longer even there?

It reminds me of Billy Wilson, back in Walla Walla. He used to marvel over the pain in the leg he'd lost in the war. A pain he felt in the long bones of the calf and foot that had been *amputated*.

No doubt this is something like that.

With all these emotions racing along my nerves, in my heart, in my *head*, I'm not paying attention to my surroundings. In a hurry to reach the privacy of my dressing room, I dodge around the electrician's big spool of cable in the corridor. When a woman suddenly steps into the hall, I am simply too close to stop on a dime.

I barrel smack into her.

Grabbing each other's arms, we perform an awkward little shuffle to keep from careening off the narrow hallway walls or ending up in a heap on the floor. "Botheration!" I snap when my right foot skids.

At least I manage to catch myself. And looking into the pretty face of the other dancer in the sister duo, I suck in my ire, my frustration, and exhale a deep breath.

Then grab a hold of all the emotions coursing through me like balls in the pinball machine they had where I sang place before last. "I am so sorry. Are you all right?

"Oh, pos-i-lute-ly, doll. Me and Clara have done more damage rehearsin' our act." A hint of Southern drawl adds softness to the modern slang, and she flashes a big smile. "I'm Dot Brasher."

"Lena Bjornstad," I reply. Then shrug. "Or Lola Baker, if you'd rather not deal with trying to keep real names straight from the stage ones."

"Oh, heck, girl, me and my sis have good memories, so what's a coupla names between new friends? Nice to meetcha, Lena."

The other Brasher sibling glides to a halt beside us. "I'm Clara," she says, clearly having heard the introductions. "Dot's sister."

"I know. I watched your act before my set. And, oh my goodness, you two were darb! Where I grew up we weren't allowed to dance, so I never learned. I do so admire those who can."

"You weren't allowed to *dance*?" Clara stares at me as if I'd said I wasn't allowed to breathe. "Why, that is just plain wicked! Where on earth did you grow up—in Hell?" She flashes a saucy smile. "Hell, Michigan, of course."

"Of course," I agree, smiling back. "But it's closer to the interpretation most people think of when they hear 'hell'—I grew up in the Blood of Christ Foundling Home in Walla Walla. That's down south of here, Walla Walla is. Well, I guess so is the other place—" I make myself stop talking for a moment. "Sorry. I'm babbling. The B of C is owned and run by a rather fundamentalist church."

I wave that aside. "I sure adore watching people who do know how to dance, though. And I have *never* seen anyone quite like you two." For the first time since coming face-to-face with Booker, a genuine smile tugs at my lips. "Not to mention my fascination with how identical you look."

And how! Dot and Clara have the exact same short, shiny brown bob, big golden-brown eyes, prominent cheekbones and, of course, long, lean dancer's bodies. "I have never met twins before."

"You still haven't, doll—I'm thirteen months older then Sis. They just breed 'em true on Ma's side of the family." Clara's laugh is bawdy and infectious. "Heck, Dot and me know all the players and *still* it's tough telling who's who among all the cousins at the Rowland family reunions."

She opens a nearby door and stands aside, gesturing me to precede her into the room. "C'mon in. Feel free to help yourself to the flask over there. And do tell what led you to slappin' Mr. Jameson."

Dot's jaw drops. "She slapped *Mr. Jameson*?"

"Right across the kisser," Clara says. "You shoulda seen it, Dot. He said something I couldn't hear and offered her a glass of champagne, and she whacked him but good, drank the champagne, then swanned away. It was the cat's meow!"

Stunned into silence by the recitation of the altercation, I follow them into a dressing room that is perhaps the tiniest bit larger than the oversized closet I call my own. Clara closes the door behind us and gives me a level look, raising one eyebrow. "Can't say how smart it was to hit the man who signs your paychecks, though."

Still feeling raw and used, I open my mouth to tell the Brasher sisters exactly why I hit Mr. Booker Almighty Jameson. But Dot jumps into the conversation before I get a word out.

"He gave you *champagne*?" She stares at me as if I'm the It Girl, Miss Clara Bow, herself. "Wow. We've seen a lotta Janes try to snag his attention since we've been here. But I can state with God's honor truth I have never seen Mr. J buy any of them a drink." She glances at Clara. "Have you?"

"Huh-uh. He doesn't mingle with the likes of us. Oh, he's always respectful and he's charmin' as can be with the clients. But the man isn't all flash and strut like most of the speakeasy owners we've worked for. He's more Joe Brooks. And I've never seen him flirt with the high hat women or the flappers who frequent the joint, either."

"More Joe Brooks," I repeat and snort like a blue ribbon winner at the county fair. Appalled, I slap a hand over my mouth. *That* was less than elegant, for pity's sake.

Then I square my shoulders, along with the so called chip Matron Davidson used to insist I carry on them. What do I care if I made a little—okay, loud—farm noise? I'm not elegant. I may play at it onstage, but that's as far as it goes. I drop my hand to my side. "Absolutely—his clothes are impeccable. Always were. But then he *is* the only son of the richest man in the town where I grew up."

The Brasher sisters squeal like they're riding one of the big wooden roller coasters at a same fair my pig noise came from. "Oh my gosh." Dot stares at me with big eyes. "So, you *did* know him before?"

In the Biblical sense, one could say. Not that I do. It's one among many facts and feelings buried deep in my Midnight File. I learned young at the Blood of Christ to keep my secrets secret. There was very little privacy, so I built my mental Midnight File. I envision it as a golden box with a strong lock, positioned deep in a closed room somewhere in the back of my mind. This is where I keep my most persistent emotions—the one's I simply cannot shake. I mentally sort through them in the dead of the night when all around me are asleep.

So, I don't say now what I'm thinking—not aloud at least. I can't control the way it whispers in my brain. "We have...history," I admit. Not, now that I've cooled down, I'm prepared to go into details about it with these women I have only just met. I do add honestly, however, "I had no idea he owned this lounge."

Had I, you could take it to the bank I never would have signed the contract. I am darn near one hundred percent certain of this.

"Didn't you talk to him when he hired you?"

"He didn't—a man named Leo Stone caught my act at the Tropics Lounge in Spokane. He bought me a cocktail after my show, and during our conversation he somehow talked me around to telling him my contract with the Tropics was coming up for renewal. Then he came back the following night and made me an offer I couldn't refuse."

I would never say this out loud, but I would have signed for far less money, just for the opportunity to play a larger, more sophisticated venue in a larger, more sophisticated city.

Clara's cheeks suddenly turn pink. "Leo is Mr. Jameson's manager." I can't tell for sure, but the careful neutrality of her voice makes me wonder if perhaps she, too, knows a little something about sharing a less than swell history with the wrong man.

Or heck, maybe she just thinks the manager is a sheik. Like

Booker—especially this new version Booker—Leo is a very manly fella.

In any event, Clara clams up once the words leave her mouth, so I find myself filling the drawn-out silence when it edges into awkward territory. "I didn't learn that until today," I confess. "Before I got here, my dealings were all with Mr. Stone, including signing the contract. Mr. Jameson wasn't even mentioned until I walked into the manager's office when I arrived here this evening."

The name had given me a jolt—I can't deny it. Aloud, however, I merely say, "I had no reason to connect the name with the Jamesons I knew back in Walla Walla."

Dot gives me a look. "How well, exactly, *did* you know him back in your home town?"

I hesitate, then say honestly, "I guess you could say he was my first love." My only love, actually. But that's a fact I feel no compulsion to share.

Those feelings turned to dust a long time ago, anyway.

"Ooh, now you're on the trolley!" Clara twirls a hand, a clear invitation to keep talking. "Feel free to share the details."

"There isn't much to share. We went to the same high school, but he was two years ahead of me. And we attended different churches. Walla Walla isn't all that large, yet it's sizable enough we likely never would have crossed paths. But his mother hired some of the girls from the foundling home to serve at a party they hosted. I was assigned to the kitchen and Booker escaped there in order to avoid both his father, who never failed to lecture his expectations for his son, and an older woman who'd latched onto Booker. She, apparently, was a non-stop talker whom, from everything he said about her, sounded like she'd feel right at home at the Blood of Christ. Apparently, she, too, believed having too much fun puts us firmly on the path to hell."

Annnd... not really pertinent, so once more I wave off the aside. "Anyway, he chatted me up easy as could be. And since I have never had a decent grasp on my proper station in life, according to Matron Davidson, I chatted right back." One of my hands involuntarily rises to splay atop the swell of my breast concealing my racing heart. "And, *oh*, he was interesting! Plus, he made me laugh." Like I had *never* laughed before that evening. I feel my smile stretch into a wide, lopsided smile. "There wasn't a whole lot of laughter at the Blood of Christ."

"And they couldn't see that might be a result when they hung a name like *that* on a home for orphaned kids?" Clara murmurs dryly. "Because, it doesn't exactly trip cheerily off the tongue."

I can't help myself, I laugh and then laugh harder still when the two sisters join in. "Oh, my," I say once we finally get our giggles under control. "I have a feeling knowing you two is going to be very, very good for me."

3

I *said*, just a minute!

BOOKER

The woman beneath me feels both familiar and brand new. The touch of her skin, so smooth and fair, is well-known. Its more-delicious-than-maple-syrup flavor is achingly recognizable as I kiss an open-mouthed trail down her throat. Starting from the spot below her jaw that once made her moan in the back of her throat.

I also remember these spiky pale pink nipples trying to drill holes through the tougher skin of my palms. Yet the breasts from which they thrust I recall being small and exceptionally firm. The lush curves currently captured by my fingers, my palms, are significantly fuller. And while they're also firm, the most minute shift of my hands sets off a mouth-wateringly luscious jiggle.

I have felt similar in other women's breasts, but I cannot recall ever feeling it from hers. The sensation gives me an illicit thrill. The body I touch is intimately known in one sense, yet as if I'm stealing liberties from a stranger in another.

The taste of her mouth is a different matter. I'd recognize it in the dead *of night in the deepest, darkest coal mine.* "Lena," *I breathe. And lower my head to rock my lips over hers.*

I wake up spitting out my pillowcase. Rolling to sit up, I mutter a few choice words under my breath and scrub at my mouth with the back of my hand.

"Shit." I reach over to click on the lamp next to the bed, then blink in its sudden glare. Sometimes I miss the softer gaslight, which electricity has been replacing over the course of the past several years. As my dream fades, irritation takes its place. The abrading rub of anger has its own weight of familiarity to it.

Once I realized Lola was Lena last night, it didn't take long for wrath to replace my initial rush of happiness. She has some damn cheek accusing me of promising to write her, then not following up on my promise. I wrote her two or three letters a week, faithfully. *She* was the one who never wrote back.

It doesn't help my temper that following our argument last night, Lena was never alone. God knows I kept track. Frustration at not being able to pull her aside to set the record straight, was exacerbated when I missed seeing her leave the club. So, I ended up drinking too much. I'm not hung-over, exactly. But my head has definitely felt better.

Stewing again over the way she'd had the last word, and damned if I intend to let it ride, I throw back the covers and go in search of aspirin and a hot bath.

M y righteous anger loses steam when I storm into the club, and belatedly remember it's far too early for any of the performers to have arrived. I stop and take a deep breath. Well, shit.

Then I square my shoulders. I have a lot of other stuff to do, so I might as well accomplish something while I wait for Lena to show up. I stride straight through the darkened lounge to my office. When I enter it, I find my manager, Leo, rifling through one of the piles of papers on the partner's desk we share.

"Afternoon, Sarge." I toss my hat on the coat rack. "What are you looking for?"

"The damn electric bill." Straightening the pile of papers he'd been searching, he glances up at me. "I could've sworn I paid it. Apparently not, though, because I sure as hell didn't enter the bugger in the ledger. Or file it in the Utilities folder." Scrubbing his fingers over the raised scar running from his temple to the middle of his cheek, he scowls at me. "Why you thought a senile old warhorse like me could manage your fancy club is beyond me."

"Maybe because you invest damn near as much strategy in running the joint as you did in keeping us alive in the trenches." My former sergeant has a habit of talking as if he's seventy years old instead of the somewhere in his early-to-mid-thirties he actually is. "It's one bill, Leo. Here." I hand him a pile from the several peppering the desk and pick up another stack for myself. "You look through that one and I'll go through this."

Leo found the bill he sought in the second stack he pawed through. "Well, hell, I remember now," he says. "I had just opened this when we got word our whiskey shipment was ready up in British Columbia. By the time I arranged for our fellas on Whidbey Island to pick it up and run it to our truck on the mainland, the bill was buried beneath a shitload of papers and slipped my mind."

"So it turns out you're not senile, after all. Just busy."

"Yeah. Good to know." He flashes one of his rare smiles, but quickly sobers and pins me in his steady gaze. "What's this I hear about you and the singer I discovered on my trip up to visit my cousin Elmer? I heard she slapped your face. What the hell was that all about?"

Shit. The last thing I want is to get into this with anyone but Lena herself. And yet... "Do you remember when you asked me, back during the war, why I joined the Army?"

"Sure. You said you got caught in your old flivver about to get lucky with some girl. And that your old man pulled strings to give you the bum's rush out of town and into the University of Washington two weeks before classes began."

I shrug. "Then you likely remember, too, that I went straight to the recruitment center to enlist." I meet Leo's gaze. "Lena was the girl in the car with me. We were high school sweethearts." And, God, she had meant so goddamn much—hell, *everything*—to me.

"No shit?" Leo sits down hard on the guest chair. "And you didn't *recognize* her?"

I try not to wince at the incredulity he doesn't bother to scrub from his tone. But facing it squarely, I have to admit Lena had a right to be pissed off last night when I failed to even identify who I was trying to seduce. Piled as it had been on top of her laundry list of other offenses I'd purportedly committed. "In my defense, she's changed dramatically."

Then, my shoulders stiffen, because I really hate to say this next part after my lame duck attempt at defending myself. "I brought her a glass of champagne."

"You shot the first salvo in making an advance on an *employee*?" He gives me a searching look. "That's not like you."

"I know." I shrug like it's no big deal. Because it's not. It is no goddamn big deal at all. "She took umbrage." Mostly over other items on her list of my offenses. "We are, however, going to have a little talk about professionalism when she gets in."

"Good plan. It doesn't pay to let slapping go unaddressed." Leo's mouth quirks up slightly. "Unless it's a cat-fight between two women. Gotta admit, I wouldn't mind seeing that."

Lena's voice sounds out in the hall a few hours later as she and the Brasher sisters clatter past my office. I leap to my feet before my better judgment overrules a near-overwhelming urge to track her down *now*. The last thing this joint needs is every employee within hearing range throwing in their two cents worth. Or, God forbid, taking sides. The upcoming conversation is one best carried out in private.

The trouble with waiting, however, is the way it gives my temper time to stage a repeat performance. I turned myself inside out trying to contact Lena after I enlisted and didn't hear a thing from her in return. Now she's accusing *me* of not writing? By the time Dot and Clara hit the stage for their first act, I have once again worked up a full head of steam.

I cover the distance between my office and Lena's dressing room in less than a minute flat. Once there, I give its sturdy door a set of authoritative raps. Lena's response is muffled, and I don't bother requesting clarification before turning the knob and pushing the door open.

"Hey!" She snaps. "I *said* 'just a minute!'" Clearly irate, she swings around to look at me from her makeup table.

My feet flat-out quit on me, grinding me to a dead halt. Because, Jesus.

The lone article standing between Lena's body and my gaze is a black silk wrapper. Its thin fabric hosts a flock of spread-winged birds I assume are cranes, given the craze for all things Oriental these days.

But who the hell cares? Her seated twist-around has widened the black wrap's lapels between those unbound breasts, exposing spectacular, pale-skinned cleavage. It's all I can do to not let it command every scrap of my attention.

Because, *damn*, she looks good in that.

Lena stares back at me, apparently equally shocked. Then, following my gaze, she jerks the two sides of her wrap together. The better coverage can't disguise her generous cleavage, but it does restore a few of my brain cells. I take a deep breath, then slowly exhale it.

And get myself back on track. "We need to have a little talk about professionalism," I say coolly. "Slapping your boss is anything but. Do anything like that again, and you will not like the way I retaliate."

"I had a darn good reason to smack you, considering all your lies."

"No, Lena, you didn't. You're all indignant about supposedly not getting any of the dozens of letters I mailed you—"

She makes a sound like a tea kettle about to set off its whistle. "There is no *supposed* about it, you bimbo!"

Swell, now she's calling me a *tough guy*? Everyone knows that's pretty much a synonym for mobster. I breathe deeply again, then manage to say calmly, "Yeah? Well, where were all your letters to *me*, Lena? You're pretty vocal about not receiving the ones I damn well sent. Funny thing, though. I never got so much as one from you, either."

She surges to her feet. "And where was I supposed to send them, pray tell? In Care of the postal gods? You said you'd send me an *address*, remember?"

"And...what?" I move in on her. "You broke your legs? Lost your voice? You couldn't bestir yourself to go ask my mother when my letters failed to reach you?"

"Ask your—?" Lena takes an incensed step in my direction. "You waltzed off first to college, then to *war*, and left me to face everyone with my brand-new reputation as the Quiff of Walla Walla!"

That word from her lips, coupled with the sheer agonized outrage on her face, freezes me for a moment. The town branded her a *slut*?

I'm still reeling when she recovers enough to step in and stand on her tip toes to thrust her face so close to mine my eyes cross. She drills a finger into my chest.

"You think I was going to call on your *mother* with a newly minted, Booker-endowed reputation trailing after me like the stench of ground beef left in the sun?"

"People called you a *slut*?"

"Yes, Booker, they called me a precisely that—among other, equally lovely slurs. What the hell did you expect when Millie Long-mire caught us with my blouse unbuttoned and your hand up my skirt?"

"Not that." The truth was, I'd been so miserable dealing with my own humiliating removal from town, I hadn't stopped to consider the ramifications to her. I'd ached for her, yes. But— "It never occurred to me you had been left on your own to face down small town gossips."

"Millie was one of the biggest gossips in town," Lena snaps, "but it never *occurred* to you she might spread what she'd seen all over tow —" Cutting herself off, she steps back. Seems to gather her dignity around her. "Nevertheless, *that* was what I dealt with. So, don't tell *me* how unprofessional it is to have slapped you. If you ask me, I had enough provocation to beat you senseless."

My temper erupts again. "You know what the trouble is with getting on your high horse, Lena?"

She arches a pale eyebrow. "No, but I'm sure you're dying to tell me."

"It is a long way down when you tumble off. And I would hesitate to claim the moral high ground, if I were you. You left town with my best friend!"

She doesn't bluster, as I expected. Hell, she doesn't look the least bit embarrassed, let alone get defensive. Instead, she looks me in the eye and drawls, "Yes, Booker, I did. And I would do it again in a heartbeat. Will supported me when *you* waltzed off and never looked back."

I am so furious over the way she stubbornly clings to that fucking *fiction* when it's the farthest thing from the truth. I'm even more frustrated because she sounds as though she honest-to-Christ believes the shit she's spewing. So I grab her, thrust my fingers through her hair and use my thumbs on her cheeks to tilt her head back. And shut her up in the only manner I know how.

I kiss her.

And her mouth. God, that *mouth*. It's my dream all over again, only this time I'm wide awake and it's real. Hell, I have kissed my share of women since leaving Walla Walla as a teen.

I couldn't recite the names of nine-tenths of them if you held my feet to the fire.

Never have I forgotten Lena. God knows I tried, more than once. Yet I did not, *could* not, forget her. And with a single touch of my mouth to those pretty, pretty lips, our old chemistry explodes.

It's not just me, either. When I wrapped my hands around her head, Lena grabbed my wrists and I was sure this was it, she was going to rip them away in no uncertain terms. Determined to get what I can, while I can, I twist my mouth over her soft, plush lips, opening them to my tongue.

And the next thing I know, she's on her tiptoes and using the leverage of her grip on my wrists to strain again me, that unfamiliar soft, lush body plastered to the harder planes of my own so tightly a stray *thought* couldn't slide between us. Her breath sloughs in rough rhythm against my lips, into the cavern of my mouth. And all I want is to breathe in when she breathes out.

I whirl us a half turn and back her against the wall next to her dressing table. Without relinquishing her mouth, I release her head and skim my hands down her amazing curves. Cupping her ass, I haul her up.

She jerks, but quickly gets her bearings and wraps her legs around my waist.

Turns out she isn't nude beneath that siren wrap after all. But when the crotch seam of a filmy pair of French knickers aligns perfectly with the erection straining the fly of my slacks, we both suck in a breath as if we'd touched naked skin to naked skin.

I lift my head to look at her. The midnight-blue rimmed, lake-blue eyes gazing back at me have darkened several shades, and vivid color stains Lena's cheeks. She returns my regard from beneath half-mast eyelashes. Slicks her tongue over her bottom lip.

I groan and rock my mouth over hers once again.

I'd just instigated a slow grind against her when a tap sounds at the door. Lena startles against me, then unlocks her legs from around my hips and squirms to be let down. Small distress sounds whisper in her throat.

"Shh," I murmur almost silently against her mouth. "Shh." I draw my head back slightly to look at her.

The room is beginning to darken and her front teeth gleam from between her parted lips. I glance fondly at the left incisor, ridiculously pleased to see it still at a slight angle to its center-tooth neighbor. I can't stop myself from going in for another taste.

Lena's hands cupping my jaws block me—not to mention her calm-voiced, "Let me go."

Even stated in a low whisper, she sounds pretty damn sure about what she wants.

I set her loose and step back.

The knock sounds again. "Lena," one of the Brasher sisters call. "Are you in there?"

"I'm running late getting ready for my number." Lena has to raise her voice to reply but she sounds completely confident—even as she presses a hand to her diaphragm and struggles to control the tempo of her breathing. "I'll come by your room after the show, okay?"

"Be sure to, 'cause Clara came up with a darb idea for what we can do tomorrow before work. See ya later, alligator." And the sisters' footsteps continue down the hall.

Lena turns to me. "You need to go."

"I think we should tal—"

"No. I need you to go."

So, I do. She *is* late getting ready for her act. And this was a huge mistake. It's a good thing my hoofers interrupted.

I might not have thought so in the heat of the moment, but... yeah. Sure.

It is a damn good thing.

Hell.

Fortuitous, even.

4

There will be no more kissing

LENA

I wake up in a cold sweat late the next morning, thinking the same thing I fell asleep thinking: *Ohmygoodness.*

Ohmygoodnessgracious.

Oh. My. Goodness. Gracious.

Agnes!

Except for the top sheet, all my bedding is on the floor, a testament to my tossing, turning, sleep deprived night. Okay, for those of us in the club entertainment industry, a night's sleep is a relative term, starting with the milkman's four am run about the time we arrive home and ending whenever we wake up. Still, that period is our version of a night's rest and I, for one, would be a whole lot happier not to have lost mine.

Reluctantly giving up any hope of a return to dreamland, I roll out of bed just before noon. I collect my bath kit, throw in the new tube of Pepsodent toothpaste and bar of Lux soap I bought at Woolworth's yesterday, then head for the communal bathroom down the hall.

I have to admit I've harbored some regrets about passing on a sweet little apartment on Capital Hill when I was looking for a place in Seattle. I'm not sure why I didn't grab it, really. I had sure liked it. Yet, I had instead moved into yet another Women's Residence. Even though I would have had that lovely little space all to myself. *And* been closer to Will.

"For pity's sake, girl, that is neither here nor there now!" My regret over not taking the place no longer *matters*. In fact, it's just as well I didn't sign a lease on the little studio apartment up on Capitol Hill. At least this way I won't be breaking *another* contract when I leave. Not to mention only having to forfeit a few days rent.

Still, I'm dead tired of always having to share bathrooms and strictly scheduled meals or having to be back under lock and key by nine pm. Well, all right, that second matter doesn't really apply. I am grateful that Mrs. Rodale, who runs the joint, grants me a break on the curfew rule because of the nature of my employment. The woman looks down her long nose at me for working in a speakeasy. But she did waive the curfew and give me a key so I am not locked out when I arrive back here at the crack of dawn.

But *that* no longer matters, either. Because I cannot possibly stay on at The Twilight Room now. Not when Booker. . .not when I felt so. . .

Well. It's simply not thinkable, is it? I load some of my new tooth-paste onto my brush and start scrubbing my teeth furiously.

I sure wish Will was around, though. He's my best friend. Okay, he is my one and only genuine, time-proven friend. I would love to lay all my feelings out for his input. Tell him about my sneaking, unwelcome hunger for Booker's kisses, my anger and confusion over feeling *any*thing positive for the man at all. Booker had some nerve introducing himself to me as if I were some stranger. When I was seventeen, he told me repeatedly that he *loved* me. Oh, how he told me!

I think the very least he owed me night before last was a glimmer of recognition.

I don't discount how much my body has changed since our days in Walla Walla. Lord knows, I love to eat, so I gained weight once I left Blood of Christ and began getting meals with honest-to-God flavor. But for pity's sake, my face, while softer and rounder, remains the same.

I spit the toothpaste foam into the sink, then rinse my mouth and the sink bowl. Raising my head, I study myself in the mirror. Am I overreacting?

I truly don't think so, but Will would know. Will has a way of cutting through the garbage to find the bottom line in a situation. Especially the kind that jumps the rails the way this one has. Maybe it's even within the realm of possibility he'll tell me I'm overreacting. He might even say I *don't* have to leave this job, which was supposed to be a huge boost to my career.

On the other hand, he might say *cut your losses, girl.*

But Will is in New York City, attending appointments with *Life, Collier* and *Judge* magazines, where he's pitching his work and presenting his marvelous portfolio. He also scheduled an interview with an ad agency about a possible contract to provide illustrations for a couple of their clients. And if that isn't enough to easily eat up more than twenty-four hours a day, he intends, should he have any spare time left over, to take his personal portfolio around to the top five art galleries he'd most like to see host a showing of his work. Not the commercial illustrations. His art.

And I am happy for him, because this is a huge opportunity, and Lord knows no one deserves it more. Unfortunately, it is not so great for me. While he's on the other side of the continent, I feel as though I've been thrown into the deep end of the pool. With no lifeguard on duty.

None of which is Will's fault, of course. But I'm drowning here.

Hoping to shut down all the clatter and clamor in my head, I haul my pile of toiletries down the hall to get ready for the day.

I arrive at the club early, prepared to tackle Booker, and beyond irritated with myself to realize how uneasy I am. I'm not usually the Nervous Nellie type, but I am definitely on edge and want to get this over with.

When I don't spot him in the lounge, I head directly to his office. Stopping at its door, I shake out my hands, draw a deep breath, hold it for several seconds, then slowly exhale. I hate that my heart is beating like the drummer's entire kit when the house band gets to wailing mid-*King Porter Stomp*. Understanding for the first time what it means to gird one's loins, I suck in yet another deep breath and give the solid wood door a good, strong rat-a-tat-tat.

"Enter."

I almost laugh. Because, who *says* that? Most people would say *c'mon in* or ask who's there. Matron Davidson used to snap *Come*, in a tone both cold and brusque, but then that was her to a T. And in her defense, Matron never claimed to be a charmer.

So I can honestly say I have never heard anyone say *Enter* before. I turn the knob and let myself in.

Booker is hunched over his desk, his tie hanging loose and his tailored jacket over the back of his chair. He's scribbling something in a ledger book and looks industrious as all get-out.

For all of ten seconds. Then he glances up, sees me and tosses his pen on the blotter. His chair creaks as he sprawls back in it. He swings his big feet up onto the desk. "Huh," he says. "Didn't expect you to show your face so soon."

"Why wouldn't I?"

"Figured you'd dodge me until the impact of the kiss we shared faded."

Oh, you fat-headed, miserable...

Swallowing my temper, I manage a creditably nonchalant shrug. "Guess it wasn't as memorable for me as it was for you."

"Ouch." He drops his feet to the floor but remains seated. "Still, interesting supposition. Maybe we should test that theory."

And, darn it to hell and back, I realize right then and there if I quit I will promptly negate my big *Hey, doesn't affect me* stance. I will pluck out my eyelashes one by one before I'll let him know that maybe, just *maybe*, his kiss did rattle me. Perhaps it even affected me enough to think the two of us had the potential to burn down the club.

No. *No,* dang it! I square my shoulders. The kiss had been nowhere *close* to setting the joint on fire. Coaxing forth a few curls of smoke, maybe. But hardly in the neighborhood of torching the speakeasy. And if quitting without losing face is no longer on the table, I can at least use the words he threw at me last night to try to slant this gawd-awful push-me/pull-me the two of us share in my favor.

And see how *he* likes it. "So, let me see if I understand this correctly. It's okay for you to whine about professionalism when I deliver an itty-bitty, much deserved slap—"

"Itty-bitty, my ass," he mutters. "It damn near swiveled my head around my neck until I could see where I had been." His sudden frown slants his dark brows toward his nose. "And men—former soldiers, by God—do not *whine.*"

"—but at the same time," I press on as though he hadn't spoken, "you appear to have no difficulty believing it somehow *is* professional for you to press unwanted advances on me?"

He leans into the desk. Picks up his pen again and twirls it between lean fingers. "Oh, let's have a little truth between us here, shall we." He clearly doesn't consider that an actual question. "My... advances, as you call them...were far from unwanted."

I realize my nerves have settled nicely and raise an eyebrow as I give him the *maybe looks* can *kill* stare I adopted when I was thirteen. I have utilized it to my advantage ever since. Its steady refusal to waver, along with an accompanying lack of expression, tends to unnerve people enough to prevent them from digging too deeply into my own messed up emotions at any given moment. "Believe what you wish," I tack on for good measure in a bored tone.

And manage not to crow when I see the slightest twitch of uncertainty cross his face.

The look quickly vanishes and he squares his shoulders. "It's a good thing you didn't come here tonight to quit," he says coolly. "Because we really would have a problem then."

Oh, God, did he suspect I had? I inhale a slow, stealthy breath and keep my expression bland. "Would we?"

"Damn right. Slapping me was strike one, doll. Slapping me in my own establishment, in front of other employees was strike two. Quitting on me would have been—"

"Yeah, yeah—strike three." I buff my right hand fingernails against my breast and study their pretty shine. "Seems to me, either way the bottom line is I'd be out."

"True. But you signed a binding contract. Breaking it two nights into your employment would have been the height of unprofessionalism. And had you done so, I would have sued you into the poor house and saw to it you were blackballed from ever singing in Washington State again."

Looking into his eyes and listening to the flat, assured tone, I believed him.

Good Lord has he changed from the boy I once knew and loved! Young Booker had been full of fun. Oh, he'd been less than happy about his relationship with his father, because the two of them butted heads on a regular basis. Yet, looking back, I can see he hadn't been nearly as mature as the two of us considered ourselves to be at the time. Because even as he'd performed small acts of rebellion, he'd had a difficult time flat-out standing up to Clyde Jameson.

I doubt *this* Booker would have the same problem.

Which, I suppose goes without saying, seeing as we're standing in his obviously successful speakeasy.

I am suddenly glad I didn't lead with my resignation as I originally intended. My heart is trying to pound its way out of my chest at the thought of what I'd dodged. Angry about it and the shiver racing down my spine, leaving a crop of goose-bumps in its wake, I call on every muscle in my body to stiffen my spine. It helps me grow the tiniest bit tiny bit taller, my backbone more rigid than the Smith Tower.

And I might have thrust my chin up a bit. "Why do you feel the need to tell me this, Booker? Have I mentioned the word quit?"

"It's always a good plan to get the more likely possibilities out on the table. I know you, Lena—or at least I used to. You were one of the most focused people on the planet. You knew you wanted out of Walla Walla and had concrete ideas how you might achieve that." He gives me a puzzled look, then shakes his head. "Singing was nowhere in the plan back then, but clearly when you decided it was your ticket out of town, you worked to make it happen."

Booker drops the pen and slaps his hands down on the desk, half rising to lean across it. Suddenly he seems far too close, and it takes everything I have not to startle back in my chair.

"But while you had drive and were results oriented," he says in a low voice, "you were also impulsive, particularly when your dander was up." One muscular shoulder rises and drops as he looks me in the eye with deadly earnestness. "So, now you know where I stand on the seriousness of a contract."

"Yes, goody, goody, gumdrops." I say it with a bite of sarcasm. And yet...

He isn't wrong—and darned if it doesn't make me a little weak in the knees to realize he *does* remember things about me, even if they aren't my more flattering traits. I do allow my temper to take me places it shouldn't at times. And I have always found it difficult to back down from a confrontation.

"Glad we're on the same page." Apparently choosing to disregard my tone of voice, Booker surges to his feet in a single fluid movement. "Now that's settled, let's put this other business to bed. Where do you get this shit I never wrote you?" He gives me a hard stare. "I wrote you three or four letters a week."

"I never received a single one from you! I can understand one going astray. But all of them?" I shake my head in disgust. "*Please.*"

Still, a tiny part of me wonders why Booker insists so hard he wrote me. If he didn't, it seems he would just shrug and tell me to get over it. Say *It is what it is.*

"Well, I wrote 'em. Right up until my mother told me you had left town with my former best friend."

"Oh, some best friend you were!" Okay, getting all worked up again isn't going to help. I pour real effort into shoving my indignation into the darkest cupboard in the dustiest corner of my mind. Usually the Midnight File isn't this difficult to access at a moment's notice. I finally unearth it, however, and as I shove as much of my anger into as I can I promise myself I *will* display some self-control. "You called *him* when you joined the Army." I manage to say the words calmly. Still, I wish I hadn't emphasized *him*. I sure as heck don't want Booker thinking a heartbroken girl still lurks somewhere inside of me, moaning, *Not me—you didn't call* me.

But frustrated, on the other hand? Too right I'm frustrated. I know darn well if Booker Jameson had truly wanted to get hold of me back then, he would have. I do not give a good God dam—er, *darn*—that the Blood of Christ's party line was located in Matron's office and used exclusively for business. If he had truly cared about me the way he said he did, he would have found a way to contact me.

I give myself a stern mental shake and mutter on an exasperated exhale, "Stay on track." I draw in a deep breath, let it out, then face him again, my expression arranged in as composed a mask as I can arrange it. "You called and Will headed straight to Seattle to join the Army with you. So, don't tell me you didn't know how devastated he was when influenza swept through his boot camp. Will was only partly recovered when they shipped him home, Booker, and he darn near died. It did kill any chance he had of joining the war. But did you even once write him?"

Guilt flashes across Booker's face, but I refuse to relent. "He was the one who finally got me an address to write to you, you know. He went and asked your father for it." I stared Booker in the eye. "Did you know his mother got sick and Will gave up his college scholarship to care for her?"

"No, I didn't." A muscle jumps in his jaw. "When did you two get so pals-sy?"

"When we ran into each other at the opening of the new courthouse and got to talking. We discovered we had heaps in common." I give Booker a look making it clear his abandoning both of us was chief among my commonality with Will. And, indeed, it may have started that way. But our initial chance meeting soon evolved into a dearly cherished friendship with Will. Our chance meeting became one of the biggest blessings in my life.

Recalling myself to the present, I finally use the brain God gave me. Booker, this man whom I no longer trust and who did not live up to his promises, is now my boss. And he's right, I did sign a contract for the next twelve weeks, so I am well and truly stuck.

Squaring my shoulders, I adjust my attitude on a quiet exhale. "You are right," I admit quietly. "I haven't been professional. So, I apologize. I will try very hard to be more so from now on. But that means no personal questions or comments. My life is my business, yours life is your business, and I propose we each stay the heck out of the other's." I pin him with the diluted version of my *May you die* stare. "And that kiss was a onetime experiment. There will be no more kissing." Stepping closer to his desk, I thrust out my hand. "Deal?"

He just stares at it for what feels like several drawn-out seconds, then reaches across the desk and grips it. He looks as if he's about to argue.

Apparently, I'm mistaken, however, for he abruptly gives me a terse nod. "Deal."

His hand is hot and calloused, and I wonder when the latter happened. Young Booker was always incredibly hot-skinned; I can't believe I'd actually forgotten that. But his hands, while hot, also used to be much softer. And smaller, I'm pretty sure, because I sure don't remember them swallowing up my own the way the one holding it now is doing.

Shaking off the thought when it begins to feel as if Booker might hang onto my hand a bit longer, I pull my fingers free, and step back. "Good talk," I say briskly.

And get the heck out of there.

5

Who the hell *are* you?

BOOKER

"Oh, hell no!" I surge to my feet. Damned if Lena gets to dictate terms and just waltz away. I catch up with her in the hallway where she's in full hip-swinging locomotion down the corridor, the beaded fringe on her short dress rocking briskly. Reaching out, I wrap my hand around her upper arm, swinging her toward me and bringing her to a halt. "Wait a damn minute."

Those beads whip around to wrap her left side, rebound to swipe at the right, then fall to sway with a gentle shimmy, clicking and clacking with the sudden cessation of her body's motion. Her arm feels firm and smooth and plump beneath my fingers, my palm. And considerably more smooth-skinned than I remember.

Which I suppose shouldn't be a big surprise, considering the way Matron Davidson at the Blood of Christ worked the kids living at the foundling home.

Her gaze hones in on the spot where I'm holding her in place. Then she raises those dark-rimmed blue eyes to level me with the *look* again. The one that makes me question damn near everything I have ever known to be true.

Even as it makes me pretty damn sure she has a good idea where to hide the body, should the need arise.

I drop her arm. Rub the too-familiar Lena feel off against my slacks. And look her in the eye.

"Look. I'm not going to ask again why you insist I didn't write letters I know I did. Both of us seem to believe we're in the right here, and I doubt that's going to change any time soon." I narrow my eyes at her. "But I do want to know about your relationship with Will."

She narrows hers right back. "What part did you fail to understand?" But then her eyebrows furrow in what appears to be genuine befuddlement as she looks up at me. "I told you, he's my friend."

"Your boyfriend?"

"No." She laughs, that full-bodied, don't-give-a-damn-who's-listening laugh that neither years nor distance were able to erase from my memory. "*Much* better than that. He's my best friend."

It catches me by surprise how relieved I am to hear it. I'm also a bit annoyed with the *much better than that* comment. But what the hell, I was once her boyfriend. In a time gone by, it's true, distanced by years and war and the lack of communication we have agreed to stop disputing. Or at least I think we have, when it comes to the latter.

She tugs against my grip. "So, if that's all, I'll be off."

"Yeah, sure." I turn her loose. "But just so we're on the same page, we are agreed, yes?" My voice hardens. "We are going to act professionally and get along."

"That's what we said. Professional." Lena gives me a cool look. "And nothing more." She turns on her heel and strides off again, the beaded fringe promptly reactivated by the hypnotic motion of her hips.

It doesn't escape me she didn't actually agree to anything. I watch her go and think about her parting shot. Then shake my head as I start back to my office.

Because I didn't agree to everything, either. So, yeah.

We will just have to see about that *nothing more* part.

Three nights later I'm standing at the back of the club watching Lena belt out her last song of the evening, and congratulating myself over the way this getting along business has been working out pretty well—all things considered—when a man stops next to me.

"She's great, isn't she," he says in a voice low enough not to disrupt my customers' listening pleasure.

Since it's more statement than a question, I don't take my eyes off her. "Yes." She definitely is. Lena has an ineffable something special when she sings.

I'm not sure why that surprises me. The night I met her in my folk's kitchen where I had escaped to avoid Father's relentless expectations, she'd all but knocked me off my feet. She was so interesting and full of life. Filled with dreams, fired with determination and full of intention. And here I am years later, watching and listening to the results of all that focused purpose—even though the dreams had changed in a direction I had no idea about back then. In the short time she's been here, word of her talent has already gotten around. The club is more packed every night—and we were bringing in good-sized crowds long before her advent. People no longer talk over her introduction. Instead, they applaud wildly. And profits are definitely up.

So, no, I don't want to talk to a stranger about her talent. I just want to listen to her. And watch. Because that's a treat all by itself—and I don't mean only her face or supple body. No, she has a way of wearing every emotion she wrings from the songs she sings like a beating heart on her sleeve. It sucks people in. Makes them *care*.

The fella next to me, however, clearly isn't in the no talking zone. "I love the way her phrasing incorporates the blue notes, sudden swoops, dives and surprising leaps of the great colored singers."

Okay, what he says rings true, resonating right down to my bones. And I find myself replying, "Yet she never sounds like a white singer mimicking Bessie Smith."

And when I turn, it's to look straight into my old friend Will's dark eyes. His love of jazz and blues back in high school, along with my own, was instrumental in introducing Lena to it. Before that, she had only heard and sung hymns through her participation in the Blood of Christ choir. But one song played on my Victrola, and she was hooked. A fan for life.

And looking at Will, a surge of happiness at seeing him again bolts through me.

Only to be promptly supplanted with thoughts and, worse, mental images of Will, not as he was when I knew him well. But rather, as he appears now. An adult Will who has been with Lena during all the years I have been gone. Who has been by her side to watch and presumably give his support when she decided to give singing on a professional level a try. The fella who was there when she broke into the music industry and during her burgeoning rise.

Will, who ran off with my girl while I was fighting a fucking war that did its best to crush me. While I wrote all those damn letters and missed her beyond bearing at times. Will, who has maybe kissed her. Who maybe has even...done more?

A tidal wave of...something...rises up in me. And the next thing I know the punch I've thrown is knocking Will sideways along the wall, before dumping him on his ass on the plush Twilight Room carpet.

Chaos erupts. People at a nearby table scramble to their feet, knocking drinks over. More than one woman screams, bringing more people to their feet at adjacent tables.

Will presses the back of his hand to the underside of his nose. Pulling it back, he looks at the blood adorning it generously. His nostrils are gushing pretty good.

Then he looks up at me with murder in his eyes. "You want a fight, you faithless piece of shit?" he says in a low voice, climbing to his feet. He advances on me, his right arm drawing back. His hand makes a much more sizeable fist than I recall from back in our high school days.

Then he shoots a glance past me. Before I can turn to see what he's looking at, someone shoves me aside. And Lena is suddenly in my face.

"What is the *matter* with you?" she demands, but doesn't wait for an answer before turning away. She brushes past me, pausing at the table around which people are still ineffectually milling about. She sweeps up a clean, folded linen napkin, dips it into a glass of champagne on the table and presses it to the bottom of Will's nose. "Here, keep this pressed there to staunch the flow." Her voice is a universe gentler than the one she used to address me. Twining her arm around Will's, she hugs his biceps against the side of her breast. Strokes the back of his hand with gentle fingertips. "C'mon. Let's go get you fixed up."

Without sparing me another glance, they walk away, heading toward her dressing room, I imagine. The thought of the two of them back there by themselves gets my feet in gear and I follow—stopping only long enough to instruct Millie to put new linens on the jostled table and replace their drinks on the house.

Before Lena and Will reach the only indoor access to the backstage hallways not involving the use of the stairs on either end of the of the stage, Sally rushes up to them, her breasts and cigarette tray bouncing. "What can I do to help?" I hear her ask.

Lena, still clutching Will to her side, barely slows her stride. "Could you bring some ice to my dressing room?"

"You got it, sweetie."

"Thanks, Sally. You are one fine woman."

"Awww!" My cigarette girl laughs and veers off toward the bar.

I vacillate for a moment or two. I should probably circulate among my guests and make sure they've all settled back into the club's normal routine in the wake of my outburst. But my urge to find out what the story is with Lena and Will is stronger than my desire to placate the paying guests.

Which is kind of a first for me. But, fuck it. With an impatient shrug, I head to Lena's dressing room.

I can hear her and Will talking as I approach the room a minute or three later. Lena hasn't bothered closing the door behind her and as I reach it I hear her say, "...and I thought you weren't getting home for a couple of days yet."

"Nor did I. But I finished my interviews early."

Will's voice is a deeper rumble than I remember. But then a lot of things have changed since the last time I saw him. I step to the side of the open door and look in.

My ex-closest friend sits in a chair placed crossways to the doorway. His head is tipped back, eyes closed, while Lena tenderly wipes blood off his face.

She frowns down at him. "Since you're here and have probably been on one train or another for a good four days, maybe you didn't get the telegram I sent. I can't remember exactly when I sent it." She shrugs. "It just said the venue for the gig I thought was such a grand opportunity turned out to be owned by Booker."

I wince a bit at the way she spits out my name with such venom.

Will cracks an eye open. "The desk clerk actually gave it to me as I was checking out of the hotel." He grimaces. "That was a surprise."

"No bananas," she says drily. "But let's not talk about him. How did the interviews go?"

"*Life* isn't interested, but I knew that was a long shot. *College* magazine expressed some interest and so did *Collier*, so I'm hoping to hear from them. The ad agency interview went great. I signed a contract to do an illustration for a Winx Waterproof eyelash darkener ad. Isn't that the one you use—*Winx the magic lash darkener, makes your lashes something, something?*"

"*Long and shadowy.* And, yes! Oh, Will, that's so exciting. You're going to be illustrating for a New York ad agency!"

"In a national campaign in newspapers across the country, they tell me. They also said if they like my work on this one there will be more like it. So. You wanna be my model? It pays eighteen dollars and they loved the idea of a blonde."

"Hmmm, let me think. Do I want to see my face in a national campaign? Ab-so-toot-ly!" Her laughter fades, however, as she looks down at his now mostly cleaned up face. "This is still bleeding. That damn bully. Why the devil would he hit you?"

Shit. You know Lena's mad if she swears. All those years in the Blood of Christ Foundling home left her with a lasting belief one does not curse. Well, she never seemed to mind if Will or I did. But she only swears herself when she's furious.

"Hell, if I know," Will replies. "We were talking about your talent one minute, then he turned to look at me and...pow! I took a hard-left hook straight to the beezer." He shakes his head. "I didn't even know he had that move in him."

She shakes her head as well—as if my actions are beyond a civilized person's understanding, then frowns at the blood still trickling from Will's nose. "Dang it, this is not stopping. Let me get the styptic stick."

She straightens, but Will's hand snakes out to grip her wrist. "If you think I'm letting you shove a styptic stick up my already abused nose, you've got another think comin'."

"It will help stop the bleeding."

"It's made for small bleeds, so yeah, maybe it will. Then again, maybe it won't. What it *is* guaranteed to do is burn like the fires of hell."

She makes a rude noise. "You're such an infant."

"Says the baby vamp who wailed like a banshee when I put mercurochrome on her skinned knee. It's the only time I have ever heard you hit a note that high."

"Hey, I lost several layers of skin from that knee! And what the heck is a banshee, anyway?"

"Damned if I know. But I do know they're supposed to wail to beat the band."

"Hey, Mistah Jameson."

Caught up in listening to their conversation, I jerk in surprise at the nasal voice, then glance over to see Sally coming down the hall with a bowl of ice and a couple of wash cloths. Shooting a skittish look in my direction, she gives me a wide berth as she approaches the dressing room door.

Swell. Apparently, decking a man everyone assumes is a customer has dented my reputation some. "Hey, Sally."

Lena's head snaps up and turns my way. Seeing me, she gives Will's hand a gentle pat, then rises and stalks over. Reaching for the bowl of ice and washcloths, she gives the cigarette girl a smile. "Thanks, Sally. You're a peach."

"Yer welcome, doll. I gotta get back on the floor but I hope your friend feels better real soon." She shoots me another who-the-hell-are-you look, spins on her heel and heads back to the lounge. The minute she's out of sight, I turn to Lena.

"Eavesdropping now?" She gives me a look disgust. "Who are you, Booker?" she demands before I can utter a syllable, unerringly mimicking the exact words I'd assigned Sally's unspoken disapproval. "You've changed so much I don't even recognize you anymore. And, trust me, not for the better."

I open my mouth to respond...but don't really know what to say. Because, going over in my mind what I've just seen of her interaction with Will, I realize what she told me three nights ago is more than likely the God's honest truth: she doesn't have romantic feelings for my old friend. Clearly, I only gave lip service to believing her up until this moment. But looking at it realistically—something I have failed to do up until now—the two them could have been married and had a passel of kids in the near-decade since I've seen them. I'm still ...well, not *jealous*.

But maybe I am a little irate they'd forgotten me so easily.

In the end, it doesn't matter what I might have said. Lena cuts short any possibility of having a conversation when she slams the door in my face.

6

Shave and a haircut, two bits!

LENA

"What on earth *happened* to the old Booker?" I cross to Will and peel away the washcloth I'd wrapped around Sally's crushed ice. Looking at the bruises starting to bloom on my best friend's face, I wince, gently balance the makeshift ice pack back over the bridge of Will's nose. Then I raise my gaze to meet his. "He used to be *fun*. We were all friends—a trio. Now he tries to break your nose for no good reason?"

I shake my head in disbelief. "That's not the man I cried buckets over." Barely able to acknowledge the years of tears to myself, I am darned if I'll admit to Will it's possible I'm pining *still* for the young bold-hearted man I used to know.

And if I am, it's only the tiniest bit, darn it! Because I have moved on.

I shake off the niggle in my conscience over keeping certain thoughts from my best friend. Say briskly, "Until I met him, I never knew so many things could make me laugh. But Booker used to be funny."

And smart. And *oh, my*. So amazingly...something. "Are you comfortable? Is it too hot in here for you?" Something...I don't know ...magnetic. When Booker is near it's all I can do to hold my ground against the persistent compulsion my body feels to move closer. Flapping the sides of the wrapper I'd slipped on over my costume, I try without success to circulate a bit of air across my overheated skin.

"Lena." Will has that don't-even-try-to-kid-a-kidder look he's perfected over the years. And right this minute he's training it on me. The man is sporting rolled gauze stuffed up his nostrils, which makes his voice nasal and not at all like him. But the look—

Well, *that* is amazingly effective. "A blind man can see he's knee-crawling jealous," he says, and even delivered in that nasally, stuffy-nose voice, Will's tone is flat and authoritative.

Which is also effective. Until the words sink in.

"What?" My head snaps back as though he smacked me. "No, he isn't!"

"Hell yes, he is." Will nods sagely. "Booker is damn near beside himself with jealousy. He thinks you and I are an item."

I stop, startled into silence.

The thought of Booker believing Will and I might be more than simply the great friends we are—and being *bothered* by it?

Oh, dear. I'm loath to admit this, since it doesn't speak kindly of my Christian charity. But the idea of Mr. Heartbreaker Jameson feeling jealous ignites a spark of heat deep down in a part of me I haven't acknowledged in a *long* time.

Which is *not* smart, so I shove it away. Then speak the absolute truth. "That is crazy talk. I *told* him you and I were just friends." At least I'm pretty sure I did.

No. I straighten. I did precisely that.

"You know and *I* know we're not lovers." Will lifts the icepack from his nose and gingerly removes the gauze. After disposing of the soiled bandaging material, he pulls a clean handkerchief from his pocket and dabs gently at his nostrils. When its pristine surface comes away unblemished by blood, he slowly straightens in his chair. "I'm damn sure Booker thinks otherwise, though."

"Now, that just makes me mad. I could be having petting-parties with every man in town, and it wouldn't be any business of Booker's." I slather Pond's cream on my face and reach for the tissues to wipe off my stage makeup. "And why the heck would he care? He dumped me without a second thought. When I think of all the letters I wrote—" I shake my head. "Lord, what a fool I was. Oh, and get this." I pace a few steps away, then whirl to face Will again, a harsh laugh evading my attempts to keep it inside. "He claims he wrote me several times a week while he was gone, then had the gall to act all wild eyed because *I* didn't respond to *his* supposed correspondence."

Booker's claim simultaneously infuriates me and ignites a stupid spark of hopefulness.

Will stills. "He says he wrote as well?"

"Yep." I stand taller, refusing to fall into the trap Booker's claim represents. My mother left me on the steps of the Blood of Christ Foundling Home when I was not quite two years old. Not that I have any real memory of it. Still, it doesn't take that genius fella who won the Nobel Prize in Physics a few years back to track my on and off feelings of abandonment to its original source.

Dear old Mum was merely the first to teach me that people don't stick around for the long haul. People leave. Always. It's just a fact of life.

During my sixteen years in the Blood of Christ, the older girls sometimes befriended me. For a while life would feel pretty darn special. Yet, predictably, those sweet relationships always ended the same way. With me left behind as my new friend went into service or married a townie or was just plain turned out when she hit eighteen, to make her own way as the State rules dictated.

Well, I'm nothing if not a fast learner. Okay, maybe not all that fast, considering it took me several crushing disappointments at being left behind—*again*—before I wised up and stopped trying to get close to people.

Yet the evening I met Booker all my savvy flew out the window.

He was like no one I had ever known and I simply had no choice but to take a chance on him. He's twenty-two months older than me, and I knew from the first he would be leaving for college in a few brief months. Yet we spent every moment we could steal from our day-to-day routines in order to be with each other.

I fell head-over-heels in love with him, juggling emotions I had never even dreamed existed.

"There is something mighty damn fishy about all these missing letters," Will says, hauling me out of my memories.

I drag myself back into the now—only to find myself gawking stupidly as his words sort themselves out in my brain. "You *believe* him?"

"The Booker I knew was no liar, Lena. Neither are you. So maybe someone else had a hand in keeping your correspondence from the two of you."

"Oh, please. Who would do such a thing? And *why*?" But I take a step in his direction. And concede, "I did wonder at one time if Matron might have." I feel a glimmer of hope I truly don't want to entertain for fear it will blow up in my face. But I have to admit, "I can honestly say she wouldn't have hesitated, because she was just down-right cold and judgmental about everything. She had so many rules and restrictions it's a wonder a body could find a reason to smile at all. Not that she didn't have her moments," I add guiltily, because every now and then Matron Davidson would do something almost...nice. Warm, even. "But, Lord, she took it personally if anyone had a better time than she. And face it, darn-near everyone did."

"What did you do about your suspicions?"

I shrug. "I decided to take my letters directly to the post office."

"When the hell did all this happen?" *And why didn't you ever mention a damn word about it?* Will didn't need to actually say the words to broadcast the question loud and clear. He never did have much of a poker face.

I ignore the look but answer the question. "It was about a month before the war ended. The same day I saw Booker's mother in the post office and overheard her telling the postmaster Booker was thinking of staying in Paris instead of coming home." I shrug as if it hadn't crushed the still-clinging-to-hope portion of my heart into one big greasy, grimy pile of broken dreams. Despite everything, I had clung long and fiercely to the notion that, once the war finally ended, he would come home to me. That he would have a good explanation for why he'd never written.

I thrust my chin out. "Clearly he didn't give a hoot about telling *me*. So, I saved myself sixteen cents by not buying one of the new airmail stamps for the letter I'd come to mail. And that was the last one I wrote."

The Brasher sisters' familiar rap of *Shave-and-a-hair-cut, two-bits!* sounds on my door then, and I jump as if someone goosed me. Looking at the clock on the wall, I'm surprised to see how much time has passed. Enough for the band to have played a set of dance tunes and the sisters to finish their final two dances of the night.

I turn away to open the door and Clara and Dot tumble into the room, demanding the skinny on the rumor flying around that Booker punched some fella right in the kisser. Seeing Will himself sitting there, they look flustered for all of ten seconds. Then they ply him with rapid-fire intrusive questions, strutting, flirting and teasing him all the while.

Will, of course, fields their demands with his usual low-key ease, and even gives every appearance of being highly cooperative. I'm apparently the only one to notice not once does he give either sister a straight answer.

I hide my smile. Because, that's my friend in a nutshell. So outwardly easy-going some people make the mistake of thinking he's a pushover. But Will is no one's patsy. The man is rock solid to the core.

And he always speaks from the place his conscience dictates.

7

Open the damn door, Jameson!

BOOKER

I have only been home maybe ten minutes and am trying to ice my knuckles while simultaneously disrobing when some idiot pounds on my door. "Oh, for Cri's sake, *now* what?" Who the hell comes calling at three o'clock in the morning? Isn't it enough the night has already crept along like a moonshine-soaked turtle, while displaying damn near every shade of balled up known to man? Now *company* comes knocking at my door at o'dark hundred?

I throw back the three fingers of Canadian Club sipping whiskey I poured but have yet had opportunity to actually sip. I was a little busy getting ice for my hand, then detaching my stiff, high wingtip collar and removing my shirt studs and one cufflink with my left hand while burying my right one in the bowl I'd dumped the ice in. Pulling the latter from the frigid cubes, I gingerly pat it dry against the bedspread I'm sitting on. Setting the now-empty glass on the night table next to my bed, I climb to my feet then stalk down the hall to the door, trailing the shirt I've shrugged out of from my left wrist. I'm wrestling the final cuff link free as I reach the tiny entry.

Someone hammers yet again, shaking the door in its jamb.

"Knock it off!" I roar. "Who the hell are you, anyhow?"

"Open the goddamn door, Jameson!"

My heart performs a weird hurl-itself-at-my-ribcage maneuver. "*Will?*" I can honestly say he is the last person I expected to arrive on my doorstep. Not after tonight's sideshow. Curiosity alone is enough to have me reaching for the knob.

I open the door.

My former best friend strides past me, his wide shoulder catching me in the collarbone and sending me staggering back. Okay, fair enough. Rubbing the spot he slammed, I follow him into the living room.

"Long time, no see," I say with a bite of sarcasm layered atop the manners I was raised on. Then, watching him drop into a chair in my living room, the sarcasm grows deeper. "Please. Sit your ass down. Make yourself at home."

"Done that. Thanks." He looks up at me. "Interesting look."

I glance down and shrug. I have yet to change out of my dress slacks, and my bowtie is still neatly tied. Having finally rid myself of my shirt on the entry floor, however, from the waist up I'm dressed only in the tux tie and my undershirt.

Well, too damn bad. "My house. Dead of night. If you want sensibly dressed, come back at a reasonable hour."

He shrugs right back at me. "Got any hooch?" The words no sooner leave his mouth than he barks out a laugh. "Of course you do. You own a damn juice joint."

I study him. Is he my rival now for Lena's love? My thoughts on the latter have been all over the map tonight. One minute I'm thinking yes. The next, no way in hell. My bottom line at the moment is: what does she see in him, exactly?

Sure, Will has always had an easiness in his own skin I envied. Before I discovered it for myself, I had to spend fifteen months in European trenches and woods, then more than five years forging my way through the clubs of Paris, learning everything I needed to know to eventually run my own business. My one-time friend is a little battered right now because of me, but I suppose he's nice enough looking with his tall, rangy build, dark eyes and sun-streaked brown hair. Shit, how would I know? Men don't consider that sort of thing about each other.

Clara and Dot sure as hell couldn't stop talking about him, though, when they left Lena's dressing room for a quick drink at the bar before heading home. Truth be told, I was relieved when the dancers finally left.

I look down at my clenched fists, and slowly straighten my fingers until I'm no longer sporting bloodless white knuckles. I remind myself Will has never approached anything close to movie idol handsome. And his money likely isn't the attraction. He was never dirt poor like Lena back when we all lived in Walla Walla. But he had been a lot closer to her income bracket than my father's. And from what I overheard outside her dressing room earlier, he's taken those drawings he was always working on and turned them into a career as an illustrator. I'm guessing it's probably a decent living, but I doubt it has him rolling in dough. So what is it, exactly, all the women see in him?

What does *Lena* see?

Of course, the details people like my father would consider drawbacks never seemed to matter as much to the ladies. And Lena wouldn't give a damn if Will was rich as Croesus. She sure hadn't given two shakes about my wealth or lack of it. She would appreciate Will's creative mind, though. Women almost universally found him interesting. So my money is on Will's easygoing confidence being his biggest drawing card.

Yeah. I can easily envision Lena liking a confident man.

Will follows me to the dining room where I cross to the bar I've established on the sideboard. Snatching up another highball glass, I splash a couple fingers of the rye whiskey into it. I start to turn away, then appropriate another glass and pour some for myself.

I hand Will his and carry mine back to the living room, where

Will sits down again in his easy chair. Dropping onto the couch across the small, low table from him, I shoot him a level look. "So, what are you doing here at—" I glance at my watch "—three-goddamn-twenty-three in the morning? If you're wanting an apology —well I guess I might owe you one."

"You think?"

His lack of expression riles me. "Look, what did you expect to happen when you came waltzing into my club? Could I have handled my goodbyes better back then? Yes. And I should have talked about going to war with Lena first. But I did try to call her at the foundling home and I sure as hell kept my promise to write to her. She's the one who couldn't be bothered to respond. So, I concentrated on two things: staying alive and being a good soldier.

"A week or two before the war ended, I broke down and wrote home to find out what Lena was doing and maybe discover why the hell she hadn't written. Mom's letter back to me was short and sweet. She said, I am so sorry dear, but Miss Bjornstad left town with your friend Will." I stare him down. "You might as well have gutted me."

Will doesn't display an iota of guilt. He merely raises an eyebrow at me. "Why would you care? You were gonna go to France to live in Paris anyhow. Or so Lena overheard your mama telling the postmaster."

"I was already in France. In September of Eighteen, the 1st Army *was* the attack on the Western Front at Saint-Mihiel."

I scrub my eyes with the heels of my palms, then drop my hands to grip my knees. I would give a bundle to be all cool and composed. But it's late, I'm fried and I just don't have it in me. I instead blow out a breath and simply tell Will the truth. "I felt betrayed on all fronts to hear you and Lena were together while I was fighting that fucking awful war. So, yes, rather than come home I went to Paris. I had to earn my own living for the first time in my life, and I liked it there. It's where I fell in love with clubs and cabarets. They were such an antidote to the war."

I look Will in the eye. "War wasn't anything like the glorious adventure you and I envisioned. It was constant mud and fear. It was infected feet from standing in water up to your calves in the trenches and seeing fellow soldiers get blown up in front of you out in the fields. It was airplanes strafing the ground all around you and fighting off tanks with a goddamn machine gun." I suck in a breath and shake off the old nightmare. I give my one time friend a small half smile. It's the best I can manage at the moment.

"So, yeah," I admit. "I liked the night life in Paris. It saved my sanity and gave me purpose. And since I was making a living, saving and learning a lot, I stayed until the beginning of last year when I was ready to implement my plans to open my own place. But I tell you what, Will. While I'd flirted with the idea of living in Paris, I didn't make up my mind until I got that note from my mom about you and Lena."

"Wanna know the big flaw if you're using that as your reasoning?" Will asks easily. "Lena and I weren't together." Clearly seeing me open my mouth, he waves a hand. "Yes, we left together," he says. "After mama died, I came into a bit of money and shared it with Lena so we could both get a fresh start away from that damn small-minded town. But she and I...? Booker, we have *never* been anything but good friends."

My heart is suddenly trying to drum its way out of my chest. But I suck in a deep breath and slowly, *slowly*, exhale it.

Then give Will a slight nod. Because... "I might have caught a hint of that earlier tonight."

"It better be after you decked me, asshole."

"Yeah. It was sort of beginning to sink in you had had nearly a decade to get married and have yourself a passel of babies." I ignore the way the thought of the latter in particular hollows me out. "Then I went backstage to talk to you and maybe apologize for punching you. Instead, I heard you two talking. And it didn't sound lover-like. You didn't call each other pet names." A thought that hadn't occurred to me earlier sends the right side of my mouth kicking up in a half smile. "And Lena never once offered to kiss your nose all better."

Will gapes at me. "Why the hell would she wanna do that?"

"Because once, in the park back home, we watched a woman

clean her little fella's hands in the drinking fountain after he skinned them up on the sidewalk. When she was done, she patted them dry with her handkerchief and said, 'Let mama kiss it and make it better.' Then she carefully kissed each one. Lena was completely taken with the gesture."

"I can picture that. God knows she had no one, growing up, to give her any kind of tenderness, let alone taking the time to kiss her ouchies, as my mama called them when I was little." Will smiles fondly.

I clear my throat. "Yeah. A while after that incident I cracked my crazy bone against the door jamb of the Feed and Seed and Lena kissed it better." I remember being touched and totally aroused, thinking of other places I could ask her to kiss.

I'm smart enough not to say as much aloud, but, hey. I was an eighteen-year-old boy at the time. Or maybe simply saying I'm male is all that's needed to justify my youthful thoughts. I take a sip of the Canadian Club.

And spray it all over myself when Will murmurs, "If I'd had a pretty girl say that back then, I would have been seriously tempted to point out some other body parts needing a good kiss better."

I pull a clean handkerchief from my slacks pocket. Dab at my chest and thighs. And scowl at Will. "Jesus, man, give a fella a little warning, would ya?"

Will shrugged. "You can't tell me the thought never crossed your mind."

"Of course it did. I figured you'd lay me out cold, though, if I mentioned it in conjunction with Lena."

Will winced. "Yeah. I'd rather not rub those two thoughts together. She's the closest thing I have to a sister." He throws back the rest of his drink and sets the glass on the end table. "Speaking of which, what is the deal with all these missing letters?"

I'm exhausted and not tracking anywhere near an efficient level. Consequently, I don't exactly sound brilliant when, in answer to Will's question, I meet his eyes, one of which is—*shit*—turning black and swelling shut, and say, "Huh?"

"I know Lena never received a single letter from you, Booker. And

I know how badly it busted her up inside. But I'm going to tell you the same thing I told her. I have never known *either* of you to lie to me or each other. You have both always been straight shooters. Yet here we are, with the two of you insisting you wrote the other. Damn, man. Doesn't it strike you as strange that so many goddamn letters went missing? You were always aces with numbers, Jameson. And you and Lena were tighter 'n ticks at the time you left town."

Will tunnels his fingers through his hair, holding it off his forehead as he studies me through the eye that's not swollen. "Given that, what are the fucking odds not so much as one letter got through from the two of you the entire time you were gone?"

8

Don't know whether to scratch your watch or wind your ass

BOOKER

I feel my jaw drop as I stare at Will. I always thought that was just an expression, but I actually have to firm mine up. "Shit." My brain feels as if it's been flooded with light. "I should have thought of that, myself. But who the...?" *Well, who else, genius?*

"Dad," I say grimly.

"Considering the bum's rush he gave you out of Walla Walla after you and Lena got caught necking in your old Model T, it's a reasonable theory," Will points out. "I don't imagine he's thrilled with your speakeasy, either."

"To say the least."

Will's shoulder hitches infinitesimally. "On the other hand, I raised the subject with Lena while she was mopping me up earlier, and her gut reaction was the iron-fisted Matron who ruled the Foundling home."

"Or the two of them acted together." I get up to grab the fifth of whiskey out of the dining room and bring it back to the sitting area.

After splashing a couple more fingers into our glasses, I leave the bottle on the table between us. "I wouldn't put it past the old bastard. He probably "donated" money to the foundling home, only to immediately turn around and say, 'By the way, could you do me one little favor?'"

Every muscle in my body has tensed and I am so goddamn angry I could spit enough nails to build a new addition to the speakeasy. It takes every ounce of willpower I possess not to snatch up my car keys, jump in my car and drive the nine plus hours to Walla Walla for a showdown. God knows it's long overdue.

"What do ya plan to do about it?"

Good question.

Wait. Fuck. Will's talking about Lena, not my issues with my old man. Plowing my fingers through my hair, I blow out an exasperated breath. "Not much I can do now, except make a pact with Lena to at least treat each other civilly. We've paid lip service to the idea since she got here, but maybe this time we can actually put some muscle behind our efforts."

He looks at me like I'm an idiot. "That's it?"

"What did you expect? A helluva lot of time and water has washed under that bridge."

Except...

The words no sooner leave my mouth than I realize Will was wrong about me not being a liar. If I didn't this minute look an old friend in the eye and do just that, at the very least I'm a champion at deceiving myself.

Let's call a spade a spade here. Will demanding the odds of not one piece of the correspondence Lena and I claim writing ever reaching the other shined a light on a realization I should have ...well, realized on my own.

And, the answer *zero* is a game changer.

So, I am full of shit, claiming my relationship with Lena is water under the bridge. So full of it, it isn't even funny. Truth be told, I considered her mine within hours of first clapping eyes on her when we were teens. Add to that my body's reaction every time she's anywhere in my vicinity, both then *and* now?

Well, an idiot can see I still believe she is. And *that's* in addition to me throwing punches with next to no provocation. I have rarely been a hothead, and I quit acting on impulse around the time I discovered war is not glorious at all, but rather muddy, bloody and most soldiers' personal dance with the devil.

I square my shoulders. "All right, so maybe saying Lena and I are through is bullshit. I have no idea where we'll end up, but I do know this much to be true." I look Will in the eye. "I'm going to do my damnedest to get her back."

A crooked half smile reshapes his mouth. "Now, *that* sounds more like the Booker I knew." He immediately pins me with a hard look. "But understand this, buddy. If you hurt her, I will beat you into the ground."

"If you really think I would do that you clearly don't know whether to scratch your watch or wind your ass. Still—" I give him a terse nod. "Message received loud and clear."

"So, what's the plan for getting her back?"

Yeah, that is the question, isn't it? "Well, like I said, I'm going to start out trying a little faith-based interaction with the woman."

"And...?"

Shit. I'm not happy with the idea of telling him I have no concrete ideas at this point. I'm not about to lie to him, however. So, I settle on a shrug. "Guess I'll figure it out from there."

9

Valentino? Or Fairbanks?

LENA

Three evenings later

"Oh, for God's sake, Dot," Clara says as the dancers and I barrel through the Twilight Room's entry. "I am not quarreling with you over this anymore." Her long-legged strides lead the way through the empty lounge. "I merely said the man is hotsy-totsy!"

To no one's surprise, Dot ignores the no arguing decree. The Brasher sisters could argue to a standstill the sun coming up in the east—while changing sides mid-argument. "Rudolph Valentino is hotsy-totsy," she says. "Douglas Fairbanks is...well, I have to agree the man is mighty swell. But he is no Rudolph Valentino." She turns to me. "What do you think, Lena? Fairbanks or Valentino?"

"I'm more of a Rod La Rocque girl, myself. Did you see The Stolen Kiss?" My heart gives a little flutter, even though it must have been four, five years ago since the movie hit the silver screen. "I saw that one seven times. It was so romantic!"

"Oooh," Clara squeals. "I loved that movie, too! He was romantic."

I pat my hand over my heart. "I can hardly wait for his next, the one coming out in December."

"Lena!" a male voice commands. "Come in here for a moment."

All three of us stutter to a stop and I turn back to the office we just breezed past.

The one I so very carefully hadn't glanced into.

"What's this about?" Dot asks in a whisper.

I give my shoulder a twitch and shake my head. I can guess, but I have no way of knowing for sure. My stomach suddenly doesn't feel so hot, though, because I have a horrid feeling my suspicion might be true.

The sisters give me identical sympathetic grimaces and continue toward the hallway to our dressing rooms. Blowing out a quiet breath, I reluctantly walk back to the office and poke my head through the open doorway. "You wanted to see me?"

Booker barely skims a glance over me before returning his attention to a pile of papers on his desk. "Come in and close the door."

A shiver runs down my spine. Ever since Will introduced the possibility of someone other than Booker and me being responsible for us not receiving the other's letters, I have done my best to avoid the club owner. I bite my lip and move as slowly as I dare. Because, darn it, there is a part of me deep inside I've guarded for years. A part that wants nothing more than to believe in Will's theory. Yet if this notion of his does turn out to be true—

Well, it means my immediate future is at stake. I have been outrageously mouthy to my employer. Not to mention—swallowing hard, I step into the office and ease the door closed behind me—slapping Booker's face in front of a lounge full of customers and his other employees. It's a wonder I'm still working here at all.

Chances, are, I won't be much longer. Oh, sure, I managed to dodge Booker for the past few nights, while doing my utmost to give great performances to build a bit of credit on the plus side of my Twilight Room let's-keep-Lena-employed ledger.

I didn't try to fool myself into believing staying one step ahead of him would last forever, however. I knew good and well I was on borrowed time.

Now he's caught up with me, my future as the speakeasy's canary could very well be about to change.

"Take a seat."

Doing as I'm told, I perch rigidly upright on the edge of the chair facing Booker's desk.

"Will came to see me."

My heart begins pounding even faster than it had when he first hailed me. "He did? When?" Except for a brief telephone call to make sure he was doing all right the day after Booker decked him, I have neither seen nor heard from Will. He'd mentioned that in order to make room for his new projects, he'd be up to his neck completing the jobs he had set aside to go to New York.

Booker levels a look on me. "You know, the other night—or I suppose early morning, if you want to be literal." He shrugs, since we both know how speakeasy time goes. When one doesn't go to work before nine p.m—and often later—the hours after midnight are all considered the same night.

I raise an eyebrow at him. "The night you punched him in the nose?"

Had I blinked, I would have missed Booker's slight wince. But to his credit, he merely nods. "Yes. He came over to ask why I never questioned the fact every damn letter we both swear we wrote went missing."

"Oh. He said the same thing to me as well." I sit straighter. "Did you really write me several days a week?" I'm not even sure at this point what I hope to hear.

He meets my gaze squarely. "Yes. I did. You, too? You wrote me as often as you said you did?"

"Ye—" The word sticks in my throat, rendering me unable to get out even a simple syllable without croaking. Okay, so it turns out I was wrong. I did want to hear Booker hadn't forgotten about me entirely, which was sure as heck what it had felt like. Booker occupies most of my mental Midnight File already. Now, finding out he hadn't dumped me, that he had truly loved me all those years ago, cleaves a huge swath through everything I'd believed. Confusion swarms my brain like a disturbed hive of bees, and I don't have the first idea what to do with the knowledge.

Do I laugh like a loon or lament every single thing I lost?

I square my shoulders. Now isn't the time to think about it. Clearing my throat, I nod. "Yes. I wrote." I merely look at him over the cluttered expanse of his desktop for a moment before clearing my throat again. "Will said something else to me that night—something I might eventually have thought of myself if I hadn't spent all these years gathering what I thought was undeniable proof you're an ass. He said the Booker he remembered wasn't a liar."

I lick suddenly my dry lips. "I didn't want to hear it at the time, yet...he had a point. The Booker I knew back then wasn't." I hesitate, then add in all honesty, "I'm working on the believing you still aren't part." I shoot a glance at his neutral expression. "I imagine you're doing likewise with me."

But what if he's actually thinking this is the perfect opportunity to get rid of me? To give me the boot without having to admit he's embarrassed he ever had anything to do with someone like me in the first place? Maybe he simply doesn't want the girl from the foundling home around reminding him of a youthful indiscretion he wishes he never committed.

Booker tosses the pen he's been slowly rolling from one finger to the next on the desktop. "That brings me to what I need to say." He seems to grow taller in his seat. "You and I have had a conversation already about showing each other civility and professionalism. Yet, we haven't particularly done so."

Oh, God, this is it. The *'We both know it's you who hasn't kept up your half of the bargain, who has been neither civil nor professional, so pack your bags and go'* talk. Drawing in a ragged breath, I brace myself.

Only to blink at him in momentary confusion when he says, "I think it's time we both work harder at it. Do you agree?"

Trying not to sag beneath the relief of a dawning realization he is not firing me, I nod. "I do." Then I simply look at him.

Apologize! my self-preservation angel screams from one shoulder. It's not that hard, Lena. Open your mouth and say 'I know it's been me who has been the most discourteous and I'm sorry.'

But Matron might have had a point when she'd lectured, with mind-numbing regularity, the perils of me being bullheaded and stubborn. It doesn't help there is a self-righteous devil on my other shoulder insisting while Booker may have written, he still left not merely our hometown, but the entire damn country, without so much as a word to me. That he left me to worry myself sick he would be killed on some far away field without even having said goodbye. It's not easy to simply erase nine years of carrying the dagger of betrayal in the bottom-most, bloodiest part of my heart. Not when that disregard of me finds a new tender spot from which to draw blood every time I think of the disrespect he showed me.

Joining up to go off to war was better than being with me?

This is the question that has long occupied the largest corner of my Midnight File. The one that hammers at me constantly.

The one I never talk about. Not even to Will.

I feel like I've been suspended in amber for an age, while all this races through my head, but actually it's only been seconds. Even then, all I manage to limp out is, "It's kinda...hard...to do a complete turnaround on a belief I've held for nine years." Then I pull myself up to sit yet more erect. "But I will work on it." I meet his level blue-eyed gaze. "I will work very hard to do unto you as I would have you do unto me."

Booker's mouth, normally so hard these days, softens with a small smile. Maybe my evoking the golden rule reminds him of something the Lena he used to know would have said.

Which I suppose it is. My shoulders twitch in a small shrug. What can I say? You can take the girl out of the Foundling Home, but you can't simply erase sixteen plus years of the foundling home's preaching.

"Can't ask for more than that." Booker studies me a moment. Is that...disappointment I see?

If so, he merely says, "Was that the Brasher sisters I heard out in the hall with you just now?"

As I nod my agreement it was, I decide the "disappointment" was either my imagination...or wishful thinking on my part.

"What were you girls talking about?"

Either way, I'm grateful for the change of subject. I probably shouldn't be surprised he heard us; we hadn't exactly been quiet. "We saw Don Q, Son of Zorro at the Orpheum this evening and Dot and Clara cannot quit arguing over who is the best leading man: its star, Douglas Fairbanks Jr, or Rudolf Valentino."

"I thought Valentino was dead."

"Oh, he definitely is. Dot's been mourning his passing for almost two months now. But she maintains he'll forever be a legend."

Booker quirks a brow. "And what side did you come down on?"

"Neither. I'm stuck on Rod La Rocque." As a flash of heat steals up my neck and across my face, I mentally curse my ancestors for giving me such fair skin. What on earth possessed me to tell Booker Jameson, of all people, about my crush on a Hollywood leading man? Must I really voice every thought to pop into my head? Goodness gracious Agnes. I pine for the day when I adopt a little classiness.

At least I managed to keep to myself my old fantasy of the movie idol sweeping in to rescue me from the life turned gray after Booker left.

I do my best to rise to my feet in a calm, casual way. It's not as easy as it sounds with this itchy impulse to leap up and run as fast and far from Booker's office as I can get.

He stands too and I try to ignore the way he always seems to take up every inch of available space whenever he's near.

Oh, the heck with it. When in doubt, brass your way through it, I always say. "Well." I sidestep the chair still brushing the backs of my knees. "I'm glad we cleared the air. I should get going. I have some, um, things to do before my first set."

His hands slap softly atop the desk, making me jump even though the sound was barely audible. Balancing his weight on the tips of his fingers and thumbs, he stares at me searchingly for a moment.

I wonder if my thoughts are written all over my face. Hoping to mask my inner turmoil, I manage the Foundling Home smile. The one I learned to slap on young when I was paraded in front of couples looking to adopt. I know how to sell it. Know how to make this smile look the next best thing to real.

Booker, however, doesn't appear to buy it. Or perhaps he's simply unaffected by it. Either way, he straightens and turns his attention to the calendar pinned on the adjacent wall.

It's no secret he keeps employee scheduling, employee's birthdays and every single appointment or delivery pertinent to the club on the thing. He has to turn his head to get a good look at it, so I have a moment to study him unobserved.

There's a catch in my chest every time I see anew the man Booker has become. Not that there aren't still traces of the boy I once loved. Bone structure like that, in the lean angles of his jaw, the sharpness of his cheekbones, doesn't just change.

But the adult Booker is stronger than his teenaged self, both in mind and body. He's more...hard boiled. More honed down to the bone. And he carries himself with a confidence he didn't have a full grip on back in the days when I thought I knew everything there was to know about him.

I'd bet my bottom dollar he doesn't give two figs about his father's opinion nowadays.

Booker turns back to me and I quickly drop my gaze to give my fingernails an intensely interested inspection.

"You remember you have a fitting for your new gowns at Frederick and Nelson a week from tomorrow, right?"

I swallow hard. Whether at the sudden change of subject or in anticipation of new clothing, I am not sure. But it's a lifeline and I grab it. "Yes, at four p.m. I have the seamstress's name in my purse."

Considering how beside myself excited I am about this, I'm proud of the breeziness of my reply.

But, oh, my golly! Except for a single gown I received from the management at the Tropics, I have always supplied my own stage outfits. And the one from the Tropics' had been a hand me down.

Booker, however, supplies up to five gowns for any singer deemed to bring increased profits to the Twilight Room. It was in my contract, but I'm embarrassed to say I didn't actually read it all that carefully. I was too impressed with the money I'd be getting. It was much, much better than I had received from any other singing gig I've ever had. Besides, the lounge always seems full to bursting to me, so I have no idea how Booker determines these profits. From the money the bar brings in, maybe? I know from nothing when it comes to running a joint this big and swanky.

I don't truly care. I'm just excited about the dresses. I have never in my life had one specially tailored to fit my body, never mind five dresses all at the same time. It makes me feel like Mrs. GotRocks.

I look up to see Booker studying me, his expression—well, I can't really tell if that's satisfaction I see or something entirely different.

I'm suddenly awash with an overload of emotion seeking an outlet, which in my case unfortunately usually means uncontrollable tears. I would rather chew rusty nails than let Booker see that, so I murmur a hasty excuse to hurry me out of his office.

Before I say or do something to give away my sincere befuddlement and complete and utter lack of sophistication.

10

Are you even listening to me?

LENA

I have managed to dodge Booker for four nights now. I am slowly coming to accept neither of us was at fault for the missing correspondence. What I can*not* seem to move beyond is the old resentment, which resurrected the minute I discovered my dream job was in the very joint Booker Jameson owns.

The mere thought of it has me churning up a full head of steam. I would love to say it's a simple fix, a mere matter of turning down the heat beneath the boiling kettle that is my bitterness. But no matter how many times I have gone through this, how many promises I make to myself to move *on* for pity's sake, my fury over the way Booker dumped me refuses to go away. It will cool down. It will even sleep for long periods of time. But darned if it doesn't refuse to lay down its weapons and just walk away. I *know* I oughtta be over it by now. Heaven knows I'm not the teenaged girl I was then.

Yet, every time the memory resurfaces out of the wreckage Booker left behind, every time I think of the sheer betrayal I felt when he left me flat, I am somehow still caught by surprise. Before him, I had gotten over the abandonment of my mother. Heck, that was more the idea of it than the actual leaving me, anyway. Because when she left me on the steps of the B of C, I was too young to have more than a hazy impression of a woman singing to me. I had even grown accustomed to being repeatedly deserted by the kids who'd befriended me in the orphanage before they had to move on. But I had honestly believed Booker was different.

Turns out he wasn't. Having to learn that lesson finally made me wise up. It made me quit expecting anything from anyone. Well, except Will—I refuse to paint him with the same brush.

The missing letters apparently weren't Booker's or my fault. But when it came to going off to war, Booker did so willfully. He had a choice. He chose to go to a continent far, far away without uttering a word to me about it. Just left without a single discussion, as if my opinion didn't matter.

It doesn't take a genius to understand it wasn't merely my opinions that hadn't mattered. No, sir, why stop there? *I* hadn't mattered. Not one. Damn. Bit.

Well, never mind. I stomp out the flames of my righteous indignation and tuck its not quite cold ashes into the dustiest chamber of my Midnight File. This one with fireproof walls and its own extra sturdy lock and key.

I truly don't want to fight with him anymore.

But neither do I like the idea of spending any more time in his company than I absolutely have to. I made myself a few vows when he marched off trailing my bleeding heart behind him. Not that I foresaw *this* situation as an option back then, but I did swear I was through putting myself in positions that allowed people to take pot shots at my heart. Never again. And I'd determined I would make something of myself through my singing.

Yet here I am. Juggling my two old vows, which are pretty much pitted against each other now I'm working for Booker. It's just too darn difficult. In fact, it's starting to become more and more obvious I should—

"Are you even listening to me?"

I blink and give Clara an apologetic grimace. "Sorry, my mind wandered for a second there. What did you say?"

"I need to stop at the five and dime. I'm out of rouge and my knees have been throwing a tizzy fit."

My eyebrows shoot up. "Talking knees. You dancers have such interesting body parts. Still. Rouged knees are all the rage. So, Woolworth or Kress's?"

"Either works for me." Clara's brow wrinkles. "Don't you think it's odd that two stores selling basically the same stuff to the same people set up business right across the street from each other? Seems to me they would make more profit if each had its own territory."

"Like these eight blocks are yours and those eight are mine?"

"Yeah, something like that." Clara abruptly cuts loose a belly laugh. "I'm sure they're sorry as can be they're not following my business plan. Seeing as how I'm so educated in fi-nance-seez and all." She flashes a big grin. "They probably weep over their loss all the way to the bank."

Dot dashes up to us just then, her lightweight coat unbuttoned and flapping behind her. "Sorry, sorry," she says as she approaches. "I didn't mean to hold up the show. MacDougall is having a sale and it was a crush in there."

Clara lights up. "You find any bargains?"

"Did I...?" Dot holds out a shopping bag. Gives it a shake. "Who's the undisputed queen of the bargain basement deals in this family?" she demands.

"That would be you," Clara concedes and the two women laugh uproariously, then dive in to inspect Dot's purchase.

I shake my head at their antics, but smile along with them. I so like these girls. In the short time I've known them, they have been nothing but fun. And so nice to me. They don't say one thing while actually meaning something entirely different. Next to Will, they have to be the most genuine people I've met in...

Well, an enormously long time. What makes it exceptionally nice is never once have I felt them working an agenda. That's nothing short of a marvel, considering some of the operators I've rubbed up against over the years. I have worked some joints—a few of them barely one step above a dive, others more elegant—where getting stage time was downright cutthroat. I swear to heaven a great many performers would kill their competitor's granny if it meant fifteen more minutes onstage or somehow otherwise boosted them another rung up the ladder.

I'm proud of having earned my spots with my voice, rather than playing the old slap and tickle game with the far too many men who trade in sexual favors for a spot in the lineup. It was tough for a while, but word got around after the time a particularly handsy manager refused to take no for an answer and I sang my way down the street to another bar. By itself, that would likely have landed me on the dole. But a parade of Mr. Handsy's patrons followed me as if I were the Pied Piper—and the other bar owner was impressed enough to hire me on the spot.

I smile, but shake off the memory. Dot and Clara straight out adopted me from my first night at the Twilight Room. They regularly invite me to join them in their before work activities . They have also had me over to their apartment, which is so high class compared to my Women's Residence room. I have been there twice to listen to the brand new NBC National broadcast on their equally new wireless. And they're trying to teach me to dance. I'm far from a natural, so that's kind of a riot all by itself.

The Brasher girls make me feel special, yet they act as if including me in whatever they're doing is the most natural thing in the world.

I'm not used to this feeling, as if I'm part of a sisterhood. As if I *belong*. It's been an age since I gave up attachments at the Blood of Christ. I had to. The lows when they regularly ended after the thrilling highs of the beginnings kept getting more and more painful. I'm trying to be an optimist about Clara and Dot, though. Because the way they've included me sure feels swell.

Kinda splendid, actually.

Today we're on a shopping spree. Well, Dot and Clara are. I'm mostly luxuriating in their enthusiasm rather than doing any real shopping of my own.

As if she can read my thoughts, Dot suddenly turns to me. "Don't think I haven't noticed you're not buying anything, missy," she says sternly.

I shrug. "I'm copacetic."

"Oh, hell, no. Not if you aren't participating, you're not. You haven't bought a single new thing since we met—and face it, doll, your wardrobe could use a few updates. Isn't Mr. Jameson paying you enough? Sis and me's paychecks are pretty damn generous, compared to some of the juice joints we've worked. But maybe he doesn't pay singers on the same scale?"

"Oh! No. I mean, yes!" I sound like a total idjit and am unable to do anything but stand there for a moment, my hands dangling uselessly at my sides as I gaze at both sisters helplessly. "This is more money than I've ever made in my life. Anywhere. *Ever*." Okay, I just said that. Still, it bears repeating.

"Then why aren't you buying anything?"

"I don't know. I just...I guess I've been on a strict budget for so long, I can't quite believe I actually have money left over after I pay my bills. I can't seem to pry my grip off my purse strings." I shrug helplessly. "It's ingrained in my bones to save for a rainy day."

Clara nods. "Lord knows there's always one of those around the corner. But, Lena..." She slings an arm around my shoulder and hugs me to her side. "...while I understand more than you might think about putting money away for that rainy day, you also gotta treat yourself sometimes. You have to celebrate the good times as well as put aside money for the bad ones. Because you *are* making good money right now." She looks me over, her gaze settling on my old worn cloche. "So, let's go find you a new hat, sister, 'cause that one has gotta go." She nods at Dot. "My trip to Woolworth can wait a while longer. We need to go back to MacDougall's."

We do exactly that. Heck, we not only shop at MacDougall's, but also go to the new Rhodes Department Store. We listen for darn near half an hour to the man playing piano requests from prospective buyers wanting to hear a song from the stacks of colorfully illustrated sheet music. At one point, I even sing along. I can't help myself. I just love *Bye Bye Blackbird*.

I don't feel so silly when Dot and Clara break into dance when the pianist plays *I'm Gonna Charleston back to Charleston*.

The sisters are much bolder than me. When the crowd around the pianist applaud enthusiastically, Dot says, "If y'all wanna hear more of Lola's singing or my sister and me's dancing *annnnd* the best band in town, stop by The Twilight Room. You won't be disappointed."

As we head once again to the five and dime, I can't stop checking out my reflection in the store windows we pass. I'm wearing the most beautiful cloche in the history of the world. Dot says its midnight blue color brings out my eyes and, although Matron Davidson would smack my knuckles with a ruler for my immodesty, I have to agree. It really does. A half inch band of bronze satin edges the curve of the cloche's brim from ear to ear. Four skinny bands sit behind the broader one and another four repeat the pattern nearer the crown. A big bronze and copper feather is pinned at a jaunty angle on the right.

I feel prettier than I ever have in my life. I never *knew* how much fun it could be to shop with friends who only want to laugh and have a good time with you. If I end up following the urge to pack up and move on that started itching at the back of my brain again after my talk with Booker the other night, I will sorely miss The Brasher sisters. *So* much.

Maybe I should talk to Clara and Dot about my impulse to run. Except...

I already know what they'll say. They have been dogged in their insistence I become "more than friends" with Will. Since the one and only time they actually saw him, they have been pushing for this. They think he's the cat's pajamas and simply cannot fathom how a gal can be "just friends" with a fella. According to them, it's unnatural.

But if I can't get them to listen to me when I tell them that will never happen, because Will and I are the best of friends who might as well be brother and sister because we simply do not, and never will, think of each other *that* way—

Well, I certainly can't share with them that Booker and I have resolved our beef. For the most part, at least. The Brasher girls are dyed in the wool romantics and I know darn well they would cast Will aside as my soul mate in a heartbeat in favor of laying odds on my chances with Booker. And as much as I'm starting to...well, not love them dearly exactly, because that is just begging to have my teeth kicked down my throat. But I sure do like and admire them. Okay, I adore them. And I love spending time in their company. I've laughed more with them in the past several weeks than I have in—heck, I can't remember how long, precisely.

It's not as if I've been totally friendless aside from Will. I have gotten to know all kinds of other singers and the nonperforming women who staffed the various dives, bars and lounges I have sung in across the state. I have even been downright friendly with a few. But never have I had an honest to goodness bosom bow type girlfriend. Now suddenly I have two. Two women who are boisterous and fun and outspoken. Really outspoken. These girls definitely have opinions.

If I admit Booker and I are no longer at war, I won't ever, but *ever*, hear the end of the catalog of my so-called possibilities for a crafted just for me happily ever after with the fella. I can't deny part of me gets all atingle at the mere thought of such an outcome. The wiser, battle hardened part of me who barely made it out of my previous relationship with Booker alive, however, knows that particular train left the station a long time ago. And I won't be buying a ticket if it rolls back through again.

Not after having been left battered and bruised...but one heck of a lot savvier than the starry-eyed girl I used to be.

The Twilight Room employs a lot of females. I haven't taken an actual head count or anything, but between the cocktail waitresses, the coat check and cigarette girls, the cleaning ladies, client photographer and the talent, as Leo Stone, the office manager Booker calls Sarge, tends to refer to us stage performers...

Well, add those all up and there is a goodly sized number of us. And Lord knows I have heard these women oohing and ahhing over Booker often enough to realize every woman I work with considers him an ab-so-loot sheik. I doubt a single one of them would understand what a risk it would be for me to think of Booker as anything other than my employer.

Well, *I* grasp the problem for what it is. Long ago I gave Booker Jameson everything I had to give. Wholeheartedly, I did that.

And just look how well it turned out for me.

I adore my singing gig in his club, and I'm due to get fitted for all those lovely, lovely dresses in just a few days. The idea of surrendering either opportunity makes me want to howl like a pack of dogs at the moon. At the same time, I can feel anxiety starting to twine its way up my spine and belly crawl through my innards. It hasn't taken up permanent lodging in either place yet. But it's only a matter of time before it does. Which makes me think maybe I had better consider my options.

Not that I have a wealth of them. The smart money would probably opt to protect myself. To hand in my resignation and get as far away from Booker as I can. He has already warned me he'll blacklist me in this state if I violate the terms of my contract with the club. But I could always try my luck in Chicago or New York. Somewhere, *any*where, I won't run the risk of seeing Booker on the almost every darn day basis I currently do.

And yet—

Will is here. So how smart can it be to travel across the country, leaving behind the best job and closest relationship with other women I have ever had? How clever to place myself a good five plus days by train away from my only time-proven friend?

My good mood is rapidly being taken over by clammy hands and a pounding heart. I need to talk to Will *now*. Looking up the block, I focus in on the clock on the sidewalk in front of Ben Bridge Jeweler. If I leave for Will's apartment right away, I'll have, well, perhaps not adequate, but at least a bit of time before I have to have my bottom planted in my dressing room chair to put myself together for my first set of the evening. Time well spent if Will can help me put my options in order. Or at least talk me off this growing pile of anxiety.

I stop outside Woolworth's door as Clara pulls it open. "I've got something I need to do."

"You're finally going to see Will?" Dot demands. "Now you're on the trolley!"

Darn my thin skin! I can feel the heat and color just beneath it spreading from my chest to my forehead.

"Oooh!" Clara nudges her sister. "She is!"

"But not for the reason you two think!" I shake my head. "One of you has really gotta make a play for him, yourself. Will is never going to be the Sheik to my Sheba. It is just not going to happen."

"Aww, we're just razzin' ya." Clara laughs, then waves goodbye as she and Dot enter the store. I watch for a second as they quickly disappear into its depths.

Moments later, I hop a trolley to Capitol Hill.

I don't have the first idea if my best friend will even be home, but I shrug off the possibility Will might not be. At this point I can only show up and find out. But I think positive thoughts. He often paints this time of day because he likes the late afternoon and early evening light through the northern facing window of the room he uses as a studio.

When I arrive at his brick building a short while later, I climb the stairs to his third floor walkup and rap on the door. I wait, but no one answers. I knock again.

Once again there is no answer. "Come on, c'mon!" This time I pound. But I already know Will is not home and, blowing out a sigh, I rest my forehead against the solid wood of his door. Okay, perhaps that favored northern light is a bit closer to twilight than I cared to admit.

Accepting I won't be receiving the comfort I'd been counting on from my best friend, I slowly straighten. I turn away from the door even more slowly, as though if I procrastinate long enough, he will somehow magically appear.

Quite clearly that is not going to happen, and I finally walk away. On leaden feet, feeling as though I'm forging a path through molasses, I trudge down the hallway, then make my way down the stairs. I prod myself to take one step at a time, one foot after the other, until I find myself out on the street once more.

Where, with a final glance up at Will's darkened window, I turn and start walking toward downtown and The Twilight Room.

11

Creative types move to their own beat

BOOKER

Christ, the woman is slippery! How's a fella supposed to get his girl back when he can't get within ten feet of her?

Since our last conversation several days ago, I have kept my eyes peeled for Lena. Not that my watchfulness has done me any good.

Not a damn bit. Aside from when she's on stage, Lena might as well be a shadow glimpsed from the corner of my eye. By the day after our talk, I'd already lost track of how many times I would have sworn—*sworn!*—I saw her in my peripheral vision. Yet, time after time, the instant I whipped my head around to face that hazy silhouette head-on?

She wasn't there.

Too restless to sit still a moment longer, I shove back from my desk and stand. To hell with this. Tonight is the night. I am through waiting—I'll track Lena down if it takes me the entire damn evening. Filled with renewed determination, I stride out of my office and head toward her dressing room.

When I arrive a minute later, however, no one answers in response to my somewhat overenthusiastic pounding. Opening the door, I peek in, but it's as unoccupied as I anticipated. I pull the door closed again and check the Omega Swiss watch strapped to my wrist. In addition to keeping damn fine time, the watch was a gift to myself the day I opened my club. I smile, because I suppose it's a reminder I am making a success of myself, by myself. The piece is a talisman of sorts.

I know Lena's in the club—I heard her come in with the Brasher sisters while Leo and I were discussing how pleased we are so far with Kusak's, our new glassware vendor. They are a huge improvement over the last one. But my time check also made me realize it's too early for Lena to be getting ready for her shows. She is no doubt visiting with Clara and Dot. Those three have been thick as thieves since Lena's very first night.

I hear laughter from behind the sisters' door as I approach. One giant stride brings me within reach and I give it a good hard rap.

Something I seem to be doing a great deal of tonight.

The laughter on the other side quietens. A second later the dressing room door is whipped open.

Clara blinks up at me for a second, but quickly hides her apparent surprise. "Hey, there, Mr. Jameson. Can I help you with something?"

"Is Lena here?"

She blinks again but immediately composes herself with a shake of her head. "No. She had an engagement."

Denial and rage compete in my gut like a knock down bout between ice and fire. "What?" I demand.

"Well, I s'pose it's not an engagement so much as an...appointment? She said something about meeting with Henry Boggs, anyhow. You know, to talk about one of the new numbers she's introducin' next week?"

"Of course," I agree, ignoring the wash of relief. As it happens, I actually do know something about this. Henry caught me at the tail end of last night's shift. He had a question regarding one of Lena's new songs and wanted permission to talk to her about it. Of course, I agreed. I even joked he didn't need my permission to do his job. I also admitted I appreciated him taking the time to keep me informed.

I might have a slight issue with control when it comes to the Twilight Room. What can I say—I've had my hand in every aspect of the business. Except for the building itself, I have built every bit of it from the ground up. This club is my baby.

Thinking about that conversation now, I acknowledge being kind of surprised at myself. Considering the game of hide and seek Lena's been playing with me, ordinarily I would have already considered ways to capitalize on such an opportunity. As owner, I can sit in on any discussions I damn well want to between my band leader and my singer. Lena can hardly walk away from her appointment without looking unprofessional.

I mentally wince. Because while it's within my rights as the Twilight Room's owner, sitting in just because I want to be near her would be woolly ethics on my part. *I* am the one who insisted we treat each other with professionalism. I'd damn well better honor my decree.

If I'm being honest, though, had I known last night what time Henry meant to meet with her, I can't be a hundred percent certain I wouldn't have horned in on their discussion. Guess I'll just have to live with never knowing if I took the high road...or simply knew Henry hadn't, in all likelihood, had a firm timeline in mind himself when we spoke. I have learned over the years that creative types tend to move to their own beat. More often than not, they work under timelines and deadlines of their own making.

Seeing Clara still looking up at me questioningly—and her sister doing the same from an overstuffed chair deeper inside the dressing room—I drag my attention back on task. "Thanks, Clara. I'll catch up with them backstage."

"You betcha, Mister J."

She was closing the door even as I turned away.

12

Not my usual after-set experience

LENA

"I'm sorry, Henry; I know I should just shut up and agree." Yet I can't seem to force myself to do just that. Instead, with a sense of urgency I lean in, reaching out to touch his arm. For a good fifteen minutes now, the two of us have been arguing about the single line change I want to make in a song I had quickly sung for him last night.

Heaven knows, the band leader has probably forgotten more about music than I will likely ever know. Still, I desperately want him to say yes to my version. "I hate fighting with you, because I so admire your work. But I just can't seem to accept no for an answer. Please. Listen one more time." I sing the contested phrasing again, making it drop low for the last few bars where the original song ended on a higher note.

I didn't even know those things had specific names until Henry told me what I was talking about were a major fall and minor lift. Accordingly, when he sits now with his eyes closed, I don't interrupt. The band leader deserves my respect. He is always willing to answer my questions and has been teaching me the names of techniques I have picked up over the years spent listening to others.

Finally, when I can't stand the suspense a moment longer, I cross my fingers hopefully, even though I have sung the same section the same way several times already. I try not to sound wheedling when I ask, "Can't you see it's more dramatic?"

He cracks an eyelid. "I do see it, Lena, and personally I love the change. So maybe we should take this to Booker. It's a cover of a popular song—and one thing I know about popular songs is changing one in any way can blow up in our faces. Folks tend to get testy when their favorite tunes are sung differently from what they expect to hear."

"I know. I honestly do understand the risk we take." And God knows the last thing I wanna do is involve Booker. If I have to, however, I will. Because... "I also believe with all my heart *this* is the part our audience will find themselves humming instead of the popular version." *I* sure as the dickens can't seem to get it out of my head.

"She's right," a deep voice says behind me, and a bolt of lightning zings through me, searing my nerve endings. I whip around in my seat.

Booker is standing on the edge of stage left, not far from where Henry and I have been sitting on a couple of chairs we'd dragged behind the backstage scenery so we could hash out the details of this song with at least an illusion of privacy.

"I am?" I blurt, caught by surprise. Booker is agreeing with *me*?

His eyebrows raise. "Have you changed your mind about the drop?"

"*No!* Of course not. It's definitely the direction we should go in. I guess I just never thought *you* would agree with me over Henry." Heat crawls up my face. "That is—Henry has a lot more experience than I do in the business, and he knows all the right terminology and reads music and whatnot."

"While you," Henry responds, "have a passion and natural affinity for music that transcends mere music education."

Electrified, I beam at him. "I do? It *does*? Transcend means... to rise above?"

"Yes, or go beyond." Henry grins and reaches into his shirt pocket for a cigarette.

"He's right, you do," Booker agrees. "The change you fought for is a perfect example. It's unexpected, and that's exactly the type of thing the audience you've been drawing in with increasing numbers every night has come to expect from you."

I beam at him as well, thrilled right down to my toes with the compliment.

For a moment, however, I'm not sure he even notices. He has a funny, faraway expression that makes me think he might be looking inward. Slowly, he murmurs, "*Expect the unexpected.*" His eyes sharpen and he grins back at me. "I think that would look damn eye catching on a reinforced poster on an easel board outside the club. Something crisp and clean—maybe just Lola Baker in big letters and a photo of you with the tagline under it."

"Oh, *my*. Really?" A big poster featuring *me*? The mere thought tickles my heart. It sounds so glamorous. Like I'm some kind of celebrity or something.

"Yes. We'll need to get a new photo done of you, though. The one you gave Leo doesn't have enough clarity, so let's see if Elsie can capture a live shot of you singing," Booker says, naming the woman he pays to roam the Twilight Room taking photos of and selling to the speakeasy clients.

"Could we wait for one of the new gowns to be completed?" I ask hesitantly. Booker's already offering so much, I know shouldn't ask for anything extra. But...the dresses!

"Yeah, sure, not a problem. We'll start with the candid shots. If those don't work out, we'll have you sit for Elsie." He turns to Henry. "So, how much work is this change going to cost you?"

Henry lights his cigarette and shrugs. "Not that much. I have to change the sheet music in one spot, but that's a matter of minutes. If I had to hand print a copy for each of the fellas it would be more labor intensive. Lucky for us, I only need one for myself." He favors me and

Booker with an engagingly lopsided smile. "My band is a lot like Lena, here. They're short on education in music theory, history and composition, but long on talent and intuition. Most times I only need to play changes for them once and they're on the trolley."

He turns to me. "I'll leave you in Booker's hands and go talk to the boys. You two don't need my input to hammer out details for his promotional idea." He rises to his feet, then pauses mid step to look down at me.

"You did good today, kid, fighting like a demon for your vision. Don't ever be afraid to do it again exactly the way you did with me. You refused to give ground, regardless what you believed about your music education versus mine. Your willingness to stand your ground for something you believe in that strongly is part of what makes you such a good musician."

I probably look like an imbecile, standing here with my hands clasped together atop my breasts and giving him a huge, goofy smile. I am just so awed, so delighted, I can't help myself.

Booker laughs and gives me a nudge. "Come on. Let's go to my office and discuss my promotional idea."

"Okay." But glimpsing the position of the hands on his watch, I make a sound of disappointment. "Ohhh! I can't. I need to get ready."

He glances at his timepiece as well. "I guess you do. How about we have a drink after your final set and discuss it then?"

My practical side says no. The less time I spend in Booker's company the better. And yet...a poster. On an easel. Featuring me, as if I'm some big star like Blossom Seeley or Bessie Smith! In a brand new, tailored specifically for my body gown. "Okay."

"Good. Meet me at my table after your last set."

A few hours later, as I make my way to Booker's table at the corner of the dance floor, I find myself half nervous, half excited. To my surprise, several people stop me as I weave through the packed tables. This is not my usual after-set experience. And it is one I'm not quite certain how to handle, since ordinarily I head straight to my dressing room to change into street clothes after my last set. I do my best, however, and eventually make it to Booker's table slightly breathless, but a survivor of my first tiny brush with fame.

Pushing aside a folder on the tabletop in front of him, he rises to his feet and holds the chair he vacated for me to take. I murmur a *thank you* as we navigate the sit, but not quite until he pushes in the chair dance I always find so awkward. The seat is warm from his body heat, however, and in the oddest way comforting.

Booker, of course, is cool as a cucumber as he negligently raises a finger to summon Millie and pulls out the chair on the left side of the table for himself. He sits, then turns his attention back to me, sliding a comprehensive glance over my face and what he can see of my upper body. After taking his sweet time about it, he treats me to a downright wolfish smile.

What the heck is he up to? Whatever it is, it's working.

Because, just like that, my vague irritation with him turns into something more heated. Something far more dangerous to my peace of mind. Good Lord. It has been years and years—nine, to be precise—since I have experienced this delicious feeling deep between my legs in the company of a man. Crossing them, I squeeze my upper thighs together in an attempt to dispel it.

Without noticeable success, unfortunately. "You didn't have to give me your chair. I know this is your regular seat."

He shrugs a tuxedo clad shoulder. "It will give you a better view of the stage."

Tearing my gaze away from the one he's pinned on mine, I look out at the floor in front of us, which is rapidly filling with dancers.

"I see you garnered some admirers on your way across the room," he says beneath the sound of the band playing a foxtrot.

Dancers circle the floor and I pull my fascinated glance away from the grace and style of one couple in particular. It is not easy, though, because my *gosh!* They could give Fred and Adele Astaire a run for their money! Warning myself to stay on track, I replay Booker's comment in my head. *Admirers. Stopping me to talk.*

"I did," I finally say. "I don't know how well I handled the attention, though, since being recognized by someone who isn't the usual half-drunk barfly is sort of new to me. I do know I was a bit clumsy at freeing myself from some of the conversations."

"Just thank them for the compliment and sign an autograph if one's requested, on whatever they thrust your way." He sits straighter. "Unless it's my good linens. If anyone offers one of the napkins for an autograph, do me a favor and tell them you don't feel comfortable ruining the club's linens."

I choke on a little laugh, but have a feeling he's only half kidding.

"Then move on," Booker continues. "You have no obligation to become entangled in a series of rambling conversations."

"Easier said than done," I mutter.

"Here's a tip for you. Keep your objective in sight—it helps move you past people without allowing them to catch your eye."

"Except tonight several people called me by name." Or at least the stage name I'd chosen. I'm still a little unnerved and a lot delighted by it. I try to not to let either emotion show on my face. "It's kinda hard to ignore."

"It is more difficult, yes. Sometimes you don't have the time or inclination to stop, though. If that's the case, give them a nod and your best smile, but keep moving toward your objective." Suddenly Booker grins. "Which in this case was me." He stabs the folder with the tip of one long finger and drags it between us. "I worked up a rough draft of what I'd like to see on your poster."

I sit taller in eager anticipation, but Millie arrives at the table before I can reach for the binder. "Hello, I'm Millie, your waitress," she says, shooting me a cheeky smile. "What may I get the lady and gentleman this evening?"

Booker raises his eyebrows at me and I order a Mary Pickford as if it's an everyday event.

"Good choice, doll." Millie turns to Booker. "Would you like your usual, Mr. Jameson?"

"Yes. Thanks, Millie."

She gives him a wink, then sashays off.

He turns to me. "Why am I not surprised you like your drinks sweet." It's not a question and if his crooked smile is anything to go by, he's quite amused by me.

I shrug and answer honestly. "I'm not wild about the taste of most booze. The pineapple and maraschino cherry juice helps disguise it. Plus, I have a sweet tooth, so I just plain like it." Having given up any embarrassment over my lack of palate a long time ago, I reach for the folder. "I'm dying to see what you came up with," I admit and flip it open.

"I'm far from an artist, so it's rough," Booker warns as he hitches his chair closer to the corner of the table nearest my seat and leans in. He moves the paper so it mostly faces me, but is slightly angled to give him a not entirely sideways view, as well. "The finished product will be twenty-four by thirty-six inches. I thought we'd do the background in a deep red and use the same bright gold lettering that spells out the name of the lounge on the awning. Maybe use the color in a border as well. Then it's pretty much as I described it earlier. Lola Baker across the top here in large lettering, then your headshot placed at a slight angle, with the tagline beneath that."

"Expect the unexpected," I murmur. And smile hugely as the ramification of what Booker is doing here fills me. Will has supported me from the moment I decided this was what I wanted to do with my life. But as much as he believes in my talent, he doesn't truly understand how the variables in this business can make or break a singer's chance of success.

Booker knows. He also clearly cares about the bottom line. So, if he's willing to bestow these perks on me: the dresses, the poster, I have to believe he thinks I'm going places.

Lord above, how I've searched for this exact vala...valad— someone to tell me he believes the same thing I do. For years, I have longed for an assurance I am dead right to follow the little voice in my head whispering this is not a pipe dream I'm chasing. That I am *not* wasting my time on something that is long on wishful thinking and short on reality.

And Booker just handed it to me on a silver platter. No one can take the excitement of this moment away from me.

Millie brings our drinks as the dancers vacate the floor, and I watch from the corner of my eye to see what kind of a tipper Booker is. As someone who has cocktailed while waiting to get hired as a singer, I'm pleased to note he's a generous one. Then Henry leans into the mic to announce the Brasher Sisters and I clap in delight as they dance out onto the stage.

While I have seen them dance dozens of times by now, it has always been from the wings. Never have I watched their performance as a part of the audience. This whole sitting at a premier table with the club owner, sipping a fabulous, fancy cocktail while watching the entertainment the way a paying guest would do is even better. And so much fun.

Heck, who am I kidding? *Fun* is far too pale a word. Sitting here like one of the swells is utterly *marvelous!*

I have been mesmerized by Dot and Clara's talent from my very first night here. I didn't think I could possibly find it even more enthralling, yet seeing them now from almost center stage I find I do.

Their second dance is a hysterical routine where Clara acts as if she can't master the steps Dot shows her, and I laugh uproariously. When they finish with a flourish of amazing footwork, I clap and clap until my hands bloom with heat. Smiling hugely, I turn to Booker as Henry launches the band into a soft rendition of The Original Memphis Five's *Henpecked Blues*. "Aren't they just the most *talented* women you have ever met?" I sigh happily. "You were so smart to hire them."

He studies me with an expression I can't quite make out. "They are definitely brimming with talent," he agrees.

I feel amazingly comfortable with him for the first time since the old days in Walla Walla. Planting my elbow on the table, I prop my chin in my hand. "Whatever made you decide to open a club like this? It suits you—but it is definitely not anything I ever heard you mention back when I knew you."

A faint shadow crosses his eyes, but perhaps it's my imagination, for he flashes me an easy smile and says, "I worked in a couple of clubs in Paris, made my way into management, then eventually had the opportunity to buy the last club I managed. When I decided to come home I was lucky to sell it for a high enough price not to have to ask my father's help in opening this one. The old man has made no bones about how he feels when it comes to my speakeasy."

"Ah, well," I say. "It's good to earn stuff for yourself, anyway."

His eyes light up. "Yes! It is." He reaches across the table and picks up my hand, his thumb lightly rubbing the tips of my fingers.

I feel the effects down to my *toes*, for pity's sake, and have to concentrate like crazy when he continues, "It means so much more than having it handed to you."

Then his gaze drops to my mouth and I watch his eyelids go heavy. He leans into me.

Oh, my God! Is he going to *kiss* me? In front of all these people, including those I *work* with?

I push to my feet and nearly trip over them trying to step away from the table. "Thank you so much for the drink and showing me what you're going to do with my poster," I say breathlessly. "I think it's going to be the most darb thing ever. I really have to run, though." Without another word, I whirl on my shoe's kitten heel, then try like the dickens to saunter away nonchalantly.

It shouldn't be so difficult to do. All I should really want is to run away as fast as I possibly can. Instead I feel a huge, shameful, yet nearly overriding, desire to throw myself into Booker's arms.

What the devil is the matter with me? Have I not learned a damn thing?

13

She has breasts. Work with them.

BOOKER

"Goodness, gracious, Agnes. What are *you* doing here?"

I set aside the folder full of paperwork I've been trying to work my way through while perched on this uncomfortable as hell, fussy little chair. A snooty Frederick and Nelson saleslady installed me in it maybe ten minutes ago, then left me to it when I requested privacy to work.

Does it compare with my office? No, not by a long shot. But the well-designed alcove outside the ladies' dressing rooms is workable for the short haul. It's fairly roomy and almost private. At this moment that equates to me, a table almost too small to qualify for the title, another ornate little chair and a large triptych of full-length cheval mirrors. And while the lighting is designed to flatter women, and consequently is not as bright as it could be, it's getting the job done.

Watching Lena approach, I'm sidetracked for a moment by that lush body in motion. Tearing my gaze away sooner than I like from the jiggle of her breasts and swivel of her hips, I check out her expression.

She doesn't look real happy to see me.

Well, too bad. I rise to my feet. Answer her question. "Exactly what it looks like. Approving the gowns you selected and overseeing their tailoring."

"I don't need supervision to buy a few gowns!"

"And yet it's my money paying for them. My club we're outfitting you for. Haven't you figured out by now I have my fingers in every damn aspect of The Twilight Room?"

Lena makes a face at me, but quicker than I would have given her credit for, she smooths the irritation from her expression. In a voice lacking the slightest hint of preaching, she merely says mildly, "You swear too much."

"One 'damn' is hardly excessive."

I swear I can hear the sigh she doesn't sigh. But once more her tone is even when she says, "I'm talking about the overall collection I've heard since my employment began." She raises delicate eyebrows at me. "Don't forget in order to get almost anywhere from my dressing room, I have to pass your office."

I scrub a hand over my face and nod. "In that case, you may have a point. The US Army is proficient at teaching a guy an impressive range of swear words."

She blows out a *pffft* that is amazingly skeptical for such a brief, breathy non-word. "*Please.* Don't you go blaming Uncle Sam for your unfortunate vocabulary. You forget I was there when you and Will swore your way from one end of Walla Walla to the other. And that, Mister, was *long* before you joined the Army."

Her pithy observation startles a big belly laugh out of me. I give her a nod once I regain control. "Okay, you've got me there."

Before I can take the step in Lena's direction my impulses are urging, a different woman from the one who brought me back here trundles a rack into the alcove. More than five dresses hang from its top bar, I notice. In addition, stacks of boxes in various shapes and sizes cover the bottom shelf. She drapes a cloth measuring tape around her neck and turns to us.

"Good day, Mr. Jameson," she says, looking at me before turning to Lena. "And you must be Miss Baker. Thank you for choosing Frederick and Nelson for your wardrobe needs. My name is Alice. I will be your floor lady and seamstress this afternoon." She gestures toward the chairs. "Please. Make yourselves comfortable."

I motion for Lena to sit, then pick up the folder from my own seat and settle in with it balanced on my lap.

Alice unclips pince-nez glasses from a brooch designed to hold the armless spectacles when they aren't being worn and pinches them in place. "Allow me to first show you the gowns Miss Baker has chosen." Meeting my gaze, she waves a languid hand at the rack. "As you can see, I brought a few extras in case her choices aren't precisely what you had in mind. I understand Miss Baker is a singer in your lounge?"

"She is. You should drop by the Twilight Room some night to hear her. She's amazing."

Lena gives me a pleased smile, but for all the attention the saleswoman pays my invitation as she rattles through the padded hangers, I may as well not have spoken. She selects a navy gown scattered with gold and silver stars of various sizes that appear to be sewn on, then beaded. The theme carries out in additional clusters of tiny beads that show like constellations against a midnight sky.

Alice opens the closest dressing room door and hangs the gown on a hook inside. She returns to the rack and rummages through the stacks until she locates the box she seeks. She hands it to Lena. "Here you go, Miss Baker. This bandeau binder will make the gown hang correctly—and is more comfortable than binding yourself with bandages."

"Oh, hell no." I jerk upright in my stupid little chair, knocking the already forgotten folder on my lap onto the floor. Papers spill out and strew in a dozen different directions. When Alice starts to stoop to pick up the ones at her feet, I wave her off. "I will not see Lena strapped down until she looks like a boy. She has breasts. Work with them."

Blinking, the tailor turns to Lena. "I thought your name was Lola."

"Lola is my stage name." Lena gives Alice a little smile and an even smaller shrug. "I used it to hold the dresses, since they're for work. My real name is Lena."

"I like it. It's even prettier than Lola," Alice says, for the first time sounding halfway human. I had forgotten that about Lena, how proficient she was at charming uptight people into loosening their grip on the stick up their rears. "Did you wear a binder to try this on?"

Lena nods. "The saleswoman insisted."

Alice turns back to me. "Then I am not at all certain this size will work."

I manage to say calmly, "If it doesn't, find her one that will and tailor what's necessary to make it fit." It takes effort to swallow my impatience, but Jesus. It's not like I'm asking the woman to figure out how radio waves cause voices to emerge from her Atwater Kent.

Alice does that sigh thing women have perfected over the years to let a fellow know he's an idiot. But she gives Lena a deferential smile, which also looks genuinely friendly. "This way, Miss. I have you set up in Room One."

When they disappear into the room, I pick up the scattered papers, restore them in their proper order to my folder and go back to work. I sign a contract with the new glassware vendor Sarge found down on Rainier Avenue. Kusak's Cut Glass Works has been supplying stemware to Frederick and Nelson for twelve years.

"And, hey, if it's good enough for Frederick's," I murmur, then chuckle. Because, talk about stating the obvious.

Seeing as how I'm sitting in the middle of the damn store, prepared to drop a bundle on gowns for my singer.

The real reason, however, is that we've already bought an order from Kusak's on a trial basis and both Sarge and I were very impressed.

I've dashed off a quick check from my personal checkbook to my favorite charity and am in the midst of pouring over recipes for some of the recent cocktails gaining in popularity when Lena comes out of the room again.

Glancing up, I freeze. Then, without looking, I set my folder on the tiny table, and don't even blink when it promptly falls on floor, once again scattering my papers. "Now, *that* is what I'm talking about," I murmur.

The dress is cut straight across the tops of her breasts, and would have had nothing to display if I had allowed Alice to bind them. As it is, the fit, while flattening Lena's natural curves somewhat, has more than made up for it by the resultant mouthwatering cleavage shoved above the neckline.

The rest of the ankle length dress hangs straight. The center, however, is cut up to just below the knees in a slightly M-shaped hemline that is partially filled with fringe to give it additional flare. The straps keeping the dress up are formed by sheer panels of inverted V-shaped fabric. And a series of little eighth-inch ribbons wrap the entire length of her left arm, connecting another sheer, spider-web type contraption sewn into the side seam of the gown.

"Raise your arm," I instruct.

Lena sweeps it up and to the side with a theatrical flourish, displaying an abbreviated one-sided butterfly effect.

"Ho-ly shit," I whisper and bend for the folder to set it back on my lap. "You look absolutely—" *Good enough to eat. Downright juicy* "—gorgeous."

She beams at me. "Isn't it the prettiest?"

"The dress is stunning," I agree. "You did a grand job selecting it. But Lena, it's you. You are the one who makes the dress. Not visa versa."

"I heartily concur," Alice says. "And Mr. Jameson, you were correct in not binding her. Lena's natural curves in the straight lines of this dress are a refreshing change from the boyish silhouette so prevalent today. She looks very womanly without appearing the least bit trashy."

"*Yes*. Well stated, Alice—that is exactly the look I was going for." I smile at the tailor and sit back. "So, what's next?"

14

Smoldering like a banked fire

LENA

W ith each new gown I try on, it becomes a little harder to walk out into the alcove and parade it in front of Booker. If I were a gold digger, this would be one of the best days of my life.

I muffle a snort. Who am I fooling? This is a darn fine day, regardless. I have to pinch myself to make sure I'm not dreaming. To make myself believe all these gowns, each one of which seems even more impossibly beautiful than the one before, are going to be *mine*.

I never owned a single piece of clothing that wasn't a hand me down before I left the B of C foundling home. For the longest time after, it still remained a rare day I could afford to buy anything new. And when I did manage to save up the funds, it was a single ready-made purchase at a time, unless I was buying staples like soap or toothpaste.

It never occurred to me to expect more.

Over the years, I've studied other singers I admire. And one of the things that's jumped out at me from the beginning is how each one has her own style. Not merely their singing style; they all seemed to have their own fashion—oh, beans, what, what, what is the French word the fashion writers like to use?—*panache* as well. I watched the way their selections helped set them apart. How it imbued a status that drew the audience's attention.

It took me a while to find what worked for me. Having grown up with the austere uniforms of the Blood of Christ, I had a heck of a time with the first few dresses I was handed to wear onstage. I will never forget the very first one. It was a cheap, used gown cut low on top and high on the hem. Having spent most of my life up until then covered from neck to ankle, I broke out in horrid red blotches upon seeing myself in the mirror. Then I used so much powder trying to cover the redness up, I could barely sing that night for inhaling the clouds of talc it put into the air every time I moved. But when I protested to the manager after the show, I was told to take it or leave it, because my choices were simple. I could wear the gown, or I could look for a new job.

I love to sing—and even more to eat—so I wore the gown.

Breaking into this business is a huge, on-going learning experience, but luckily I have always liked learning new things. The lesson that paid off the most was giving in to the spirit of a tune. I came to understand each song needs adjustments, because the emotional tone of music changes between one melody and the next. And each tone calls for a different...presentation, I believe the word is, which also varies from song to song. I get to play a wide range of roles onstage, depending on what I sing. Roles that range from earthy, to vamp, to angel, to tease. Every single one has the ability to take me out of myself. I love that.

Up until now, I had exactly two stage-worthy dresses of my own to play all the different roles. Still, sewing is something we did a lot of in the foundling home, so while I have rarely been able to afford enough fabric for a dress, I can almost always find remnants on the cheap. From those, I've made a variety of accessories to change things up. To give the gowns different looks that add believability to each role. Over the seven years I've been doing this I have gotten pretty darn good at making my two gowns—three, after last year at the Tropic—do the work of ten.

Now here I am, about to be the proud owner of not one, not two, but *five* brand new gowns! *New* is not a word I get to use often. And that doesn't take into account the sheer number of accessories Alice keeps pulling from her never ending stacks of boxes. She has affixed fancy little hair bands and cloches on my head, has tugged long, silky gloves up my arms. She's attached jewelry to my ears and around my neck and wrists. All to demonstrate to Booker how the pieces complete the look of the gown of the moment.

And he keeps giving the majority of them the nod.

So, yes, this is far beyond anything I could ever have imagined.

Yet, thrilled as I am with all this bounty, Booker is turning me into a nervous wreck. Okay, not a wreck, precisely. And nervous isn't the correct word I'm searching for, either.

But I know this much. Booker is making me edgy. *Aware.* God, so *aware.* Of what exactly, I'm not quite sure. But I am definitely aware of him.

Maybe it's because he's dressed less formally than usual. Instead of his usual bespoke suits, today Booker has on a white collarless shirt, tweed slacks and suspenders. And his shirtsleeves are rolled up. I don't know why I'm so fascinated by the sight of his strong forearms and hands, but they definitely have my steadfast attention. Maybe it has to do with the way the former is feathered with dark hair. He usually looks elegant and sophisticated. Today he looks... Rugged. Physically competent. And, oh, my.

So darn *male.*

It's likely this virility that has me on edge. And it was made worse the last time I came out by the way he crossed his hands behind his head, his elbows and strong thighs spread wide as he leaned back in that undersized chair they've put him on. Well, that male display in addition to the fact there is simply something about the way he sits there looking me over every time I model a new gown. Something unnerving—and a little bit titillating. Because, that *look.*

I swear, it's as if he's The Sheik and I'm the fair Englishwoman he's contemplating sweeping onto his horse and spiriting away to his tribal home in the desert.

"Oh, for gosh sake, Lena!" I mutter under my breath—and beneath the tenting of the gown currently covering my head while Alice cautiously maneuvers its skirt down my body. "Can you *be* any more fanciful?"

"What's that, miss?" Alice asks around the pins in her mouth as she clears the fabric from my face. Plucking them from her lips, she returns them to their nearly empty little case. They are all that is left after she used the rest for the two adjustments Booker asked her to make in this gown.

Or, more like decreed. Which plays into this stupid, yet nevertheless persistent, Sheik imagery playing in my head. But not nearly as much as the manner in which Booker has been smoldering like a fire banked, yet still a long, long way from extinguished.

"Oh, for—" I fling these silly thoughts aside as Alice lowers the rest of the dress into place. "It was nothing really," I reply. "Sorry, I'm just talking to myself." I shake my head. "I'm afraid I do that far too often."

Alice's face lights up. "As do I! When someone catches me at it, I simply admit to what I've done, then say it was a mighty fine conversation."

A tickled laugh bursts from my throat and I beam at the other woman in delight. "Oh, I will have to remember that the next time someone catches me having a 'mighty fine conversation' with myself."

Over the course of my appointment here, Booker has put the kibosh on two of the dresses I selected ahead of time. Or I guess one and a half would be a more accurate description at this point. The first was a pale pink number I'd chosen, which he pronounced an unflattering shade that washed me out. The current gown, whose fit Alice is carefully adjusting so as not to prick me where she's pinned it, is the last of the extras she originally included. Booker vetoed it as well, then changed his mind and asked her for these adjustments and to show him again. After a moment of fluffing and straightening its fit here and there, she sends me out again.

I walk right into that look again. His gaze covers me from neck to ankle, then slowly climbs back up again, pausing on some exceedingly personal territory on its way. When it reaches my face, he shakes his head. "No."

Just no. I blow out an exasperated breath and stalk back into the dressing room. Where I close the door behind me perhaps a little harder than I needed to.

Alice helps me out of it again and hangs it on the door hook. Then she gathers the final dress, the one she made a special trip to collect after telling Booker she thought she had something he would very much like in light of the direction he has taken us this afternoon.

She stoops to pool the hem of the gown's short train on the floor in front of me and lowers the skirt portion atop it. Keeping hold of the bodice's short sleeves and a couple straps whose use I can't quite figure out, she manages to further drop the gown enough for me to step into the space she arranged in the middle without treading on the fabric. Somehow, she simultaneously prevents the entire gown from forming a big black and tan puddle atop the dressing room carpet.

Once she has me lined up with the way she's lain everything out, she slowly works the dress up my body. The first stop is at my waist, which it turns out has a cunningly disguised side zipper where the gown's black bodice meets its golden-tan, sparsely patterned skirt. When she zips it up, it fits my hips like a glove before flowing to the floor in a widening A shape that rounds into a small train in the back. The black top has a fairly modest V in front once the sides are wrapped first across one breast and tied at the waist on the opposite side, then repeated on the other. It gaps a bit until Alice lifts the two black straps I wondered about. They attach to either side of the neckline, and Alice crisscrosses them over my chest, then lays them over my shoulders. Moving behind me, she crosses them again and fastens each band to the opposite side of the deep V in back. She also fastens a thin beaded chain across the widest, upper portion of the V.

Then she turns me toward the narrow full length mirror behind me.

"Oh." I stare at my reflection. "Oh, *my!*"

In all honesty, this dress probably has more fabric than most of those I've tried on today. It has short fluttery sleeves, the V in front isn't all that deep and it contains no sheer illusion fabric to show my legs from my ankles to above my knees like in the gold dress Booker approved.

And yet...

My God. *And yet.* "Oh, my," I whisper again.

"Wait here a moment," Alice whispers back and steps out of the dressing room, leaving the door slightly ajar.

"Mr. Jameson," I hear her say. "Before I have Lena step out, I would just like to say this dress is quite different from the rest we have had her model today. It is not, perhaps, as up-to-date as the rest. Or perhaps it's the vanguard of the next big thing—I'm not really certain. All I know is, it hasn't been our biggest seller precisely because it isn't in the boyish style currently so popular. I, of course, believe that is the very thing you will like about it." Alice raises her voice. "Lena? Come out, please."

Taking a final look at myself in the mirror, I raise my chin, then turn around.

And darned if I don't throw a little extra swing in my hips as I saunter into the alcove.

15

She could bring one of those eunuchs to his knees

BOOKER

Lena strolls out of the dressing room and my heart stops. The damn thing literally *stops*—I am ninety-damn-nine percent sure of it—before picking up again at an elevated rate.

"Fuuuck," I breathe, then glance guiltily at the women. Luckily, neither appears to have heard me. But Christ on a cracker. That gown, on that body...?

I am pretty sure it could bring one of those eunuchs I've read about in the Orient to his knees. Couldn't elicit an erection out of the poor buggers, since they've been uniformly castrated. But in all other ways, I'm betting Lena would have them at her feet.

The front of her gown by all accounts should appear modest. And yet the slight V between Lena's breasts displays a hint of their inside curves. Then there are the narrow black straps, contrasting starkly against her pale skin as they rise out of the wrapped front to bisect her breasts' gentle upper curves, as well as the sweep of her chest and delicate collarbones. And nothing can disguise the fact those beautiful breasts are unrestrained beneath the top, not one damn millimeter of them constricted by artificial means.

Then there's her hips. I draw a loop in the air with my index finger. "Turn in a circle for me." I lick my bottom lip and my voice involuntarily drops to a lower register when I add, "Slowly."

She does and I suck in a breath. The back of her gown is all but nonexistent. The long, smooth trench of her spine points the way to hips and an ass that take my breath away. Both are deliciously rounded, a fact highlighted by curve hugging fabric and the stylistic leaf-like patterns curving over portions of them. There is also some zig-zag border thing going on that frames the splendid anatomy and the occasional black diamond shape in the soft folds draping to the floor from where the material widens beneath her butt. But while I'm sure the additional flourishes add to the total appeal, I don't give them more than a cursory glance except for where they emphasize Lena's curves.

I have only done this gown thing for two other singers, and then only allotted two dresses each, since the rise in business wasn't as remarkable as it has been with Lena. Okay, maybe the fact Lena has been given damn few, if any, pretties in her life factored in to my decision. But only by one gown. Maybe two.

The point is, I sat in on the other singers' fittings as well. It's just good business. I know what I want for my club and the best way to get it is to direct it from start to finish.

But this is the only time I have ever sat shifting in my chair, hiding a damn hard-on at every little glimpse of skin. Every womanly curve. How the hell has my control been reduced to the level of a fourteen-year-old boy's?

"This one definitely," I say and wave Lena back to the dressing room. Not until the door clicks shut behind her, do I draw a full breath. My brain is not currently firing on all cylinders, but I know one thing for sure. Come hell or high water, I am getting Lena back.

Back in my life.

In my bed.

16

We thought the joint was on fire!

BOOKER

Lena's final fitting was yesterday and the department store just delivered the dresses to my office. As the delivery man walks away, I spot Roger, one of my stage crew, passing by and call out.

He sticks his head in the doorway. "What can I do fer ya, boss?"

Roger is a big, burly fella and I indicate the large, bulky package sitting on my desk. "This just came for Lola. Take it to her dressing room for me, will you?"

"Sure thing." He swings the awkwardly shaped if not particularly heavy package up to balance atop his beefy shoulder and heads out. Figuring that's that, I'm displeased to discover I can't seem to settle down. The numbers on the ledger page in front of me just look like so many squiggles. After a few minutes tick by with no improvement, I head toward Lena's dressing room as well, berating myself all the way.

I'm losing my edge. Here I had another golden opportunity to present myself to Lena in a positive light. And what did I do instead?

Sent Roger to deliver her gowns instead of taking them to her myself! "You're not exactly genius material, Jameson," I mutter as I charge down the hall. Maybe I should have attended university after all.

I'm approaching the corner where my hallway T's with the corridor hosting the dressing rooms when I hear Lena yelling the Brasher girls' names. Poking my head around the wall, I see her running down the hallway. I grin, both at her enthusiasm and because she runs like a girl, all legs and coltish technique, her arms and hands inefficiently flailing. She is still shouting Clara and Dot's names in urgent tones as she directs them to "Come on, come on, *get out here!*"

They do, but probably not in the manner Lena expects. They bolt out into the hallway though their dressing room door. Both women are wild-eyed as they jerkily try to look everywhere at once to get a take on their surroundings.

When they find the passage empty—and threat free, I'd wager—Dot stops dead. Hands on her hips, foot tapping an impatient, rapid tattoo, she hones in on her friend. "What the hell, Lena? We thought the joint was on fire!"

"No, that would be me! One look at me tonight in one of my new gowns and the audience is gonna be running for the fire extinguishers to make sure I don't go up in flames, I'll look so hot!"

I can hear the laughter, the pure joy, in her voice. It makes something warm and satisfied expand in my chest, just like it did the night she had drinks with me at my table. Her open joy with me then, simply because I had supported the change in her song she'd been damn right in wanting, had been a treat to see. And there had been something moving about her pure delight with Dot and Clara's dancing and the band and the proposed poster and—well, bloody near everything, really.

The sisters whoop their delight. Deciding to take that as my cue to cut my losses before I'm caught eavesdropping, I pull my head back behind the wall where the hallways intersect. Feeling more grounded even though I didn't get to talk to Lena, I head back to my office.

Barely have I traveled more than a couple of steps, however, when I hear Clara say, "Well, let's go see 'em. We'll have to decide which one you wear one tonight when we go out dancing."

I stop dead. Lena's going dancing? In one of the dresses *I* provided? My jaw gets so tight my teeth hurt.

"Oh, I doubt Booker would like me wearing one of the new gowns to another speakeasy! He bought them to enhance his club, after all."

"That's my girl," I murmur under my breath.

"He gave them to you, didn't he?" Clara demands.

"Well...yeah."

"Then it seems to me they're yours to wear wherever you wanna. You said it was in your contract."

Huh? I retrace my steps to look around the corner again. There wasn't anything in the contract about—

"Oh, not the wearing them part," Clara clarifies as if she'd read my mind and makes an erasing gesture with her right hand. "I'm talking about Mr. Jameson providing them in return for you upping the sales here. That pretty much makes it a straight-up barter in my book. Which, in turn, makes them yours to do with whatever you want."

"Don't listen to her," Dot chimes in. "I vote for you wearing something not quite so glam. We're goin' to a club that draws a lot of the officers and pilots from the new Naval Air Station at Sand Point. My plan is for *me* to wow them. Your attention-grabbin' bubbies can steal my thunder at the best of times." She pokes Lena's left breast. "I certainly don't need them all decked out in a slinky dress on top of it."

Oh, hell, no! Damned if I'll allow Lena to surround herself with a bunch of fly boys.

I wince. Because *allow* might not be the word I want to use—at least not to her face. Pulling back into my own corridor again, I thunk my head against the wall. Slow and measured, once, twice, three times I tap my forehead against it. What else is a fella to do? I sure as hell can't think of a single good outcome should Lena ever hear me linking that word to her.

"Oh, you don't have to worry about me," Lena says and I strain to hear, because it sounds as if they're walking away.

But that doesn't make sense. Lena's room is closer to this end of the hallway than the sisters' is. Then I shrug. For all I know they just decided to lower their voices for privacy. And the bottom line is: I want to hear. Stiff-arming myself away from the wall, I step back to the edge of the intersection again.

"I invited Will to join us," Lena is saying. "Trust me when I tell you the big palooka is worse than an older brother when it comes to men throwing lines my way. Still, he'll drive! He said he'll meet us out front. I'm guessing we'll go out together, but if for some reason we don't, look for an old black Ford. And, please. My breasts aren't *that* attention grabbing."

I snort and hear Dot say, "Yeah, they pretty much are. They might not be in fashion, but men just love the bejebers out of bubs like yours."

Hard to argue with that. I can't say I'm happy at the thought of other men admiring Lena's breasts, though. Even if I kind of counted on their appeal when we were arranging her gowns with Alice. But that was for impact from the stage, not up close.

Up close those beauties are off limits.

Just before I hear a door close, I hear and the muted murmur of voices and realize the women must have gone into Lena's dressing room. I hear a muffled, "Oh, my Gawd!" in thrilled tones. Laughing out loud, I head back to my office. I need to find out what club Dot was talking about.

Because, if Will's going to be there with Lena, I damn well plan on showing up, as well.

You did good, kid

LENA, later that evening

Lord above, it's been almost a half an hour since I finished my last set and I swear I can *still* feel the blood hissing through my veins like so many champagne bubbles. I've been practically beside myself with exhilaration ever since I left the stage. It added an extra little swing to my hips that still has me darn near strutting.

I can't honestly claim I'm shocked by my excitement. Tonight has been so much fun. For my performances, I picked the tan and black, form-fitting, low backed gown to wear. And if sliding into *that* hadn't been breath-stealing enough on its own, I also wore all the accessories Frederick and Nelson's Alice had selected to go with it: the long black gloves—one topped with a beautiful Eisenberg crystal bracelet —and the stunning little jet-beaded headband with a woman-of-mystery cheekbone skimming veil and a poof of black and gold feathers fastened to the side by a silver dollar-sized jet studded button.

Even more thrilling than the glamorous beyond belief clothing, however, was debuting the blues number Booker agreed I could sing my way as my final song of the night.

And. Oh. My. Gosh! We brought down the house. When my very last note trailed into silence and the audience erupted in applause and cheers, I automatically turned to Henry to see what he thought. He'd been so fabulous about Booker siding with me, but I've run into men before who give lip service one moment, only to turn around and simmer in their resentment the next.

I should have known Henry would be a class act all the way. He gave me a big, toothy grin and two enthusiastic thumbs up. Seeing it, I impulsively covered the short space separating us to give him a hard hug.

"You did good, kid," he growled in my ear as he hugged me back. And if that wasn't enough, he caught up with me while I was making my way back to the dressing room and presented me with what he said was a standard bottle of champagne.

I'm on my way to my dressing room when I see Booker headed my way. He's carrying a bouquet of flowers and walking fast in big, ground-eating strides. I'm just stepping to the side to keep from being bowled over when he reaches out and swoops me up in his arms and spins us around.

And oh, God. His heat surrounds me and I can smell the starch in his tuxedo shirt. Can smell his skin. Lord have mercy, of all the things I remember about Booker, the scent of his skin tops my list of the never, ever forgotten. It's a healthy, vital male scent that is his alone.

"Did you *hear* that audience, Lena?" he demands, tucking his chin in to grin down at me. "I thought they were going to rattle the damn ceiling loose! And Elsie tells me she won't know for sure until she develops her photos, but she's ninety-nine percent confident she got some fabulous shots while you were singing your last song!"

He slows the spin and slides his arm out from under my thighs to set me on my feet. "These are for you," he says and hands me the flowers. "I *knew* that song sung your way was going to send the crowd out there into a frenzy." Then he gives me a slap on my rear, making me jump and let loose an embarrassing squeak that hits high C.

"Best thing Leo ever did, hiring you!" he declares, and strides off laughing.

I rub my bottom and blink at his retreating back until he's gone from sight. Goodness gracious Agnes! I'm not quite certain how I feel about that encounter.

I laugh out loud. Okay, I know exactly how I feel. My heart is pounding, my mouth is dry, and yet I have a big smile on my face. Because I feel like I just caught a glimpse of, had a moment with, the old Booker. Everything from sweeping me up, to his laugh, to the bottom slap was exactly the fun, spontaneous Booker I knew before the war. And I can't deny it, it feels good.

Oh, my gosh, oh, my golly! This has been one of the best nights of my life, the ab-so-loot berries.

And I have a feeling our after-hours night out will be just as good.

Long time Joe, whataya know?

BOOKER

Feeling like a million bucks, I leave Leo to count the day's take for me. I shed my tuxedo jacket and cummerbund, change out my shirt for a slightly less formal model and put on a set of braces to make me look less like a swell out slumming. I don my cashmere fedora and overcoat, then head out a few minutes early, hoping to beat the girls. Keeping my eyes on the exit, I move through the club. I am giving no one the opportunity to stop me. A minute later, I'm through the door.

"Evening Mr. Jameson."

I tip my hat at the doorman and give him a nod. "Good evening to you, Benson." I stride out to the sidewalk. Stopping at the curb beneath the canopy, I look up and down both sides of the street. The problem isn't spotting an old black Ford, I discover. The problem is too damn many of them.

I turn back to Benson. "You happen to see a man in an old black Ford park nearby sometime in the last five or ten minutes?"

"I saw Miss Baker's friend Will. He couldn't find a place in front so he walked back and asked me to tell her he will be up on the next block—" Benson tips his head to the north "—on the other side of the street."

"That's who I'm looking for," I say. "Thanks, Benson." I head in that direction.

There really is a heap of black Fords, and once I reach the next block and cross to the other side I find myself bending to peer in the windows of each one I come across. Finally spotting Will, I walk over and open the front passenger door.

"Hey," I say, bending down to look at him. "How's tricks?"

Shit. I barely stop myself from grimacing. But, really, *how's tricks?* Not exactly my usual vocabulary. Except for a few of the less ridiculous words, I have never been much on slang.

He looks back, clearly surprised to see me standing there. He merely says, "Long time Joe, whataya know?" however, and flashes me a crooked smile that is long on irony. I would put money down Will isn't a big slang slinger, himself.

"What are you doing here?" he demands.

"I hear we're going dancing."

He maintains level, unblinking eye contact. "That's odd, the girls never mentioned you were coming."

"Uh, yeah. That's kind of the tricky part. They didn't know."

Will quirks a brow at me, and when I don't respond immediately taps a smooth jazz rhythm out on his steering wheel as if he has all night and halfway into next week to wait for me to supply more information than what I've given him so far.

I shrug, feeling a bit sheepish, and climb in the car, shutting the door behind me. "I might have overheard them discussing it at the club earlier." I give my shoulders an impatient roll. I have never liked having to explain myself. But I guess if I invite myself along I can't expect the actual invited guests to just clap their hands and shout *Yay!* "When I heard you were coming with the girls, I figured my invitation must have got lost in the mail."

Hearing the words come out of my mouth, I frown and mutter, "God knows there's been a lot of that going around."

He grins suddenly, looking so much like the boy I grew up with it causes a funny *thump* in my chest, as if someone reached out of the blue to give it a light rap with the side of his fist.

"What the hell," Will says. "As long as you're here anyway, you might as well come along. The more the merrier and all that shit." Then he levels a finger at me. "But Lena rides shotgun. You get to share the backseat with the Brasher sisters." And he laughs like an asylum escapee.

I don't. Because Dot and Clara are the farthest thing from shy I can imagine. And the thought of being cooped up in a small backseat with them off the clock?

God help us all.

19

Look at all these flyboys!

LENA

Mr. Benson hails Clara, Dot, and me when we push through the front door and explains Will's difficulty finding parking out front. He tells us where Will is waiting for us and, linking arms, the three of us set out up the block. We are laughing uproariously over a slightly blue joke Dot heard from Sally when I spot Will's car. "There he is!"

We run the final steps and I haul open the passenger side door, climb in and greet Will. Dot and Clara clamber into the back.

"Well, *hel-lo* there, Mr. Jameson!" one of them exclaims.

I freeze. *What?* Clutching the champagne bottle Henry gifted me to my chest, I swivel in my seat.

And see Booker sitting, larger than life, next to the door behind Will. "What the heck are you doing here?" My heart is kicking up a storm and once again my mouth goes dry.

Booker, as usual, is cool as can be. But he gives me a grin that does wicked things to my heart rate. "Going dancing, rumor has it."

"He ran into me," Will says, giving me a little shrug. Then he lowers his voice so only I can hear beneath Dot's sudden peal of laughter. "Do you mind too much?" he asks softly. "I'll get rid of him if you do."

I'm tempted. So, so tempted. And yet—

The way Booker laughed backstage earlier keeps playing in my mind. And the smile on his face just now made me want to smile back. Plus, he has done an awful lot for me lately. It seems small to repay him by saying he can't go with us to a bar.

Then there's the matter of that generous check made out to a local Orphanage currently sitting on my dressing table back at the club.

I just found out about it before my first set this evening, when I was about to take the box my dresses came in to one of the stage crew for disposal. The check and an accompanying note were in an envelope in the box, but I didn't see it until I swept up the tissue paper and the envelope fell out of one of its folds. According to the note, Frederick and Nelson's cleaning crew found the check beneath the chair Booker sat in outside my dressing room the day we went to the department store for the first fittings. They took it to a supervisor who eventually tracked down Alice, who saw to its return. And honestly?

I would really, really like to know the story behind Booker supporting an orphanage. But it's back at the club and this isn't exactly the place to—

Wait a minute.

It's not at the club, at all. As I was closing the door before going to meet Clara and Dot, I began second guessing myself over leaving such a generous check in an unlocked dressing room, sitting out for anybody to find. I shoved it into my purse to give to Booker the next time I saw him.

Well, here he is and here I am. I open my purse to do just that—to pass it back to Booker—but then stop. This really doesn't seem like the best time to hand it over, surrounded as we are by Will and the

Brasher girls. Booker might not appreciate everyone knowing his business.

Which recalls me back to the present and Will's offer. "No," I reply in the same low tone he used. "This has been such a great night. I don't want to ruin it with bickering."

So, here I am, moments later, zooming along Highway 99 at forty miles an hour in Will's old Ford, on our way to Swannee Don's Speakeasy up in the University district. With not only he and my two bosom pals, but Booker, too, of all people. I look down at my lap.

And smile, assuring myself it's because of my stunning outfit.

I can almost believe that's my only reason. After all of my protestations to Clara about not using the dresses Booker supplied for anything other than work, I ended up wearing one tonight. I selected the short, beaded "dance-dress". It is a beauty, crafted from a yellow under-sheath cut straight across the tops of my breasts and topped with a black sleeveless dress of small-patterned, V-necked chiffon. Alternating bottom panels swirl out when I spin and are outlined with ribbons of metallic gold beading. The points of the Vs that end at the hem frame small-pattern fabric that matches the rest of the over-dress. But where they come to a point around hip height, the fabric is heavily embroidered in patterns of gold beading and sequins. Even with the fancy embellishments, however, this dress is less formal than the others that Booker—I mean, my contribution to the business!—bought me.

I had planned on changing into one of my old dresses. But every time I'd tried to figure out what I should wear for our after-show jaunt, my conversation with Dot the day I bought my beautiful new cloche popped up to haunt me. Because she was right. My wardrobe is nothing to write home about (pretending for a moment one *has* a home for that). And when I truly give the matter the tiniest bit of thought, I had likely been long overdue to make changes to the contents of my closet a good two or three years ago.

I intend to correct that. Even if it means breaking into my lovely little savings.

I don't want to go out anymore in the tired old clothes I've been wearing for ages. In fact, as soon as I can scratch up an hour or two, I'm going to grab Dot and Clara to help me buy one of those pretty every day, flower-print chiffon dresses.

Who knows? Maybe I'll even go hog-wild and buy two. But in the meantime—

Swinging around in the front seat to look at Clara and Dot in the back while carefully avoiding looking at Booker, I heft up the champagne bottle. "Say, do either of you know how to get the cork from the bottle without shooting out Will's windshield?"

"Not me," Dot says regretfully and Clara agrees champagne cork removal isn't one of her skills, either.

From the corner of my eye, I see Booker just opening his mouth when Will suddenly swerves over to the curb, making me grab with my free hand for the back of the seat. He takes the car out of gear and sets the brake. "Hand it over." He pulls a pristine handkerchief from his pocket.

I thought he would roll down his window and shoot the cork out the opening, Instead, he does something with the wire cage thing covering the cork and removes it. He then wraps his hanky around the cork and the foiled neck of the bottle and uses his thumbs to make short work of removing the cork with a soft pop. Some of the champagne foams and fizzes up through the mouth of the bottle and, laughing, Will drinks the overflow. Then he hands the bottle to me.

I drink from the bottle, as well, then pass it back to the girls. "We don't have any glasses, so we'll have to make do with this," I say cheerfully. And truly, who cares what Emily Post would say about an innocent touch of naughtiness? Well, Booker might. But I'm not going to worry about it. It adds to the night's merriment.

Will hands me the cork he returned to its wire cage and puts the car back in gear. As he shoots back out onto the road, I carefully wrap it in my handkerchief and put the little bundle in my evening bag. I'm keeping it as a souvenir of this evening. Heck, I might even keep the entire bottle. It is the first standard of champagne anyone's ever given me.

Between us, we kill off the giggle water on our drive to the new speakeasy. Dot, Clara and I do, at any rate, and even Booker downs a couple big gulps. Will merely drinks a single man-sized swallow, claiming only college boys and chumps drive blotto. I am oddly pleased by his responsibility and the knowledge I am always safe in his company. Dot nudges me and hands over the bottle.

We girls are more than a little bubbly by the time we arrive at Swanny Don's. Will finds a spot to park in the big, dark lot out front and Clara, Dot and I all but tumble out of the car, laughing as we fumble a bit before finding our footing on the graveled lot.

The thump of drums and wail of horns filters through the walls as we approach the gin joint, but it's nothing compared to when Booker opens the door for us. We're hit by drifts of smoke and a wall of sound as we step into the dim, moody interior.

Dot whoops and shimmies her shoulders. "Look at all these flyboys!" She raises her voice to exclaim over the music. "I think I've died and gone to heaven."

"I see a table," Will yells and forges a path for us through the speakeasy to claim it.

I look around as we reach the table. "This isn't near as high-class as your joint," I say to Booker. "But it's quite nice, don'tcha think?"

"Yeah, I do. They've put together a damn fine club. I like their use of wood in here."

"I do, too!" There is a lot of it—on the floors, on the walls, in the polished bar and the tables hosting small hurricane lamps—and the wood glows with a warm-toned coating. It makes it cozy and welcoming in here. The band is more raucous than Henry's smoother sound, but I bet he would say they're solid. Flappers are dancing the Black Bottom with great energy with officers and airmen of all ranks out on the floor, and there is just a nice, general feel-good air about the place.

We have barely been seated, me between Will and Booker on one side of the small table and the Brasher girls on the other, when I hear a male voice say, "Hey, doll. How's 'bout you and me cut a rug?" I look up from the drinks menu I'm trying to read by the flickering candle-light to see an airman leaning over Dot.

She flashes him a sassy smile and hops to her feet. "You bet! See if you can keep up, fly boy."

Returning a cocky grin, he offers his arm, elbow bent, and Dot slides her hand beneath it then curls her fingers back over his forearm. Before she lets him escort her away, however, she turns to her sister. "Order me a G and T if the waitress comes while I'm gone," she says and nods toward her little beaded bag on the table. "There's some foldin' money in the inside pocket." Then she and the airman make their way to the dance floor.

Less than a minute later an officer claims Clara. Then Booker rises from his chair, saying, "I'll go see if I can get us some drinks," and makes his way over to the bar.

I turn to Will. "Is it wrong of me to feel both relieved and insulted that no one's asked me to dance? I mean, I'm really nervous about displaying my not so Jake dancing skills. But...still."

"You're sitting between me and Booker, so the fellas probably think you're taken by one or the other."

"Okay, that makes me feel better."

"If you move to the other side, you'll likely be swamped."

I shake my head. "That's all right. I'm not kidding about being nervous. Especially next to those two." I wave to where Dot and Clara are dancing up a storm, far and beyond superior to the rest of the dancers on the floor when it comes to sheer talent. "The girls have only been teaching me how to dance for a month now."

"Ah, but you can sing everyone in this joint under the table." Will taps my nose. "You don't have to be the best at everything, Lena."

"That's true!" I laugh and bump shoulders with my friend. "But you know me—I *want* to be anyhow." I pat his hand. "Thanks. You always know what to say when I start overthinking things or get crazy competitive for no good reason. Still. Maybe after I have another drink."

Booker returns to the table, his hard upper arm rubbing against my shoulder as he takes his seat. I'm still sitting very still, trying to get a handle on the heat pumping through me when the waitress arrives carrying a tray with the drink order just before a second dance ends.

A couple of heartbeats later, Clara and Dot, flushed and laughing, arrive back at the table and grab up their evening bags to pay for their drinks. Booker won't hear of it, insisting the first round is on him. With an uncanny ability to read each other's thoughts, as if they truly are the twins I first thought them to be, they simultaneously jump to their feet and round the table to lean down on either side of Booker and kiss his cheeks.

And I am not the least bit jealous. No, sir. Not. The. Least. Bit.

But I might frown at Clara and Dot a little when they resume their seats.

After drinking half my Bee's Knees, the new to me drink of gin, honey, lemon juice and orange juice Booker selected for me, I get up the nerve to switch to the other side of the table when the girls leave once again to dance with new partners. Almost immediately, I'm invited to dance. Since it's the Charleston, which I have more confidence I won't muck up too badly, I accept.

And it's fun! Danny, my partner, is as bad at dancing as I am, but he laughs at himself when he goes off track and just grins at me with high good nature when I fluff a step. His easy company and the utter fun of dancing settles my overachiever nerves right down.

We have been here perhaps an hour and Booker, who hasn't danced since we got here—or even said much to anyone—is off buying us more drinks when I find myself out on the floor with an officer named Jeffry. We're shuffling slowly to one of the dances not requiring much skill, since it's mostly body-to-body, cheek-to-cheek swaying in place. Ordinarily I might have felt self-conscious being squeezed up against a man who is basically a stranger. Yet all the fellas I've danced with tonight have been quite gentlemanly. Everyone here just seems to want to dance and have a jolly time.

Jeffry is too tall to dance cheek-to-cheek with me, but we're making it work as best we can when a man comes up and taps my partner's shoulder. "Mind if I cut in?" he asks.

What in heaven's name? I rise onto my toes to see over Jeffry's shoulder. Because, I know that voice like I know my own face in a mirror.

And, yep. Sure enough. My heart beating like a kettle drum, I look directly into the light blue eyes of the last man I expected to cut in on my dance with another man.

A helluva lot more tortuous than I expected

BOOKER, a few minutes ago

I come back from placing a new order and tense when I see no one's at the table. Okay, Lena's the only one I've been keeping tabs on, and I've had to grit my teeth every time she's danced with another man. I stayed steady, though, and didn't lose my shit as we liked to say in the trenches, because the songs they danced to were all fast numbers. At the moment, however, the band is playing a sensuous torch song.

I knock back a big swallow of the bourbon I carried back from the bar. Tonight has been a helluva lot more tortuous than I expected when I decided to crash the girls' night out. Because, damn, I want Lena bad! Sure as hell more than any of the saps she's been dancing with tonight. She is *mine*, dammit! She just doesn't know it yet.

Hell, maybe I'm looking for trouble where none exists. Lena could well be in the ladies' room. I pull my chair out from the table, swing it around and straddle it.

I've barely planted my ass on the seat, when Will plops down on his. Glancing at him, I ask casually, "All the girls out on the dance floor?"

"Yep." He looks in that direction and says, "Dot and Clara are always easy to pick out, although this particular dance doesn't require a lot of skill. Oh, and look." The amused *don't even try to kid a kidder* look Will's used to great effect since we were kids returns. "There's Lena."

I can't stop myself from scanning the floor. Then I see another man holding Lena close and a red mist floods my vision. My first inclination is to stride out onto the floor and rip her from his arms.

But my mother didn't raise an animal. I take a couple of deep breaths, get a grip on my irrational flash of temper and slap on a pleasant smile. "Excuse me," I murmur, rising to my feet.

Will's brows snap together. "Booker..."

"I'm not going to do anything stupid," I assure him. I am even damn near certain I'm telling the truth. Without a backward glance, I make my way to the dance floor where I dodge through the crush of couples slow dancing. Finally, I reach out to gently tap the officer's shoulder in the age-old signal to cut in. The son of a bitch is holding Lena far too closely, so good on me, as the British soldiers I met overseas use to say.

Hell, yes—just *look* at me behaving like the adult I quickly became in Europe. It's amazing how fast you can mature when lives are at stake. I might not feel particularly civilized right this moment, but I sure as hell sound as if I am when I say, "Mind if I cut in?"

He shakes me off. "Yeah. I do."

I can't swear to what I would have done next. I like to think I would carry on handling the situation maturely.

But I can't swear to it.

Luckily for me, Lena saves me from having to find out. She raised her head when I first spoke and peers up at me now over the asshole's shoulder. She murmurs something in his ear.

The officer's shoulders stiffen, but he loosens his hold from around Lena and steps back, clearly reluctant.

She gives him a warm smile. "Thank you for the dance, Jeffry."

The other man's face softens as he looks down at her. "The pleasure was all mine. Maybe you can give me a make-up dance later?"

"May be."

He turns away and leaves, but not before shoulder-checking me on his way off the floor. I can live with that—hell, I'm kind of getting used to it when it comes to me and Lena and other men. I hold out my hand. "May I have this dance?"

And release the breath I didn't even realize I was holding when she steps in, placing one hand in mine and sliding the other up my chest to curl over my shoulder. I tug her in, closing my eyes for a moment at the sweet feel of her body pressed to mine. Then tighten my arm around her waist to tug her closer yet.

Given the volume of the music, I can't actually hear her sharply indrawn breath in reaction to our close-pressed bodies. Yet I sense she has done exactly that by the slight, but abrupt rise of her breasts against my chest before she slowly exhales. And I feel truly content for the first time in... hell, I'm not sure how long. But a whole lot lengthier period than I realized until just this moment.

Swaying and barely moving in the simple, tightly limited pattern keeping us close, I slide my hand up her back to hold her even nearer yet, my fingers splayed wide to soak in as much of her plush heat as possible through the thin material of her dress. I tuck our entwined hands against my chest.

And my heart gives a great big thump when she rests her temple against my jaw in the same taller man/smaller woman cheek to cheek alternative she'd danced in with the officer I stole this dance from. The longer I hold her in my arms, in fact, the surer I am our heartbeats are beating in sync.

A wave of her hair not far from my lips is soft and fragrant. It slides against my jaw when random strands aren't catching on the faint stubble that has grown since this morning. I have a kit at the club, but didn't even think about re-shaving until it was too late to do anything about it.

Lena doesn't appear to mind.

The dance ends far too soon. I wish it would segue into another slow number, but the band plays the opening bars to a Lindy Hop tune. Reluctantly releasing Lena, I place a light hand on the small of her back and steer her back to our table. When she refuses to meet my gaze, I bend my knees until I can look her in the eye. "Thank you for the dance."

She flashes me a tiny smile. "You're welcome. I... enjoyed it." Then she steps back. "You'll have to excuse me, though. I need to—" She jerks her head toward the hallway hosting the restrooms.

"Sure." I step back, but keep an eye on her as she heads in that direction.

Which is how I see her veer off toward the club's entrance. When she pushes through the door, I swear beneath my breath, grab her coat off the back of her chair and follow. Because, Jesus. She's going out into the dark parking lot from which men have been coming and going all night?

Yeah, *no*. Not on her own, she isn't.

Not while I have breath in my body.

21

You don't get to say maybe, baby

LENA

I need time to get myself together, but it's colder than a witch's heart out here. Goose bumps keep piling atop goose bumps up my arms and down my thighs, and I so wish I'd grabbed my coat before I came outside. Of course, had I done so, it's a pretty safe bet any one of my group not currently out on the dance floor would have been all over me. Demanding to know why I needed it. Where I planned to go with it. In other words, reaping me the precise level of attention that would stop me from grabbing these few brief minutes to myself. Moments I could really use to sort through my emotions. God knows they're all over the place.

It isn't just the past few minutes I need to get straight in my head. It's everything that has been building and *building* between Booker and me since first discovering the identities of the owner and new singer at the Twilight Room. Every small moment and larger event between us seems to keep piling atop the ones that came before. Forming one great big hazardous and overwhelming ball-up.

Still. I can't deny I was seriously overheated from that brief dance spent plastered against Booker's—*oh, my*—extremely firm self. In that regard, the cold early morning air has quite efficiently cooled me down.

A little *too* efficiently, as it turns out. Shivering, I cross my arms across my breasts and briskly rub my hands against my shoulders and upper arms in an attempt to restore a hint of warmth. Being out here freezing my seat-cheeks off is baloney—I *know* that. But darn it all, it took me *years* not to feel abandoned every time someone came and went in my life. I had finally gotten rather good at avoiding situations that made me feel that way, until Booker blew my world apart. After he abandoned me—and, face it, there're no two ways about *that* —it took me almost as long to rebuild all my walls the second time as it had the first.

Walls, which he just handily smashed down during one stupid dance. Heck, not even an entire dance, either, but rather—

"What the *hell* do you think you're doing?" An irate male voice snarls from not too far away. "Are you *looking* to get assaulted?"

I flinch, yet am not exactly shocked when I look up to see Booker bearing down on me.

Then his words sink in, and I wrinkle my nose. "Oh, don't be so melodramatic, Douglas Fairbanks. I was just looking for a minute to myself."

"Melodramatic, she says." He strides right up to me until we're standing toe to toe and swings my coat around my shoulders. Grasping the lapels, he tugs them together until the sides overlap, the knuckles of one of his warm hands lightly pressing into the inner curve of my left breast. Heat floods me once again and I wouldn't bet all my hard-earned savings it's entirely due to my coat.

He, on the other hand, isn't feeling a likeminded warmth. Not if the way he lowers his head to scowl at me is anything to go by. "This place is crawling with fly boys," he snaps and uses his grip on my coat to haul me a step closer, his knuckles pressing the tiniest bit deeper. "Men who have been goddamn *drinking* all night. No woman with half a brain in her head waltzes out into an unlighted parking lot without taking someone along as back up."

My head snaps up. "Did you just call me *stupid*?"

"Hell, no, don't be an idiot—" Booker cuts himself off with an abrupt crack of laughter. "Sorry. *That's* clearly not the best way to make my point." As suddenly as he laughs at himself, he sobers again. "But you have to admit, Lena, hanging around the dark lot of a juice joint full of fried servicemen—by *yourself*—probably doesn't rank right up there as one of your better thought-out plans."

I shrug sulkily. Still, put that way I have to admit—if only to myself —he has a point. I was so hot and bothered the possible hazards of coming out here on my own never once occurred to me. And I'm the kind of gal who usually factors in all the risks in order to avoid putting myself in the path of any of them. In this case, however, I hadn't thought beyond getting a breath of fresh air and a moment alone to drag my composure back where the darn thing belongs. Front and center.

I should be able to simply admit as much to Booker, but I cannot. I have always had a *lit*-tle problem owning up to when I'm in the wrong. It is not one of my prettier traits. Yet even knowing this, I allow an old anger to resurface and take the place of...whatever it was I felt for him inside. All I say—in a voice even I recognize as much too peevish—is, "I hate all the cigarette smoke. It stinks to high heaven and it doesn't do my voice the slightest favor."

"Yeah." Booker slides his hands to a different position on my coat, and I immediately miss their warmth. After slipping the garment off my shoulders, he holds it for me while I slide my arms into the arm holes, then buttons me up as if I'm a four-year-old. I don't know if I should be insulted he thinks I can't handle the job on my own, or just accept there is something kind of nice about being taken care of this way.

Warmth returns the moment he finishes, mostly because he promptly pulls me into a back-cracking, feet-lifted-a-good-foot-off-the-ground hug. Seconds later, as he sets me back on my feet without letting go of me, I marvel I was able to forget the way he hugs in the first place. They were once a Booker special. How could I have forgotten just how tight and warm and *real* they are? How secure they make me feel?

"That is a definite downside of owning or working in a bar if you're not a smoker," Booker agrees. "I have never understood the appeal, myself." He draws back a little, tucking his chin in to look down at me. "But is it the only reason you're out here, Lena? Because I thought we had—I don't know—a moment in there on the dance floor." His gaze is dead level as it meets my own. "Or maybe I was mistaken. Was I the only one affected?"

I so want to say yes. Lord, I *yearn* for it to be just him. But his intense gaze drags the truth out of me. "No."

"No?" His mouth curves up. "So, you felt it, too?"

I shrug. "Maybe."

"No, you don't get to say maybe, baby." Once again, he commands my gaze. "You either felt it as well, or you didn't."

"Okay, fine. I felt...something."

Booker bends his head and presses a kiss to the left side of my neck just below the curve of my jaw. "Something that made you feel...flushed, maybe? Stimulated?" His voice is low and rough, as if he has to push his words through a throat full of gravel. He shifts his head to breathe directly into the whorls of my ear, "*Hot?*"

It spurs a shaky little sigh that shudders up my own throat. I tip my head a fraction to the right to give him more room to maneuver. As much as I would rather not answer the question, I murmur, "Um-hmm."

To any or all of what he said.

With an extremely deep, extremely male groan reverberating in his chest, he crouches slightly to kiss his way down my neck. I have no idea if it's his hungry-sounding rumble or the feel of the unfamiliar stubble on his chin and jaw scratching my skin that's doing the trick.

Whatever it is, thrill bumps flash to far-reaching parts of my body. They wash a crazy pattern across my breasts, twisting my nipples into hard, aching points. From there sensation zings—as if on a direct, private non-party line—deep in my lady place.

When Booker reaches the little hollow at the base of my throat, he gives it a small lick with the flat of his tongue. Then he lifts his head and the hot, damp spot goes icy with the loss of his body heat.

He looks up at me through half lowered eyelids. Says, in what even I recognize as a sexually charged voice, "I have something for you."

The wash of disappointment his words cause promptly drowns every bit of pleasure I felt, and I stiffen in his arms. "Yeah?" I say flatly. "I've heard that one before."

Eyes narrowing, he surges to his full height, his hand wrapped around the back of my neck keeping us near. "Who the hell from?" he demands in a hard voice that somehow commands an immediate response.

"Other men wanting the exact same thing you want from me right now!" I snap back at him.

"And how many of those men have gotten what they wanted from you?"

I thrust my chin up. "I fail to see how that is any of your beeswax, Booker."

"How many?" he persists.

"Oh, dozens," I lie with a breezy flip of my hand. "Heck, maybe even hundreds."

His hand tightens on my nape. "How. Many, Lena?"

Oh, botheration! "None," I spit out. "Okay? I have refused—well, not hordes of men—but my share. Even when it meant I didn't get the job I was more than qualified for and really deserved." I shove my face as close to his as I can , given our height differences. "I have earned every single singing engagement I've ever had with my *voice,* if you can imagine such a thing."

And I am so through with this garbage. After knocking his arm aside to make him drop his grip on my nape, I take a sizable step back. "How about you, lover boy? How many women have you gotten what you wanted from?"

For the first time since tracking me down out here, Booker looks uncomfortable, and he mumbles something I don't quite catch.

"Speak up!" I demand, then use his own method of interrogation against him as I rap out, "How. Many, Booker?"

One broad shoulder hitches toward his ear. "I don't know, exactly."

"Why, because there have been so many?" I barely take note of the half-seas-over airman and woman stumbling out through Swanny Don's front door, as I shoot only the briefest glance in their direction. I am too busy bracing myself against the sudden pain radiating out from the region of my heart.

The latter makes me so angry. "Isn't that just like a man?" I demand sourly. "Demanding 'the little woman' hold herself to the highest standards while *they* go catting around with any woman who will put up with their sorry selves?"

"Or, maybe," he says in that low, gravelly voice that sets up tingles in long-ignored parts of my body, "I was just practicing so I could get it right for the one woman who matters."

"Well, good luck explaining that to her when you find her." The thought of him with "the one woman who matters" shouldn't grind like so much broken glass in my stomach. Yet it does—and I hate it.

"Yeah, it's not going real swell so far," I think I hear him mutter under his breath.

Before I have time to process if those *were* the words I heard, he straightens. "Look, can we back this up and start over? I bought you something today to commemorate tonight's success, because I knew in my gut your version of the song was going to *be* a success. I didn't do it to get in your damn knickers."

"Oh." My voice comes out small, and in truth, that's how I suddenly feel: small. Over-reactive and petty. "I—" I clear my throat "I apologize for jumping to conclusions."

"It's clear you still have some issues with me."

That shoves the poker back up my spine in a red-hot hurry and I take another step back. Because, *really*? "Can you honestly say you're surprised by my "issues", Booker? I loved you with everything I had and I thought you felt the same way about me."

I see him about to respond and with a hissed, "*Tsk!*" I thrust a *hush your mouth* finger in his face. "This is not me bringing up the letters again. I agree there is something fishy about neither of us ever getting so much as one from the other. But you *left* me, Booker. I don't want to hear about your father spiriting you out of town without giving you a chance to contact me, either, because I accept his doing that was an impossible situation you had no control over. But your daddy didn't stick around Seattle to stand guard over you. *You* were the one who made the decision to join the Army and go off without so much as a by your leave. *You* were the one who didn't bother coming back to Walla Walla to let me hear from your own lips you were going halfway around the world. It was also *you* who didn't find a way to call me or to send me a telegram. You. Just. Left. Me." I poke a finger into his chest to underscore each word. Then take yet another step back and look him in the eye. "Without one damn word."

22

What can a girl expect from a palooka like you?

BOOKER

Shit. She's not wrong. I could argue I was so damn young, so full of beans—as well as about a thousand conflicting emotions. That I was excited about my decision to join the Army and what I was convinced would be the glory of war. But the truth is, I didn't do a single one of the things she just listed. Well, I tried to call, but when it didn't work out I didn't follow up. I also wrote my very first letter to her to tell her I loved her and let her know what I had done. But we both know how well *those* worked out between us. Other than that, I *didn't* go out of my way.

Annnnd...I guess I owe it her to actually say some of this to her, face to face, instead of trying to justify my behavior to myself.

I meet her gaze head on. "I'm sorry."

She blinks up at me. "What?"

I can't help the small smile tugging up one corner of my mouth, because it is clearer than Seattle's blue sky in summer she didn't expect that. "I said I'm sorry. You're right. I was livid with my father for dragging me to the U-dub like a ten-year-old schoolboy. And I was thrilled to be going off to war. I thought I was going to save the world from the Jerrys and have a big adventure while I was at it." I shake my head at my long-lost innocence, but it was nothing short of the truth at the time. Briefly remembering the time when I still had those beliefs, makes my sudden laugh drier than dust. "Turns out, my view of what I assumed war would be was wildly romanticized and about as far off center as it gets."

Looking at her, I realize I have a gut-deep need to win back Lena's respect. Hell, who am I kidding, to win back her *love*. And what the hey, now seems like a good time to start.

But before I can say a word, I see Lena shiver and, with a silent sigh, I take her arm. "Look, let's go inside and warm you up. I'll tell you anything, *every*thing, you want to know. We should have sat down and had a serious conversation a long time ago."

"It's too loud inside to carry on a conversation."

I grimace. "Yeah. There is that. I'm sorry if I ruined your night to dance."

She shrugs, and I have no clue if it means *Don't worry about it, not a problem*, or *Big problem, but what the hell can a girl expect from a palooka like you?*

She wouldn't be wrong about option two. I haven't once tried to woo her. Haven't taken her on a date or even shown her the smooth, savoir-faire I was known for in Paris, and have gained a reputation for here in Seattle as well, once I got the club up and running.

I look at Lena, not feeling smooth in the slightest right this moment, yet determined to set things straight between us. "Maybe Will'll let me borrow his car for a while. You and I could try to find an open diner somewhere. Give us a chance to sit down over a cup of coffee, identify any other misunderstandings we might have and deal with them once and for all." Okay, it's hardly two dozen roses or taking her to the top floor of the Sorrento Hotel for dinner and the best view in town. But it would be a start.

Lena is shaking her head even before I finish. "Who knows how long that could tie up his car?" she asks, but mildly, her voice and attitude displaying no rancor. "We have no idea when he and the girls might be ready to go home, so I'd be a nervous wreck worrying about leaving them stranded."

She suddenly stands a little straighter. "Why don't we just go in and have some fun with my friends?" she counters. "I swear I'm not trying to avoid a conversation—this simply doesn't seem like the greatest time or the place. But you could drive me back to the Women's Residence when we get back to the club. Or to a diner for a piece of pie if you know of any twenty-four-hour ones downtown. We'll talk then."

I bend my knees slightly to look into her eyes. "Really talk, Lena. No dancing around the stuff you don't want to say."

"Yes. All our cards on the table." Her eyes are solemn, and as she nods with matching earnestness, her pale, pretty hair swishes against her cheekbones. "Because, you're right. We need to have a serious sit-down. We are long overdue."

I squeeze her shoulders and step back. I want to kiss her again—quite desperately I want that. But one lesson my father managed to teach me was to know when to walk away.

"Then that's the plan," I whip her around and sling an arm over her shoulder, tucking her against my side. "C'mon. Let's get you inside before you turn into a popsicle."

23

I pay the cops good money to keep the Dry Squad off my back

LENA

Booker and I slowly cruise along yet another buttoned up downtown street. I'm not normally a pouter, but my lower lip might be sticking out a *little* as I peer at the dimly lighted storefronts and eateries. I dislike admitting this, but I was looking forward to sharing a meal with Booker again. Now, that might simply be the drinks I consumed talking. I thought I had danced most of those out of my system, but I could be wrong.

Doesn't matter, anyway, because there isn't a blessed thing open at this hour of the morning.

As if reading my thoughts, Booker suddenly shoots a glance my way, then pulls over to the curb. He looks rumpled and frustrated, worlds removed from the smooth, unflappable sophistication he usually wears like one of his dapper suits. His hat is pushed back on his head, reminding me of a bookie Will once pointed out at a horse race at the Valley Fair. Booker has long since tossed his coat on the back seat, unbuttoned the top two buttons on his shirt and rolled up his shirtsleeves. Then there's his suspenders and the dark stubble on his chin and jaw. I swear I can darn near see it growing denser by the second.

"Sorry, Lena," he says, sounding as every bit as tired as I feel. "I was sure there was an all-night café around here somewhere, but clearly I had it wrong. Let me get you home. I'll take you out for a nice dinner before work tomorrow and we can hash things out then."

I have the oddest urge to argue against giving up on our original plan. But the sheer size of my yawn threatens to crack my jaw in two, and I nod sleepily. "Sounds good. I'm worn to a nub."

A short while later, Booker pulls up in front of the Women's Residence and shuts down his Packard. Before I can tell him he doesn't need to see me to the front stoop, he's already climbed out of the car and come around to open my door and usher me out. As we reach the small landing, the front door to the Women's Residence whips open.

My heart drops when I see Mrs. Rodale standing in the opening, her hands on her hips and one foot impatiently tapping a ratty slipper against the worn thin carpet. Her expression is nowhere in the neighborhood of friendly.

Next to her are two suitcases I recognize as my own, and beside them a cardboard box, which I fear contains whatever leftover odds and ends didn't fit into my luggage. I'm glad I left my new gowns in my dressing room at The Twilight Room, because I don't even like to think about those beautiful fabrics being crammed willy-nilly in with the rest of my clothing.

Or, worse, pinched. Heaven knows theft can be a problem at women's residences.

"What is this?" Booker demands authoritatively, jabbing his forefinger at my suitcases.

Mrs. Rodale ignores him to look directly to me. "I made an allowance for you with the house curfew, missy," she says briskly, "in deference to your work hours. "But I will *not* turn a blind eye to you rolling in with the dawn after you have been out doing God knows what with your Drugstore Cowboy!"

My...what? I darn near choke on the startled laugh fighting to blow a hole in my throat. Under any other circumstance, I would no doubt *howl* at the idea of my landlady mistaking Booker for one of the shiftless fellas who hang around street corners trying to pick up girls. But the not-so-minor detail of Mrs. Rodale throwing me out on the street in the dead of the night sorta puts a damper on my sense of humor.

I draw myself up and pin the older woman with the best *I am not amused* expression I can muster. "I beg your pardon?" I demand in a tone coated with ice. "Far from being a good-for-nothing lounge-about, Mrs. Rodale, this is my employer, Mr. Booker Jameson."

"And I don't much care for your slur on either of our reputations," Booker snaps with a steeliness a hundred times more effective than anything I can drum up. "Miss Bjornstad and I have put in long hours working overtime on the new music we're adding to her sets."

Mrs. Rodale is not impressed. "Working overtime." She snorts. "Is that what you call it these days?" She uses her foot to push my belongings out onto the stoop. Then she gives me a slow up and down once-over, filled with so much contempt it threatens to shrivel me on the spot. "I run a respectable establishment," she says snippily. "And *you* are no longer welcome here."

With a final, withering stare, she steps back and slams the door in my face.

"Oh, my God!" I swing around to gape in shock at Booker. "What am I going to do?" I keep my gaze locked on his face, hoping he has an idea. I wrack my brain, then say tentatively, "Can you take me to Dot and Clara's place? I'm sure they'll take me in for tonight—and maybe even until I can find a new place."

"No doubt, but not tonight," he says. Booker hands me the box, then tucks one of my suitcases beneath his upper arm, hugging it to his side as he squats to pick up the other. After rising to his full height, he rests his free hand on my lower back and escorts me back to the car. I can feel his heat clear through my coat.

"Wait here just a sec," he says and leaves me next to the passenger door while he opens the trunk to store my luggage and the box he'd removed from my death grip. He's back in literally seconds to help me into the front seat with all the care he might show something precious. Or an invalid. Then he rounds the hood to climb in the driver's side. He starts up the automobile but turns to me instead of putting it gear. "The Brasher girls are bound to be sound asleep by now. I'm taking you to my place."

"Oh, but—" I am amazed he can't hear the hard thud of my heart battering the wall of my chest.

"No buts, Lena. You intend to be in any kind of shape to get things straightened out tomorrow, you need a good night's sleep." Reaching over, he sweeps a tender thumb across my cheekbone. "If you can't trust me on anything else, trust this. Things will feel clearer and not so unsettling once you've had some shut-eye."

"I suppose." I rest my head against the seat back. Then jerk upright once again as a thought suddenly occurs to me. "That *witch*! Just yesterday I paid her a week's rent!"

"Don't worry about that, either." Booker's expression, when he glances over at me, is all grim determination. "You don't have to deal with her again. I'll take care of getting your unused rent back."

"Yeah? You may have noticed she wasn't any more impressed with you than she was with me. So how do you plan to manage that?"

"The next time I land on her doorstep, I'll be accompanied by the local bull."

That has me sitting up. "A policeman?" I stare at him, my mouth dropping open, and I snap my teeth together. "Are you *crazy*, Booker? You do remember you run a speakeasy, right? I'm frankly surprised we haven't been raided during the five weeks I've been with the club. Yet you plan to waltz up to a *policeman* and demand he go along with you to confront Mrs. Rodale?" Is this what comes of growing up the only son of the richest man in town?

Maybe Booker is rethinking his no harm can come his way delusion, though, for he doesn't respond until he stops for a red light. Then he slowly turns his head to look at me. His face is all hard planes and angles in the red glow from the traffic light and the paler illumination off the nearest street light. It's flat-out all *business*, and I marvel Mrs. Rodale could have mistaken him for anything other than the highly successful man he is, let alone treated him like some down-on-his-luck ruffian. Even Booker's informal clothing is constructed of quality fabric and he commands an unmistakable air of authority only a fool would overlook.

"I haven't been raided, doll," he informs me drily, "because I pay the cops good money to keep the Dry Squad off my back. And I'm fairly friendly with a couple patrolmen." He shrugs. "It won't be difficult to talk one into accompanying me to get your refund."

"Wow," I breathe. Okay, so I was the naïve one here, not Booker. Still, how could I have known? I have worked a couple places that were raided. I was never arrested, of course, since it's not illegal to drink or sing in a gin joint, just to sell booze. But I can see now that some of the places I worked, which weren't raided, must have had similar arrangements as Booker's. Even then, the transactions had to have taken place behind closed doors. Because it certainly wasn't anything the employees ever talked about.

I rest my weary head back once more, then another stray thought breaks free and I tighten up all over again . "Remind me to check to make sure nothing was "misplaced" between the wardrobe and dresser in my room and my suitcases."

Booker's hot, rough-tipped fingers gently and much too swiftly caress the back of my hand fisted on my thigh. "Yet something *else* you can put off worrying about until tomorrow."

"Easy for you to say, Mr. Big Shot," I mutter. All the same, I must have dozed off, because those are the last words I remember from either of us. Not to mention I have no idea how we got from the red light to where I blink awake when Booker gently shakes my shoulder. Yawning, I straighten in my seat to see him squatting on a curb outside my open car door. I rub my eyes. "Where are we?"

"Home, sweet home." He surges to his full height and steps back, offering a hand to help me out of the car.

"Which is where?" I yawn again. "I wasn't paying attention."

"Yeah, that's always harder to do with your eyes closed."

I give him a look and he shrugs. "West Boston Street on Magnolia Bluff."

"Magnolia." I look around as Booker walks back to pull my luggage from the trunk. The gaps between houses are large in this neighborhood, as if plots are still in the process of being parceled up. Evergreen trees dot the undeveloped land in small stands here and there and two maples display their red leaves beneath the glow of a streetlight. "I've never been over here. It's very peaceful." I inhale deeply through my nose. "And it smells divine."

"Yeah, those are a couple of the things I like about the area as well. It's close to downtown, yet it feels a lot more like living in the country." He hands me the box holding my odds and ends again, then scoops up my suitcases as though they weigh nothing at all. "It probably has to do with the fact the neighborhood is on a peninsula with limited access."

Shutting the trunk, he gives a jerk of his chin and says, "Follow me." Then without so much as a glance back to determine if I'm following, he sets off along a narrow, paved path.

I shrug and follow as, with long-legged strides, Booker makes short work of the distance to a long set of stairs. Where else am I gonna go?

Reaching the steps, he stands aside for me to go first, and both of us are quiet as we climb it. At the top is a pretty yard hosting an even prettier house with a covered front porch. It, too, has stairs at one end, although not nearly as many as the ones we just hiked up from the street.

Booker unlocks the front door moments later and opens it. Reaching inside, he flips a switch, illuminating a small foyer. He opens the door wider with one hand and, with a tip of his head, gestures for me to precede him. "Come on in." Following me with the luggage, he tosses his keys into a decorative bowl on the small Mission style entry table against the wall.

After Booker sets my luggage out of the way against another wall, he takes the box from me to add to the pile. "Wait here a second and I'll turn on some lights." He disappears into the room off the entry and light begins spreading a glow in his wake.

I follow him into what turns out to be the living room, where I stop in my tracks. "Oh," I breathe, looking around. "This is *really* nice."

"Thanks." He shoots me a pleased smile. "I wanted something comfortably sized, but not a damn mansion like I grew up in."

"Well, you certainly got it, because this is just perfect. It has such warmth, sort of like a hug." I promptly squirm. *Honestly, Lena? A hug?*

But the way Booker's face lights up, you'd think I had just uttered the most brilliant words in the English language. "That is exactly what *I* thought when the realtor first showed it to me. I took one look and it just felt like a *home*."

It does feel homey. The ceiling is high, giving the room an open, spacious feel. The room is long and painted a cool-tone grayish green, the color warmed by all the wood trim in the windows and doorways, the baseboards and crown moldings, the mantel and surround over a tiled fireplace in the middle of the room, and in the beautiful built-in bookshelves on either side of the hearth.

"Oh, and look at this!" I walk up to the big front window. The top foot across its width is a beautifully worked leaded glass panel with an occasional pop of green, orange and gold stained glass high-lighting its pattern. I turn in a circle, trying to take in everything at once. "You're right. It does feel like a home." Not that *that* is anything I've ever had a up-close relationship with. But, *boy*, do I envy Booker this place. And I wonder for a moment what it would be like to live here with him.

Oh, no, you don't. I ruthlessly squash the thought. *No, no, no, no, no!* The idea of living happily ever after with Booker would have been realistic once.

But it has no relation to reality in whatever we can call this thing between us now. I turn back to him, but avoid meeting his eyes by gazing over his right shoulder. "Where do you want me to sleep?"

When did you quit liking sex?

BOOKER

Oh, baby. There was a loaded question. And before I can monitor the impulse, I give voice to the first thing that springs to mind: the truth. "In my bed."

I manage not to cringe—or punch myself in the face—but, shit, *really,* Jameson? I had smoother moves when I was eighteen. I haven't even taken Lena on a damn date or done so much as buy her a burger at the stand on Fifth and Lenora. But, hey, I'm sure she'll leap for joy at the mere thought of jumping in my bed.

Yeaaah...no. That is not gonna happen without some real effort—not to mention sincere wooing—on my part.

As if to underscore my internal conversation, Lena laughs in my face. When she gets control of herself she stares at me, her hands planted on her hips, her pale hair disheveled, her face rosy and those big, dark-rimmed blue eyes flashing with—*hell*—rage, probably.

"Uh, no," she says flatly. "Thanks, anyway." Her Cupid's bow lips look as though she just took a bite of something nasty. "I'm not a huge fan of nookie. And I'm *ab-so-tootly* not a fan of whoring myself for the sake of a bed for the night."

"What? *No.*" I take a giant step toward her, then stop as if running into an invisible wall when I see her jerk back. Shit, shit, shit! She's *afraid* of me? That is just all kinds of fucked up and I hold my hands up in what I hope is a *See, just a harmless fella here* gesture. "Jesus, Lena. Tell me you know I would never force myself on any woman, let alone you! Any bed you want in this house is yours, no strings attached. I *never* meant to imply sleeping in mine was a condition for staying here." I thrust my fingers through my hair, knocking the fedora I forgot I was even wearing to the floor.

Then my mind gives birth to a thought that promptly exits my damn mouth. "When did you quit liking sex?" Another thought treads on the heels of the first and my uncharacteristic verbal spewage continues. "Did somebody hurt you, baby?" The very thought has my fists curling at my sides and I take a daddy-long-legged step in her direction.

"If by hurt you mean *forced* me, of course not. It never entered my mind you would do that." She balloons her cheeks then slowly exhales through pursed lips. "And to be fair, I may have *pretended* to like it the one time you and I did...you know...the whole sex thing," she says with a shrug. "But I didn't. I always loved your kisses," she admits, and the look she shoots up at me through her eyelashes damn near stops my heart. "And I gotta admit I really liked the touching and petting part that came before—" Lena's distaste is clear in her wrinkled nose and curled upper lip "—*that.*"

"Then, why?"

Lena looks at me as if I'm an idiot, and, hell, maybe I am. God knows I'm totally at sea here.

For a second she looks uncharacteristically flustered. Then the real Lena comes roaring back, her chin thrusting a couple of notches upward as she drills me with a look that should have seared my eyeballs. "Well, come on," she scoffs. "I doubt any woman likes the action that comes after the petting. It's wicked uncomfortable and over before a girl can even recover from the way all the really good-feeling stuff was just killed dead."

I choke. "Wait. You're telling me the one time with me was the *only* time for you?" She'd been so sensual back then, it being a onetime only deal never even occurred to me. So, why does the mere thought, the *possibility* no other man has ever seen Lena, *touched* Lena, the way I did, make me want to thump my chest, throw back my head and roar like the goddamn king of the jungle?

Lena's jaw goes slack and the look she gives me is so incredulous I have no problem reading her opinion of me. She thinks I'm too stupid to live.

For a second I worry she somehow read my mind, that she saw my primal reaction to discovering she's only ever made love with me. Then she snaps her teeth together and makes a visibly concerted effort to relax the muscles in her face. And my brain finally kicks in, making me realize her response was to my question, not my primitive need to claim her.

She squares her shoulders, which make her breasts bounce, and now *I'm* the one having to make a concerted effort to keep my mind on the matter on hand. Still. Make no mistake. I am going to claim her.

'Til death do us *part* claim her.

Clearly abandoning her effort for cool and collected, she says hotly, "For God's sake, Booker, if I thought sex with you was a messy, uncomfortable waste of time, and I *loved* you then more than my next breath—" Her voice trails away, but she takes a deep breath, then slowly exhales it. And asks with genuine bafflement. "Why on God's green earth would I rush out to try it again with a stranger?"

I inch closer. "Honey, you had to have considered the fact we were teenagers when we made love. *Inexperienced* teenagers. Plus, it was your first time. From everything I've ever heard about losing one's virginity, *no* girl's first time is a huge success unless she's lucky enough to have a man who has experience and control."

"Well, it would've been nice if you'd told me that upfront," she mutters.

"Hey, I only had hearsay to go on myself at the time." I move close and tilt my head until my lips are near her ear. "But I can make it really good for you now."

"Yeah," Lena breathes, looking up at me, all baby vamp eyes and flushed cheeks. Then those eyes narrow down to dangerous little slits. "Because being reminded of all the women you practiced on is sure to get me in the mood." She shoves me away. "Don't hold your breath waiting for that to happen."

"So." She takes a big step back. "Where's a bed I can use? This night is beginning to feel forty hours long.

25

Like firing the first shot in a war

LENA

It feels like morning but is actually almost one-twenty in the afternoon when I track Booker down in the kitchen. I am feeling a tad on the disgruntled side. I admit some of my testiness centers around a need for coffee. But my mood mostly has to do with the nice day dress I donned to wear into work. I may not have a wealth of clothing, but I take care of what I do have. Yet this dress, I had to hang in the bathroom while I bathed to steam out the wrinkles Mrs. Rodale caused by stuffing everything I own in my suitcase. Even then, not all the wrinkles came out.

Seeing Booker at the stove, however, I can't help but smile. Except for his suit jacket hanging over the back of a kitchen chair, he is already dressed for work in one of his beautiful suits—this one topped with a jury-rigged apron.

I can't help but smile at the white bath towel wrapped around his lean hips and secured by a clothes peg. It protects his slacks as he scrambles a pan full of eggs, while bacon sizzles and occasionally pops grease in another pan on a back burner.

"I didn't know you cooked." I give him a glance of approval.

"Probably because I didn't when you knew me," he responds easily without turning around. "I learned a lot of skills living without staff."

"What a coincidence. The lack of staff had the exact same effect on my skill levels, too." I make a beeline for the newfangled percolator to pour myself a cuppa joe. "I *love* this thing," I murmur, smiling happily at the amazing gadget after my first sip of coffee. Then I inhale deeply and murmur on the exhale, "Sure smells divine in here."

Booker shoots me a lopsided grin over his wide shoulder. "Coffee and bacon," he agrees. "Perfume of the gods. How'd you sleep?"

"Like a baby." It surprised the heck out of me, too. I expected to have a hard time turning off all the thoughts spinning through my head when I went to bed. But— "You rich guys sure know how to do it up right. That was the nicest mattress and—omigosh—the softest sheets I have ever slept on."

Booker seems to hesitate for a moment. Well, that or I'm overly aware of every move he makes, because the next thing I know, he gives me a nod and says easily, "I'm glad you enjoyed them." He turns his attention back to his cooking but then jerks his chin in the direction of the first tall cupboard in the cabinets above the counter. The one he indicates is to the right of the sink. "Set the table?"

We sit down a few minutes later and have a surprisingly uneventful breakfast, considering how revved up the two of us can get in each other's company. "You look nice," Booker says as I get up after the meal to carry the dishes to the sink. "You going somewhere with the Brasher sisters today?"

I try to push down my small surge of guilt over not having even rung them up yet to see if I can sleep on their couch until I hunt up new lodging. But I shrug it off, because what I do plan to do is more important. "Nope. I'm going with you to collect what's owed me from Mrs. Rodale."

His hands still mid-removal of the towel around his waist. "No. Leave that to me and Officer Miller."

That is the ab-so-*loot* worst thing he could have said! "Like heck I will! Rodale kept *my* money, Booker, not yours. And not only did my newest toiletries disappear from my bath kit as well, but so did my brand-new cloche!" I'm livid all over again at the mere thought of my landlady pawing through my things and helping herself to my newest and best. The fact Mrs. Oh-so-self-righteous Rodale grabbed several of my smaller personal belongings was bad enough. But stealing my beautiful hat, to boot, after I had finally unclenched my purse strings to buy it? That's firing the first shot in a war! It is *my* hat—how could she possibly think I wouldn't notice it wasn't included in the suitcases or the box she'd shoved out the door at me? Or had she simply assumed her respectability gave her the upper hand over a woman like me, on my own and working where I do?

I shoot him a fierce don't-*even*-try-to-stop-me glare. As unfair as it might be, Booker reaps the brunt of my frustration over my ex-landlady's shenanigans. "I'm coming with you and that is the end of the subject!"

He studies me for a moment, then nods. "Okay. But if you have things that need doing before we leave, now is the time to do them. "We're meeting Officer Miller in front of the Women's Residence at two-fifteen. In fact—" He looks at his watch then gives me a hard stare, which I'm embarrassed to admit makes me all kinda tingly. How dumb is that?

Luckily, Booker's hard voice redirects my attention. "You have fifteen minutes. I do not intend to keep the officer waiting."

That gives me enough time to do up the dishes, brush my teeth and apply my lipstick, even if I have to fall back on an old color for the last item. My teeth clench all over again at the reminder my new tube is yet another thing Sticky Fingers Rodale pinched.

Still, at least I have an itty bitty hope of getting it back. And at precisely two-fifteen, we pull up behind a black squad car marked Seattle PD parked in front of my former residence. A policeman gets out of the car and Booker introduces him to me as Officer Miller. We follow him up the path to the rooming house.

Booker glances up at the dwelling as we approach the front door and swears under his breath. "The bitch already has a Room to Let sign in the window."

The look on Mrs. Rodale's face is priceless when she opens the door to the policeman's firm knock and sees Officer Miller standing there clad in his pristine uniform and a stern expression. She divides a quick glance between me and Booker, who is dressed in his usual elegant attire, before turning her full attention bck to Office Miller.

The policeman doffs his hat. "Mildred Rodale?" he says in a deep, commanding voice.

The older woman pales but recoups to say, "Yes, I am *Mrs.* Rodale. What can I do for you, officer?" As if she doesn't know perfectly well why we're here. I have to hand it to her, though. Mildred Rodale is one chilly broad.

From his chest pocket, Officer Miller fishes out the list Booker had me compile. "You are hereby ordered to return Miss Lena Bjornstad's unused rent, her new black cloche with bronze ribbon detailing and a metal leaf pin, and assorted personal grooming products too numerous to read—but which have been itemized, so I suggest you don't try your hand at keeping any. And I want you to explain why the aforementioned items failed to be included in the two suitcases and one box you packed, given that all Miss Bjornstad's belongings were in the same room. The one she rented until you evicted her this morning."

"I have no idea what you're talking about," Mrs. Rodale declares indignantly. Both her eyes and her voice, however, show the strain it must be taking not to panic beneath the unyielding policeman's authoritative demands and not at all sympathetic regard.

"Then I have no choice but to search the premises," Miller says, stepping forward in a manner that forces the matron to step back. The officer gives her a hard look. "The entire premises. And be warned, ma'am, should I go to this effort and find so much as one of the items on my list, I will arrest you for petty theft and unlawfully breaking Miss Bjornstad's contract."

"Now wait one damn minute." The older woman straightens her spine. "I had *every* right to eject her. I gave Miss Bjornstad a key and allowed her to come home past the regular curfew from the goodness of my heart, strictly due to the hours she keeps at that *place* she works at." Mrs. Rodale's upper lip curls in clear disapproval of said *place*. "But this morning it was a good two hours later than her usual arrival when this *man*—" She waves a hand at Booker, but for the first time she falters when she really takes in his impeccably tailored suit. I can actually see the impact of his breeding and air of authority sinking in as she realizes Booker is precisely who I told her he was: my employer.

She gathers herself once again, however, her shoulders squared and head held high. "When this man brought her home." The look of distaste Rodale then transfers to me would likely have made me want to crawl into a hole and pull it closed behind me, were it not for Booker's hand landing lightly against the small of my back. I know I should probably step away from his touch. I am hardly some wilting Daisy who needs tending, after all.

But I don't move.

His touch is warm, warm, warm, heating my skin against the brisk fall air even through my layers of day clothing and outerwear. Plus, the weight of his palm and long fingers resting against the base of my spine gives me a very real sense of security. That is not exactly something I'm accustomed to. But I sure can't deny I could *get* used to it in a mad rush.

Rodale turns to Officer Miller again. "Why don't you arrest *him* for selling liquor instead of harassing a hardworking citizen?"

Miller raises his eyebrows. "Have you ever been to his establishment, Mrs. Rodale?

"Of course not," she says huffily. "I am a law-abiding woman."

"Then what makes you think illegal liquor is being sold there?"

"It's a speakeasy!" she snaps, as if it ought to be self-evident.

"It's the Twilight Room," Booker refutes coolly. "A club where elegant people come to relax and enjoy in comfort the best blues by the best singer on the West Coast." His voice drops as he says that last part, and he gives me a nod and a warm smile. When he turns back to Mrs. Rodale, however, his voice is colder than a lamppost after an ice storm. "Mayor Bertha Landes, herself, has been to hear Miss Bjorn-stad sing. And if you know anything, you know Mayor Landes has continued the city-wide cleanup she began as acting mayor. I don't know if you realize Seattle was considered one of the most corrupt cities on the West Coast before her terms in office, but under her guidance it is now much more lawful. Which is more than I can say for you." He glances at his watch, then at Officer Miller. "Do your duty. We don't have all day."

"No, we don't." Miller pulls out a pair of handcuffs and levels a hard-eyed glance at the dragon of the Women's Residence. "Mildred Rodale, you have five minutes to comply with the return of the items I have already listed. If you do not comply within the given time frame, I will have no choice but to arrest you." He looks her in the eye. "And I will drag you out of here in handcuffs for all your neighbors to see."

The old biddy attempts a stare down with the man. It lasts for less than ten seconds before she looks away, sniffs indignantly, and ultimately says, "*Fine.*" She whirls away and disappears into the depths of the Residence.

Seconds before her allotted time is up, she appears with a box. She holds it out for the officer to take.

He drills her with a cold look. "Give it to Miss Bjornstad, so she can verify all her stolen belongings are accounted for."

She thrusts it at me and I accept it, then carefully inspect its contents. The minute I come across my new cloche, I put it on. I finally look up and nod. "This appears to be all of my things."

"And the unused rent?" Booker demands.

"The nine dollar bills in the envelope I handed over to her are in the box, as well.

Officer Miller pins Mrs. Rodale in his sights once more. "Be warned, ma'am, this is your one and only free pass. If I get so much as a whiff of a complaint against you, you will go to jail."

Rodale slams the door in our faces.

I turn to the officer. "Thank you so much." I touch fingertips to my newly donned cloche. "I know it's probably silly to get all worked up over a hat, but this is the first brand new, not absolutely necessary thing I have bought myself in, well, forever."

His eyes soften as he looks down at me. "You're welcome. I have a sister who often has to struggle to make ends meet, so I know how I'd feel if someone treated her the way that woman did you."

Before we all get in our respective vehicles I see Booker discreetly slip Officer Miller some money. "What do I owe you?" I ask as soon as Booker seats himself behind the steering wheel.

"What?" Booker's expression looks genuinely baffled.

"I saw you give Officer Miller some money. You shouldn't have to pay him for my stuff. How much do I owe you?"

"Fifty bucks."

My mouth drops open. I jerk upright. "Are you *crazy*? I could have paid for everything we just recovered—including a *month's* rent instead of just a week's—and had money left over!"

"Yeah, but didn't it feel good to watch that bitch squirm?"

It did. Oh, it really *did*. The tiny smile I can't bite back must answer Booker's question loud and clear, too, because he laughs.

Full throttle, exactly the way he *used* to laugh. It echoes in my heart, softening all the hard edges with happy memories.

No! I simply cannot go there. Sobering, I protest, "Why is it again I'm paying four times more than all my belongings put together are worth? Because I have to tell you, Booker, for people like me—who obviously don't run in the highfaluting circles you do—" I shake my head to rid myself of the topic detour "—well, for me, anyhow, *not* paying more than something is worth tends to make a lot more sense than scoring points against the opponent. It feels less like being robbed twice."

One lollapalooza of a brainstorm

BOOKER

My laughter dries up. Hell. It's moments like these that make me realize how much I take my wealth for granted. Sure, I have the satisfaction of knowing I put copious amounts of work into amassing it. The blood, sweat and tears I invested in getting the Twilight Room up and running translates into a far greater feeling of accomplishment than I ever had when it was my father's dough paying my way. I'm proud of what I've accomplished with nothing more than a fairly good brain and good, hard work.

Yet apparently, I still accept the privileges of my upbringing—a polish that opens doors firmly closed to those without breeding and manners—as my God given right. All were instilled in me from boyhood, so I suppose I did absorb a sense of entitlement from my parents before I learned to make my own way.

Lena wasn't born with my advantages, and God knows she has had damn little handed her. Yet, like me, she's not afraid of hard work. From everything I have gleaned, it's clear she's worked hard to get to this point in her career. Reaching across the seat separating us, I touch my fingertip to the little wave in front of her temple. I tip my head to look her in the eye. "I'm sorry. I was focused on getting your stuff back—and, yes, maybe sticking it to Rodale a little."

"But fifty dollars!"

"I gave it to Officer Miller because I like the way he handled the situation. I do not expect you to pay me back. I was just teasing, but it was in poor taste. After the war, I had to make my own way for the first time in my life and it kicked most of my big fish in a small town attitude out of me. But I guess I still sometimes take the prerogatives of the wealthy I was born into for granted."

"Oh, heck." Lena blows out a wistful breath, her features softening. "I'm just jealous. I would love to take dealing out fifty dollar bills for granted."

And that right there, Lena's honesty, her lack of self-pity and live and let live outlook on life, is exactly why I love her.

I freeze for a second. I *love* her. My honest shock has me swallowing a snort. Hell, I probably never stopped loving her.

Acknowledging my feelings for a change instead of dancing around them, I abandon my former vague, if sincere, plan to stake a permanent claim in Lena's life. The minute Plan A gets tossed, however, I assume the mantle for Plan B. It aims for the same end result, but is more realistic. It just this instant flashed through my mind and, sure, it isn't exactly fully formed.

But damned if it isn't, in my not so humble opinion, one lollapalooza of a brainstorm all the same.

I remember damn near every conversation we ever had

LENA

Booker is staring at me with such intensity, I shift in my seat, goosebumps spreading as I feel his regard like a finger trailing down my spine. My face heating up, I glance out the car window at the trees lining the street. They have begun whipping in a newly kicked up wind. Peering up at the sky, I see clouds, which earlier had been thin, pale and high, growing thicker, darker and lower by the second as they ride the wind northward.

Then my gaze is drawn irresistibly back to Booker. I manage not to shiver when I find him still studying me with that penetrating gaze. "Um, I should probably go rustle up a newspaper and see what the Rooms to Let situation is. Maybe I can check into one or two before work."

"You don't have a helluva lot time for that today," he says. When I stare at him in confusion, he adds gently, "It's Saturday, doll."

"Oh, *shit!*" I promptly cover my mouth with my fingers, appalled at my language. Then I jut my chin. Sometimes swear words are the only ones to properly cover the way a girl feels. Booker's right, of course, I won't have enough time to find a new place. Washington State has a Blue Law on the books going back to when I was a kid. It prohibits most businesses from operating on Sundays so their workers can observe the Sabbath with their families. This means bars close down at midnight on Saturdays. For those of us drawing our paychecks from the Twilight Room, the early shutdown means starting at the lounge three hours earlier than our usual time.

Impulsively, I scoot along the seat until I'm close enough to reach across Booker's hard stomach and grab his left wrist. Turning it toward me, I peer at his watch. I can't help but notice his skin is, as usual, toasty warm beneath my fingers and—*oh, my*—incredibly sleek on the underside of his wrist where my fingertips pick up the strong pulse of his heart.

Ho-ly crow. I have a sudden urge to fan myself, and touching him makes me highly aware that once you feel something like this, it is simply not possible to unfeel it.

Giving myself a mental shake, I actually read the watch face I've been wasting my time staring at, considering I couldn't state the time to save my soul. "Drat," I say again as the time finally sinks in. "Drat, drat, drat." Releasing my hold on his wrist I sag back against the seat. Try to reorganize my thoughts. "Okay, Plan B."

Booker's lips curve up and I hear him murmur, "A woman after my own heart."

Whatever the heck that means.

"I should at least call Dot and Clara to tell them what's going on. I'll see if I can stay with them until I get my room situation straightened out."

He looks at me. "Or you can just stay with me again tonight."

For a moment, I think my heart stopped. If so, it certainly isn't stopped now—the darn thing is stampeding like a herd of mules through my chest. And in a moment of clarity I realize that, *my goodness*, I want that! I probably shouldn't, but, oh, I do. The smart money says this very reaction is precisely why it's the *last* offer I oughtta accept. Straightening up smartly, I wiggle back into my space on the passenger side of the front seat. And give myself a stern warning to *stay* there.

As if he can already read the refusal I'm working up to speaking aloud, Booker shoots me a look so soft it rattles my will power. "Why not give yourself one more good night's sleep? Then you'll be fresh to jump into the hunt for a room tomorrow. Hell, we can pick up a copy of the Seattle Daily Times on our way home, so you can at least cull out the best prospects to interview on Monday."

Refuse, Lena. You need to refuse. You know *it's the only thing to do!*

It's just—

Home. My, how that word grabs me. I can feel it prying open my deepest, most heartfelt desire the way Will and I once tried to do with one of the clams we'd dug up over on Alki Point (before we discovered the trick of steaming them open). And even admitting to myself how the word is one huge trigger for me—

Well, it doesn't do a darn thing to shoo away the boatload of emotion it stirs up, now does it?

"Okay," I whisper. Then clear my throat and hurriedly add in a stronger voice, "But just for tonight."

"Sure." He starts the car and turns on the heater. "Look, I owe you a nice meal and we owe each other that talk we were going to have last night. Let's go see if they're serving yet at Top o' the Town."

I blink. Then I'm pretty darn sure I stare at him stupidly. But, oh, my God. Booker is talking about the Sorrento Hotel's seventh floor restaurant! "I would like that." I am *so* proud of the way I manage to say this calmly, as though eating at Top o' the Town is an everyday occurrence for me. Heaven knows, inside I'm spinning in circles, kicking up my heels and screaming, Yes, yes, yes, yes, *YES!*

"I don't believe I have ever been there," I murmur. Another proud moment because, hell's bells and hallelujah, I don't even wince a tiny bit at discovering my new-found talent for swooping around the truth. As if I don't know perfectly well I have never been there.

"It's settled then. Let's go."

We arrive atop First Hill a short while later and Booker parks on Ninth Avenue not terribly far from the Sorrento's elegant corner courtyard. He escorts me into the hotel and across the lobby to the elevator, which we ride up to the seventh floor.

Disappointingly, we learn the rooftop restaurant is closed and won't open with enough time for us to both enjoy a meal *and* make it to work for our early start. Well, not that Booker, as owner, can't do whatever the heck he wants. But I'm glad he doesn't suggest it. Because, how embarrassing would it be for little ol' employee me to come trailing into the lounge late in his wake?

Uh, *no*. I don't think so.

In any case, a friendly hostess directs us to an open tearoom on this floor. And since we have a few minutes while they refresh the two-person table that another party is getting ready to vacate, we brave the cold and blustery late afternoon weather to go out onto the loggia to take in the spectacular views. Getting hit in the face by the wind, I am happy for my warm, if not exactly the height of fashion, coat and the close fit of the pretty hat Officer Miller helped me recover from Mrs. Rodale.

Everywhere I look, there is something to gawk at, and each new sight to greet my eyes seems more appealing than the last. Below us to the west, lights wink on one after another in the downtown area. Beyond the city buildings coming to life, white caps churn up a froth in Elliot bay and on Puget Sound, even as one of the higher peaks in the Olympic mountains across the water is lit by a pale sunbeam breaking through the cloud cover. To the south is the amazing Smith Tower—the tallest building west of the Mississippi—and beautiful Mt. Rainier. Okay, so maybe the eastern view isn't as gorgeous as it could be, since we'd ordinarily have a pristine territorial view of the Cascade mountains. The storm clouds currently piling up against the foothills block a good portion of the range, but the taller snowcapped peaks thrust their tips through the cloud cover. That glimpse of their power and the sheer beauty of the remaining views threatens to overwhelm me.

I grip Booker's forearm. "Jeepers-creepers. At one time or another,

I have seen every one of these sights. But I have never stood in one place and seen them all at once. I think this might be the most *glorious* sight I have ever witnessed!"

He smiles down at me and lightly rubs the pad of his thumb against the small dent in my chin, another action that takes me back. He used to do the same thing all the time; he'd seemed endlessly fascinated by my chin's shallow cleft. Flooded with sudden memories, I find myself inching closer to him.

"Excuse me, Mr. Jameson," the tea room hostess calls softly from the doorway, making me take a swift step back. I feel for a moment almost as though she caught us doing something we shouldn't. But she merely smiles at us and says, "Your table is ready."

She seats us a moment later. The instant she walks away Booker shoots me an apologetic look. "I'm sorry, Lena. This isn't exactly what I had in mind."

I'm frankly delighted with the place and, planting my elbow on the table and my chin in my palm, I smile at him over the little vase hosting an artful single chrysanthemum. "I like it. The view can't be beat and it's *very* pretty, don't you think?" The latter is hardly a serious question—it's more like one of those whatchamacallit kinds where no answer is required. Because, please. The tearoom is beautifully appointed and it's hardly as if I have been to so many elegant eateries I'm going to look for details to complain about.

"*You* are very pretty," he says, his voice a low rumble that vibrates in a most interesting place deep inside of me. He lounges back in his chair with one elbow hooked round the top dowel of its ladder back.

"Aw, you." I grin at him across the small table. "You know," I add, studying him more closely, "*you* are more what I thought a sheik would be in the movies than Rudolph Valentino was. If you tell Dot, I will deny this with my dying breath. But Valentino seemed more grinning fool than a romantic hero."

No, no, no, no, no! I did *not* just say that! Now Booker is going to think *I* think he's a romantic hero. And okay, at the moment I kind of do. But danged if I want him *knowing* anything of the sort.

Too bad for me, though, since I am clearly too late. He shoots me a cocky smile and wags his eyebrows.

I'm valiantly ignoring him, when I remember his check for an orphanage in my purse. "Oh!" I snap upright. "I forgot all about this." I dig through my purse and pull it out. "I'm so sorry. This came yesterday." I explain how it arrived with the box of gowns from Frederick and Nelson.

"I wondered what the hell happened to that." Booker looks up from studying the check. "I didn't even remember writing it while I was waiting for you during the fittings until a couple days ago." He shoots me a crooked smile. "Which isn't too surprising considering how stunning you looked when you modeled the gowns." Then he shrugs. "Drove every other thought out of my head."

Pretending his flattery—and hot eyed gaze—aren't turning my cheeks seven shades of red, I hand him the note from Alice even as I tell him what it says. Then I meet his gaze head on and raise my eyebrows. "So, how long have you been doling out generous checks to orphanages?" I lean forward, my discomfort forgotten. I have wondered about this since first laying eyes on the check Frederick and Nelson returned with my box of gowns.

Booker shrugs again. "I started donating to The Children's Home once the lounge started turning a healthy profit."

"Almost right away, in other words?" Face it, Booker seems to have a golden touch, but I doubt it's because the sun follows him around just looking for an opportunity to shine down on his head. I think it stems from his tendency to consider every possibility before committing to an action. It simply makes sense to me that all his hard work would result in prompt success.

Not that I know the first thing about what it took for him to pilot the Twilight Room into the black. Or, heck, even if he actually has.

But I do know, by the big smile on his face, my assessment doesn't offend him. And I simply have to smile back. I am also helpless to stop myself from gazing at the smile lines his grin fans out from the corners of his eyes, or admiring the whiteness of his teeth as they gleam in the room's lighting.

His shoulder above the arm draped over the chair back hitches up, then as swiftly drops. "Pretty much."

"What made you choose that particular charity?"

"Seriously, Lena?" A dark eyebrow quirks. "Why do you suppose?"

I blink. Then blink and blink again, for all the world as if I've developed a sudden tic. Squeezing my eyes shut, I immediately pop them wide open again, relieved when the action halts the stupid winky-eye activity. My voice comes out just a bit too high when I say, "*Me*? Because of me?"

"Yeah. You and the godawful Blood of Christ. I wanted my money to go toward making something better than that place ." Unhooking his arm from the chair back, he leans forward. "I hated the way the matron from hell ran the B of C. It was a disgrace."

Then his face lights up as quickly as it clouded over. "You should see the Seattle Children's Home, Lena. It's over on Queen Anne Hill —I'll take you there one of these days. It's light and bright and everything I wished for you at the foundling home. Not that they don't do some things the same. The girls learn to sew, for instance same as you did. The boys are taught a trade.

"One of the interesting differences in this place, though, is that not only orphans live at the home. They also take in kids of single fathers who work in the woods or mines or are out to sea for extended periods of time. And the women who work there *smile* at the children. They're not all doom and gloom like Matron Stick Up Her—um. They *smile*," he repeats emphatically.

I hide my amusement at Booker's attempted cover-up. But, please. Like I don't know exactly what he meant to say! Clasping my hands in my lap, I hear myself admit, "I always had the strongest urge to stop at the local orphanage in the different towns where I had my singing gigs. I thought I could offer some music lessons, or, I don't know, maybe help organize a choir for the kids who were interested." I have never told a soul that. Not even Will.

"But you never did?"

"No. I just couldn't." To my horror, my chin quivers. I draw a deep breath and hold it one second...two seconds...three, until I regain my composure. My chin tilts up as I admit for the first time the true reason I could never bring myself to do the thing I truly longed to do. "I know far too well what it feels like to have people come into my life, only to leave me just when I drop my guard and start to count on them. And at this point in my career, coming and going is the nature of my work. I follow the gigs, and when you're trying to move up the ladder in this business that means going from town to increasingly larger towns." I sit straighter in my seat.

Because there it is, what I have never actually acknowledged to myself.

Yet Booker doesn't seem the least surprised. He gives me a brisk nod, as if to say atta girl!

Darned if it doesn't renew my strength without a word being spoken. Solemnly, I peer up into his handsome face. "I couldn't bear to get other kids all excited about singing, only to walk out on them just when they've placed their trust in me."

I brace my forehead in my palm a moment. Then I raise my head to look at Booker and softly slap my hand down on the tabletop. "I could *not* do that to them."

"Okay, I can see that." He slides his hand across the table until his fingertips barely graze mine. His touch is soft as a breeze, yet I feel it like a lightning bolt sizzling through every nerve in my body.

I'm so discombobulated I have to concentrate to make sense of his individual words when he says, "I recall you once telling me how hard it was when the older kids in the orphanage who'd befriended you moved on."

Then his words sink in and I sit straighter in my seat. "Oh, my gosh, you *remember* that?"

"Of course." Booker looks at me as if I'd asked a ridiculous question. "I remember damn near every conversation you and I have ever had."

And just like that, I feel the final dregs of my ill-will, the last of my hard-held grudge against Booker, evaporate like fine drizzle on hot rocks. I have been so darn angry since coming face to face with him again and didn't even realize until this minute how much it has worn me out. But now, all that energy-sucking ire is simply...gone.

Leaving me awash in the most amazing, peaceful feeling.

That's the *berries!*

BOOKER

Hearing Henry proclaim "*Lo*-La Baker!" in that deep, rich radio announcer voice he uses to great effect, I look up from the office ledger I dragged out to the lounge. I have been sitting here at my usual table, ice melting in a largely untouched bourbon as I try to find the entry that's been preventing Leo and me from reconciling the books this week. And I'm doing this by fucking candlelight, of all the idiotic ideas, because I don't want to miss Lena's entrance.

Turns out, it is worth every bit of discomfort, because as she rises up through the floor and the audience goes wild, I forget the slight thumping in my left temple from an aggravating case of eye strain, forget the annoyingly elusive forty-seven dollars and eighty-three cents we're off, the amount of which rings a familiarity bell in the back of my mind without giving me the first clue as to why. Staring at Lena, I finally pick up my watered-down drink and knock back half of it in one large gulp to sooth a throat abruptly gone drier than dust.

She is wearing "my" dress as I secretly think of it. The final selection Alice, the seamstress at Frederick's, brought out for her to try on the day we went in for her gown fittings. This is the curve hugging black and tan gown that clings to Lena's body like a lover.

I shift in my seat. Shit. Those are the last terms I need to be thinking in.

When Lena leans into the mic and sings, "It. Had to be. Yoooou," in a sultry alto, however, I almost forget the gown and the body it showcases. "It had to be yoooou."

The words, sung with searing emotion, arrow through my soul, every damn syllable branding Lena's imprint over yet another inch of me. It's always been her. It always will be. We were fated, mated, from the moment she kissed my minor 'owie' better outside our hometown hardware store.

It had to be you, indeed.

This is a new addition to her lineup. I approved its addition to her first set with Henry, but have never actually heard Lena sing the song. And, *damn*, have I missed out! She has turned it into a torch song far different from Isham Jone's original, fast paced rendition. And I feel like she's singing straight to me when she goes on in that throaty voice:

Might never be cross, or try to be boss.
But they wouldn't do.

And God help us all. I want to whisk her away *now*, this minute. Drag her back to my place. I want—

I blow out a frustrated breath. Something I can't have; that's what I want. At least not right this minute. Catching John's attention over at the bar he's manning, I signal for a fresh drink.

I love this speakeasy more than just about anything else in my life. My reverence is due, in no small part, to the fact that I turned a fairly run down space into the elegant lounge I had dreamed about for years. And I did it all by myself.

Okay, not entirely by myself. The minute I contacted Leo about coming to work for me, he left his hometown in Ohio and moved out here to help me make my dream a thriving operation. But I did it with neither my father's help nor his money.

Consequently, I doesn't bother me I spend the lion's share of my time here and have little social life outside of the Twilight Room. Tonight, though, I'm grateful it's Saturday and we'll be closing early. I keep half expecting that any minute now Lena will come tell me she talked to Dot and Clara and they insist she stay with them. Which ought to make me happy for her.

But, *damn* I don't want her going anywhere except home with me! I'm pleased when I hear Henry announce last call without Lena stopping by to make my expectations a reality.

The swells and the flappers vacate the joint after the final number and I collect the money from John at the bar, then head back to my office as the lounge begins settling down. I am just coming to the backstage corridor to my office when I hear a sudden burst of excited laughter, then chatter from what sounds like every damn one of my employees. Shit. Did I forget someone's birthday? I swear I didn't see anyone's name in today's calendar entries.

Leo looks up from tidying his desk as I walk into the office, glancing at the ledger in my hand. "You find the problem?"

"No, but we'll deal with it tomorrow. Go on home, Sarge."

"Don't mind if I do. I woke up way too early today, so it's been a long one." He blows out a breath. Grimaces. "Plus, I got another letter from Millie."

Oh, hell. Millie is Leo's faithless ex-wife, who wrote him a goddamn Dear John letter while we were fighting for our lives in the trenches. She has since decided she regrets the divorce and can't seem to accept she broke the faith with Leo in a way impossible to repair.

Amid the dwindling sounds of employees chatting as they begin trickling out, Leo grabs his hat and coat. "See you tomorrow," he says and heads for home, as well.

Minutes later, all goes quiet. I finish counting the take from the bar and put it in the safe. I'm beginning to think maybe Lena left with the Brasher sisters after all when there's a light tap on my door and Lena's voice softly calling my name.

I grin, then rein it in because I kind of fear my mouth is stretched so wide and my smile's so loopy-relieved, I look like a damn idiot. "Come in." I toss my mechanical pencil on the desk and lean back in my chair.

She sticks her head in the door and gives me a dazzling smile. *Whoa*, Nellie. I sit up.

"Hi," she murmurs.

"Hi, yourself. Ready to go home?"

I could almost swear she shivers, but maybe not, because she says uncertainly, "I am, but can I ask a favor of you first?"

Something has her damn near vibrating and I push back from the desk to stand. "Sure. What do you need?"

"Oh, my gosh, you gotta see this," she says breathlessly, stepping into the office. She thrusts something out at me.

I look down. It's a—I'm not sure what, exactly, so I narrow my eyes and actually study it for a moment. It's a wooden star encrusted with costume jewelry. I look at her helplessly. "It's, uh—

"*Beautiful*, right? I *know!*" She beams up at me, her entire face aglow. "It's for my dressing room door—see the little whatchamacallit on the back? Clara and Dot made it for me with the stage fellas' help. Roger cut the star out of some leftover pine and Ernie sanded it smooth and stained it. And just about everyone working here brought in orphaned jewelry that's no longer part of a big set. Those are called a parure, did you know that? I didn't, but it's fun to learn something new, isn't it? Anyhow, they brought in stuff that's no longer part of a parure or a set—I think a parure has to be more than two matching pieces—but stuff they hung onto in case the missing piece showed up. Isn't that the way it usually goes? The lost piece usually isn't found, so its mate sits forgotten in the bottom of whatever you use to keep your jewelry in."

She shakes her head and waves a hand as if batting mosquito netting away from her face. "Sorry," she says. "You might remember I tend to go off subject." She points to a small crystal Art Deco piece.

"So, this is the earring that was left when Sally lost its mate. This one and this one are from two different pairs of Henry's cufflinks. The tie pin here is from Benson. It didn't have a mate, of course—he just thought I would like it. Isn't that the sweetest thing?" She flashes me her delighted smile again.

Then she points at a brooch in the middle of the star. "This was Elsie's. One of the crystals fell out, so Dot cut off that part. Don't ask me how, because that couldn't have been easy. But she and Clara put so much work into this for me and I want you to hang it on my door, okay?"

This, I think. This woman standing in front of me, talking fast and barely drawing breath between words, is the Lena I remember in a nutshell. And she is still every bit as appreciative as she was back then.

During my time in France, I was often present in clubs when men presented their wives or mistresses with an expensive piece of jewelry. With the exception of the woman whose fella asked for her hand in marriage, I honest to God cannot remember any of the others displaying as much enthusiasm as Lena does for this gift from her friends. She is all but bouncing up and down with excitement over a star crafted from discarded and forgotten costume jewelry, disregarding its rag-tag origins and thrilled by the thoughtfulness of every single person who contributed to the gift.

As I reach out to take the star from her hands, I kind of wish someone had asked me to donate something. Checking the back of the decoration, I see Roger cut out a small notch and taped a screw next to it. All I have to do is put the screw in the door and its head will slip into the notch to hold it nice and flush against the door. "Let me get a screwdriver and we'll get it mounted."

Laughing exuberantly, she claps her hands. "*Thank* you!"

Ten minutes later, I step back from her door and glance over at Lena. "What do you think?"

Hugging clasped hands atop her lush breasts, she sighs. "It's just perfect."

"Well, almost," I say, pointing out a small gap between Elsie's brooch and what I learned was another, smaller brooch donated by Clara. "It needs something here. We'll have to look through my mismatched stuff when we get home."

Her face lights up. "You'd do that?"

I'm pretty sure my heart just seized, but Jesus. She sounds so damn thrilled you'd think I had offered her a diamond bracelet. "Of course. I'd like to be a part of your gift."

"That is the *berries!*" She smacks my arm. "C'mon, what the heck are you waiting for?" She whirls on the balls of her little T-strap shoes and sashays off down the hall.

29

Like something out of the picture shows

LENA

Goodness gracious, but this has been a fine day and night! First I get all of my stolen property back, plus have the satisfaction of watching Mrs. Rodale squirm when faced with Officer Miller. Then Booker treats me to that wonderful lunch at the Sorrento Hotel. Not to mention I am beside-myself thrilled with the reception my rendition of *It Had to Be You* received from the club's patrons. Henry is dead right—this *is* a song for the ages. One of which I simply cannot see myself ever growing tired.

Then there's my amazingly thoughtful gift from Clara and Dot. I am so humbled by the affection my coworkers have shown me with their willingness to contribute to my lovely dressing room door star. It makes me *feel* like an honest to Betsy celebrity.

Now here I am, taking sneaky peeks around Booker's bedroom while he rummages through the top shelf of his closet looking for his box of loose tie clips and pins, collar bars, button studs and cuff links. It's all I can do to not laugh out loud.

Because who but Booker would have an entire *container* dedicated to orphaned bits of accessories? I don't even own a real jewelry box, just the old cigar box I asked one of my old bosses to save for me when he finished his last cigar.

With pale grey walls and rich wood trim and flooring, Booker's bedroom is every bit as beautiful as the rest of his house. And since it's directly above the living room, it, too, has a fireplace. I can't get over that—a *fireplace* in the bedroom! This has to be one of the ritziest, most luxurious things I have ever laid eyes on.

Speaking of luxurious, I really want to throw myself atop Booker's bedspread and just flap my arms and legs like a kid making snow angels. My *gosh* the thing is swank, like something out of the picture shows. Its pattern, in a rich combination of bronze and silver, makes me think of some of the fancy Art Deco detailing I've seen on and inside of buildings around the state. And it looks so soft and silky-satiny, I can only imagine what it would feel like against bare skin.

"Hah! I knew the damn thing had to be in here somewhere."

I have to hide my smile when Booker emerges from his closet. Foraging through the enclosed space has mussed him up some and he looks so darn cute.

Well, okay, Booker is a good deal more than cute. But he looks younger somehow than he did just ten minutes ago.

He grins at me, waving his free hand with a flick of his long, strong fingers in the direction of the two leather wingback chairs in front of the fireplace. "Grab a seat. I'll build us a little fire and we can paw through this. See if we can find something to finish off your star." He sets the box on the table between the chairs, then goes to squat in front of the fireplace.

After building a little tipi of kindling over wads of newspaper, he pulls out a few larger pieces of wood from the cubby built into the wall next to the fireplace and swiftly assembles them in a similar shape over the kindling. He strikes a match and shoves its flame into the bottom section. The paper catches fire.

I reach for the jewelry box Booker left on the table while he's blowing the small flame into a larger one. But the man must have eyes in the back of his head. "Get your mitts off that," he says. "You and me, baby, we're going through that thing together."

He joins me a moment later and turns on the table lamp. As flames lick the kindling, which in turn adds fuel to lap at the larger pieces of wood, he picks up the box and hands it to me. "Dive in."

I remove the lid. "Oh, my, look at all of these! I hardly know where to start." I toss the top back on the table between us, then turn back to the box.

"Take out all the bits that won't work first and we'll set those aside." He flips the box top upside down. "You can put them in here."

I remove the tie and collar bars, which are clearly the wrong shape and size and their removal starts whittling down the choices. "Why do you even have some of this stuff in here? They don't look like they were ever part of a larger set." I shoot him a sly smile. "Or *parure*." I love saying that word. It makes me feel sort of worldly.

"I grew tired of them, but liked them well enough to think I might want to wear them again sometime in the future." Booker shrugs. "Like you said, though, you put the things away, and it's out of sight, out of mind. I forgot all about them until tonight."

"Well, you have some really swell stuff here. You should pick some of it to use again." Looking for a round piece, I cull out the rectangular and square cuff links unsuitable for the spot we need to fill and add them to the growing pile in the box lid. I glance over at Booker. "Okay, I think I've narrowed it down to pieces that might fit the space."

He reaches across the table between us. "Give it here. I can tell you right now some pieces in there are still too large." I give him the box and he removes several more items. Then he hands it back again. "Go to town, doll."

I grin at him, then bend over the box to begin picking through the remaining shirt studs and tie pins. In the end, I hand Booker a stylish round onyx tie pin with a tiny silver starburst in the center. It just *looks* like Booker. I also pass over three little onyx and gold shirt studs. "If the pin's too big, maybe some of the studs might fill in the space better." I grimace. "I was excited to see the star on my door, but

I should have brought it home so we could actually size things. I can be too impatient for my own good sometimes."

"We can drive back and get it, if you want."

I still. *Yes, yes, yes!* "Really?"

"You gonna be able to sleep for thinking about it all night?"

Oh, Lord, has he got my number! I shake my head.

"Grab your coat."

I whoop and race downstairs ahead of him to do precisely that before he can change his mind.

The streets are deserted this hour of the morning so no more than a half an hour later, we're back at Booker's house again with my beautiful star and a tube of glue Booker grabbed from Roger's work bench. We also have a Sunday copy of the Seattle Daily Times we picked up from Booker's favorite seller who was busily stocking his news shed with freshly delivered stock.

Booker locks the front door behind us, then tosses the paper on the entry way table and hands me the glue. "Take the star into kitchen—it has the best lighting. I'll go up and grab the jewelry." He climbs the stairs two at a time.

He's right about the lighting, and after covering a generous section of the kitchen table with a couple of layers of old newspapers I find in a box on the enclosed back porch, I lay down my door star and place the tube of glue next to it.

"Here we go." Booker hands me the four pieces we selected and sets the box with the remaining jewelry on the far end of the table. "See if they fit."

I pick up the tie pin and set it in the spot. "Oh." My heart drops. "It's...almost perfect." It fits the space pretty well, except for one tiny spot. I didn't even realize I had my heart set on this piece until a hot surge of disappointment washes over me. It doesn't make sense, because I didn't even notice the little gap until Booker pointed it out. But now I want this tie pin of his to fill it, and fill it perfectly.

When I, of all people, should know there is no such thing as perfection.

"Hey, it may still work." Booker hands me one of the shirt studs. "Try fitting this in next to it."

It slides in like it was made for the space and I squeal like a little girl. "There *is* such a thing as perfect. Oh, my gosh, you are brilliant, brilliant, *brilliant!*" I throw myself at him, rising on my toes to lay a *thank you* smooch on his lips.

At least, that was my intention. But it's as if I kissed a live wire. I feel a jolt of 100 proof, make your hair smoke, pure *heat* rocket through me from where my lips press against Booker's clear down to my—ahem—lady place. I jump back, my face on fire.

"I'm sorry! I got carried away. I didn't mean to get fresh with—" I cut myself off, because, God, I sound like an idiot. What the heck? I can handle amorous drunks without blinking an eye. But put me within smooching distance of Booker Jameson, whose kisses I have relived in my dreams for eight long years, and all my street smarts, my confidence in myself as a woman, goes up in smoke.

"Oh, honey." Gaze intent, Booker snakes an arm around my waist and jerks me flush against his hard, hot body. "You don't have a damn thing to be sorry about," he assures me.

His voice is a low and husky rasp abrading every nerve in my body. And I have a feeling I'm in trouble.

Big, *big* trouble.

He looks down at me with smoldering eyes. "In fact, you and me? Lena, sweetheart, you and I are just getting started."

And, squatting slightly, the better to align himself with my not nearly as impressive height, he bends his head and rocks his mouth over mine.

30

God, but it feels like home

BOOKER

I think I'm holding her too tight and kissing her too hard. But I have been dying to get Lena back in my arms for what seems like half a lifetime. And good God Almighty. Those pretty lips cushion mine even as her plush curves gently give beneath the crush of my harder body. Desire rattles though my bones like a runaway train. But when a sudden thought crops up in the back of my mind, I fight back the mist of animalistic lust that has me in its spell.

Shit. I just grabbed and kissed her without so much as a how's-about-it-baby. From the first touch of my mouth on Lena's, I was so consumed with the scent, the feel, the *taste* of her I have absolutely no impression as to what her feelings regarding my caveman tactics might be.

Yet when I start to lift my head, I feel her plump, pretty arms, which I'm only just now realizing are already twined around my neck, wind tighter still.

And she sighs a long, drawn out, "Oh."

So, all right, by God, it may be nonverbal but that sounds like a green light to me. Taking full advantage of the small opening her breathy word gives me, I explore the slick inner flesh of her bottom lip with a slow slide of the tip of my tongue. Feeling impatient, on edge, I coax Lena's lips open wider. I inveigle them even farther apart by nipping her full bottom lip here, helping myself to a tiny suck there. But mostly I just kiss her. Endlessly. Insistently.

I groan when the opportunity finally comes to slip my tongue more deeply into her sweet, sweet mouth. *God*, but it feels like home.

Lena must think so as well, because her fingers wind through my hair, and she grips handfuls of it with take no prisoners resolve. She opens those satiny, addictive lips a tiny bit wider yet, her tongue rising off the floor of her mouth to duel with mine.

I doubt I could feel the effect of her tongue sliding over mine more explosively were I a fuel barrel she was twirling lighted torches while dancing the Black Bottom atop. I back her up against the closest upright surface. It turns out to be the new electric Frigidaire and her shoulder blades reach its top.

I bury my mouth in the soft, fragrant crook of her neck, my jaw brushing the shoulder it curves into. I need to feel her skin. Blindly seeking it out, I God bless the fad for rolling women's stockings, as I reach firm bare skin the moment I hit her knees.

I smooth my hands up the warm, smooth backs of her thighs, hiking the skirt of her dress up, filmy fabric pooling atop my forearms as my hands move higher.

And higher.

And higher still.

Until they reach the silky leg openings of what feel like tap pants. Lena sucks in a breath as my fingertips brush beneath a leg opening to trace the crease at the top of her thighs where they meet the sweet curve of her ass.

I groan. Then promptly slip my hands the rest of the way under her French knickers. Hauling her up, I splay my fingers to lightly grip a lush cheek in each hand. My eyes slide closed in sheer appreciation.

Of the heat, of the sumptuous feel and weight of the full curves I hold.

Then Lena spreads her legs and sets me on the path to the Promised Land. "Jesus," I growl, hiking her up until I can press my cock against the soft, hot notch between her legs.

The moment I do so, I hear our urgent, ragged breaths as, together, we sharply inhale. *Feel* as the insides of her knees grip my hips. Rubbing up against that little piece of heaven at the apex of her fabulous thighs, I smile savagely against her warm-skinned throat as a moan vibrates beneath my lips. I chase the little quiver with the flat of my tongue, which sets off another tremor. Then yet another, fainter one.

For a moment, the room is silent aside from our rough breathing, her faint moans and my own guttural groans. Then the fridge suddenly kicks in, making Lena start. I slowly lift my head.

Hell. We're in the damn kitchen—not exactly the ideal place for what I have in mind. Reluctantly, I set Lena on her feet again and step back.

Swaying slightly, she blinks up at me. "Booker?"

She looks so damn cute. Those clear blue eyes, rimmed in exotic navy blue, are heavy-lidded. Her cheeks are flushed, her hair's all mussed and her lips are swollen from my kisses. I sweep her up in my arms.

Where she feels so damn right.

"We need a more comfortable spot." *God, baby, don't change your mind.* Hoping to prevent precisely that, I kiss her again.

Attempting to control a woman through seduction is hardly the stuff of heroes. I'm pretty damn sure, however, I'm gonna lose my mind if Lena decides all this heat between us is going nowhere. And, face it, given her opinion of sex, courtesy of my pitiful teenage performance, that's a very real possibility.

But when I raise my head once again, she dazzles me with a dreamy smile. And presses an openmouthed kiss against my temple before sliding her lips over to my ear. "*Nifty*," she breathes.

I grin so hard I probably look like an escapee from Western

State insane asylum, and I take the stairs two at a time up to the second floor. Not an easy feat sporting a raging hard-on, lemme tell you.

Which is why I need to rein things in a bit before I literally go off half-cocked. Lena already believes sex is for the birds. That's a direct result of my younger self doing precisely what I need to avoid in the here and now. Because, going at her with all the savoir faire of a dog covering a bitch in heat will sure as hell never change her mind and win her heart. I have to be smart about this...which is impossible if I allow my dick to run the show.

When I carry her into my bedroom moments later, low flames are still flickering from the fire I built before we left on our run to the club to fetch Lena's gift. Firelight infuses the room with a soft, warm glow and creates soothing, ever shifting patterns against the nearest wall. I stride straight over to the bed and toss Lena upon it.

A startled whoop escapes her, then she laughs as she lands in a sprawl on her back. She promptly wings her arms and legs in and out against my spread.

"Are you making a *snow angel* on my bedspread?" I demand, biting back the huge laugh fighting to escape me at her antics.

Only to have Lena immediately stop. "*Nooo.*" She shoots me a sheepish smile. Strokes her hands against the spread with such sensuality I'm dying to feel them bestow the same attention to my body. "Well, maybe," she amends.

Then she laughs with uninhibited gusto. "Okay, fine, I am. The minute I saw this beautiful thing, I wanted to fling myself down and make a snow angel to feel its satiny, silky fabric against as much of me as possible. And oh, my gosh, Booker. It is *every* bit as grand as it looks!"

"And you look mighty fine lying on it, baby." On my hands and knees, I prowl up from the end of the bed to join her on the bedspread, rolling onto my side next to her. I prop myself up on a forearm. Now that Lena's brought up the subject, I realize the bedspread really *is* a sensual treat. I can't believe I never truly appreciated just how much of one before this morning. I smile down at her.

Hook a rogue hair off her cheek with my unoccupied hand. "Hello, gorgeous."

"Hi, yourself, handsome."

I bend my head to kiss her neck once more, and smile against her soft skin when she lifts her chin to give me better access and more room to move. Pushing back again, I track my gaze from the neckline of Lena's chiffon dress to her T-strap shoes. "When the hell did you get this body?" My hand outlines her curves an inch or so above her body. "You weren't built anything like this back in Walla Walla."

Lena snorts. "They didn't starve us at the Blood of Christ, but they sure could have shown a little more Christian charity in the size of their portions. Although, to be honest, the flavor—or lack of it— doesn't really support the larger portions idea." She grimaces. "Truth is, until I started spending time with you and Will, I had no idea how good food could taste. But once I was exposed to honest to God flavor and pleasing textures—well, let's just say the minute I left the B of C, I started seeking out more of it. I ate what I wanted to eat instead of tolerating slop like the foundling home served up." She gives a flat on her back little shimmy. Flashes me a grin that takes my breath away. "And as anyone can plainly see, I ate a great deal more of it."

Lena shoves up onto her elbows, a position that thrusts her breasts out. To stop myself from getting grabby, I sit up and slide down the mattress to kick off my shoes. I remove hers, as well—then unfasten her left silk stockings and slide it down her leg and off over her foot. I stretch back up to press a kiss to the soft, firm skin I just bared. Then reach for her right stocking.

"In order to make a living while waiting to get my first singing gig in the lounge I was interested in," she continues breathlessly, "I waited tables at a few restaurants." Throwing her head back, she laughs in that way I remember, full-throated and without a speck of self-consciousness. "Heck, I waitressed while waiting to get my second, third and *fourth* gigs, as well."

Freeing an arm, she smooths her hand over a rounded hip. "The food was grand, and little by little all of it seemed to land on my breasts, hips and butt."

Lena glances away, for the first time looking self-conscious and without a second thought, I abandon her second stocking down around her ankle to sit up and pay attention. An instant later, however, she returns her gaze to my face. "It made me wonder what my mother's figure was like. Was she built the way I am now, do you suppose? Or was she more like I was back in Walla Walla? Or, heck, I could take after my father's mother or an aunt for all I know." Lena looks wistful for a moment, no doubt at the idea of relatives somewhere. Then she shrugs.

I return to my previous position alongside her on the bed and pull her onto her side to face me. "Whoever the hell you take after, I doubt she was anywhere near as perfect as you are."

"Aww." Lena presses her cheek against my chest.

"I'm serious," I insist, because I am. Dead serious. "You were beautiful then and you're even more so now."

Slinging an arm around my neck, Lena pushes up onto her other forearm. All those lush curves coming to rest against me radiate a heat that sinks clear down to my bones.

Then she raises her head. And kisses me.

And this time it's filled with some pretty damn serious intent.

31

Master of all my pleasure

LENA

I adored kissing Booker back in the day. Before we met, I knew from nothing about this smooching business, but it didn't matter. I have the exact same feelings I remember: an enticing sizzle of energy that streaks like lightning from my lips to the pit of my stomach—and lower yet. We were good together back then. I have no doubt it was largely due to Booker being an expert kisser.

And yet, *this*, this thing between us, right here, right now—it's even better. And *ho*-ly crow.

I have no words.

I'm in Booker's arms—or, more truthfully, he's in mine. I felt him start to pull back and it was as though my entire body stood up to scream a denial. The moments following his pullback are a blur. But I do know it was me, this time, left trying to hang on.

I had no trouble pinning the responsibility on Booker when he had his hands on my butt. (Hands. On my *bare* butt!) He didn't simply put them under the skirt of my dress. He slid his big mitts beneath my knickers, to boot.

Heat crawls up my face at mere recollection. Okay, fine. I can admit, if only to myself, this burning in my face (as well as other places I'd just as soon not dwell upon) stems from how much I actually like having his hands on me.

That's about as far as my thinking power will stretch, however. All these uncharacteristic emotions roiling in my head have left me with maybe two brain cells to rub together. I simply cannot think clearly with all these emotions, these *sensations,* sizzling through me. Lord, the man has a sweet touch! The truth is, I can barely breathe. Every inch of my body, where it touches Booker's, feels scalded. Which is darn near all of it. The front half of me, at any rate.

Oh, who am I kidding? The whole shebang is like a gigantic overly stoked furnace. No bananas—I expect smoke to start curling up between us any second now.

Then Booker groans deep in his throat and wrests back control of the kiss. And not only are our bodies smoking, I'm now pretty sure the few thoughts I've managed to hang onto are at this very moment floating away on a poof of thin, grey vapor.

The next thing I know he's rolling us over and I'm flat on my back, sprawled out against his lovely, lovely bedspread once again. Booker props himself partially over me, a heavy, muscular thigh thrown over mine to pin me in place.

His eyes have always been a lighter blue than mine, but they are unusually dark when he pushes up onto his palms to look down at me. In fact, they contain so much heat I'm surprised they don't raise blisters in their wake as he slowly rakes that intense gaze down my torso.

And, at this very moment? I'm sort of loving the forcefulness of his regard, where it settles on my breasts. At the same time, I feel ten kinds of self-conscious, and I cross my arms over them, hoping to disguise the way my nipples are suddenly poking spikes into the stiff brocade of my brassiere. Okay, they probably don't even show, the fabric's that solid. Still.

"No," he commands roughly, getting his knees under him in order to reach for my wrists. Straddling me, he presses my hands against the coverlet on either side of my head. "Let me look. I have imagined this so often and for so damn long. Don't take away the first opportunity I've had to feast my eyes."

I have no idea where my sudden courage comes from, but I shake my breasts at him. Or as much as one can, wearing such a binding garment.

Booker growls. He honest to God *growls*. Then he shifts his entire body down and slips his fingers inside the deep V neckline. I have no idea how he knows about the modesty piece, which can be left out or buttoned in to avoid showing too much skin. But within seconds, it's been removed.

"Jesus." He scowls down at the rigid barrier of my brassier. "It's like a damn fortress."

One that apparently holds no power to keep him away, because the next thing I know he's worked the stiff fabric below my right breast. And before I have even a second to worry about my sudden exposure, he's lowered his head to tease the nipple, which has been pressed back into my breast, into pointing in the right direction again. Once it is, he sucks it into his mouth. His eyes locked on mine, he scrapes the firm point between his teeth.

"Oh. My. Gawwd!" A crazily intense feeling zings from the stiff tip where his lips provide such wondrous suction, spearing straight down to that feminine spot deep inside of me. Swear to heaven, I think my already fairly prominent nipple grows a bit longer yet. I squeeze my thighs together.

Booker lifts his head, his lips releasing my nipple with a soft pop. He pushes back to trace his forefinger along the half of my dress's neckline still in place with his free hand. "I haven't seen this before. Is it new?"

I shake my head. "Clara lent it to me. I was telling her I wanted to get something like it and she said I should try it out."

"Pretty. How do we get it off you?"

I freeze. Dear lord, do I really want that—to strip off the dress in front of Booker?

I'm surprised I've gotten to this point, and there's a good chance I'll talk myself out of something even more intimate. I don't take chances on a personal, put yourself out there where you can get crushed kind of way. Not anymore. Not since Booker left me behind so many years ago.

Not to mention my long ago experience getting naked with the guy. Heck, we didn't actually even get naked back then. We were in his flivver out by the onion fields, so it was more a matter of rearranging our clothing. Do I really want to take another chance on him?

And yet...

The question isn't even fully born before I find myself pushing Booker aside. He swings his left leg over to join its mate and sits back on his heels beside me as I sit up. My sudden tension takes off for parts unknown as, from there, I roll up onto my knees.

"You have to pull it off over my head." Facing him, I hitch the hem up to a point where I, too, can sit back on my heels without having to worry about trapping the fabric. Then I raise my arms so he can remove the dress.

I'm pretty certain I do want this. My body feels crazy restless and I ache in places I had no idea could *feel* the things they're feeling. I want to see where indulging this urge takes me. I clearly remember making out and petting. And, lordy, but I loved that part. The actual sex was far from swell, but I did love the kissing and petting stuff leading up to it. Apparently, that's called foreplay—at least according to one of the waitresses at my gig before last.

So, I'm gonna do it. I'll tolerate the Booker-inside-of-me part in order to experience once again the glorious foreplay I still remember so well. It's been years. But I've never forgotten the truly fabulous moments before things went south.

Unlike me, there is zero waffling on Booker's part. Taking me at my word, he rises onto his knees in front of me and gently works the dress off over my head. He tosses it aside.

A wordless protest involuntarily sounds in my throat and he halts mid reach toward me to study my expression. "Shit. You're going to worry about wrinkles in Clara's dress, aren't you?"

"She *lent* it to me. That means she trusts me to return it the way I got it. I can't give her beautiful dress back to her all balled up."

"Gotcha." Booker climbs off the bed and snatches the dress up off the floor. He gives it a brisk snap to straighten it, then swiftly and competently folds it into a smooth little square. He places it atop the nightstand.

Then he dives back onto the bed, grabs me and rolls us until he is flat on his back and I'm somehow sitting astride his lap.

Smack dab on top of an extremely hard ridge pressed up between my legs.

Booker stares up at me. "I'm definitely doing something wrong if you have time to worry about the state of Clara's dress." He hooks a hot hand around my nape and tugs my head down. "Kiss me."

I inhale sharply when I lean down to do exactly that and feel Booker's hardness rubbing over a spot *very* happy with the attention. I cup his cheeks in my hands and lower my mouth to kiss him. Mimicking his actions, I rock my slightly open lips over his and search for his tongue with mine.

And immediately make a rough noise deep in my throat. Holy, holy crow. I am steeped in so many simultaneous sensations I hardly know what to do with myself. Booker's mouth is hot and damp, his tongue aggressive and knowledgeable as it duels with mine. His early morning stubble scratches lightly against my palms and I slide my hips back to feel that rigid length glide along the furrow between my legs once more. Only a scrap of fabric separates me from the slacks separating *him*. Fabric that is growing embarrassingly wet. The movement also makes my bare shins slide against the magic bedspread's satiny fabric.

Booker's long-fingered hands slap down on my butt and his fingertips curl to grip it in a take no prisoners hold. He uses it to guide my movements atop his...pecker, the boys in the B of C used to call it. But that seems so boyish.

I lift my mouth off his. I've heard a lot of different names for that particular body part over the recent years, but I don't have a clue which one to go with. "When you think of this—" I grind against his length, and the sensation promptly firing through me darn near sends my eyeballs rolling back in my head "—what do you call it?"

"My cock, my dick. Hard-on. *You* can call it whatever your little heart desires."

"Pecker?" I murmur.

Booker grimaces. "Except that. Little boys have peckers." He lifts up against me. "You can call this bad boy a cock. Or Master of all my pleasure." He grins up at me. "That would work."

"Sure." I roll my eyes. Lightly slap his chest with the flat of my hand. "Hold your breath waiting for that to happen."

"Oh, Booker," he moans in what I'm sure he considers a feminine voice, "I need the Master of all my pleasure. Neeeeeed it, I tell you!"

"You idiot." But I laugh. He sounds so much like the boy I used to know. Then I have to go and blush, darn it all.

His eyes light up in the dim, fire-lit room. "You *do* blush all over," he says, reaching up to attempt sliding the other, too small cup of my brassiere aside. I hate this thing; hate the way it squeezes me down. But I needed the flattening effect to fit into Clara's dress.

"Why women wear this shit is beyond me," Booker grouses, reaching behind me to unhook it. He slides it down my arms and tosses it aside.

And, even leaving me half naked, he hears no protest from me this time. Breathing a sigh of relief, I stroke back into shape the breast Booker hasn't already had his hand and mouth all over. I've heard women who have bound their breasts for years complain their bubbies never returned to their former perky life. It's not hard to understand why.

"Here." Booker peels my fingers off my breasts and replaces them with his rougher skinned hands, cupping my breasts in his palms. "Let me help you with that."

"You are such a charitable fella." It is no easy feat keeping my voice steady when every glide of his slightly rough skin over my nipples robs me of breath. Without thought, I shift atop his slacks covered cock once more. And moan deep in my throat.

Booker's groan sings a rugged two-part harmony with mine. He shifts his hands to cup the bottom curve of my breasts, then stares at them like he's serving them up on a silver platter for his—what do the carnival barkers say outside the girly shows? Delectation! Like he's serving them up on a silver platter for his delectation.

"Damn, you're pretty," he murmurs.

My skin heats up again and he smiles up at me. "Yep," he murmurs, his voice somehow sounding deeper than usual. "You definitely blush all over."

I don't know how to respond, so I do what I do best—redirect. "How come I'm next to naked, but you still have all your clothes on?"

"Excellent question." Sliding me down to perch on his thighs, he sits up and starts removing his shirt studs.

I brush his hands aside. "I'll get these. You undo your cufflinks."

Between the two of us, we remove Booker's dress shirt collar and peel him out of the shirt itself. He pulls the hem of his white undershirt out from under his pants waistband and raises his upper body several inches off the mattress to tug it off over his head.

His skin gleams with health in the firelight and I gawk at his bare torso in ab-so-toot fascination. His arms and shoulders are muscular, his chest and stomach so hard and firm. His chest hosts a fan of fine dark hair which arrows down between those distinctly separate muscles in his abdomen to disappear beneath the waistband of his dress slacks.

I follow the trail with a fingertip and find the hair unexpectedly silky.

Booker lifts me off his thighs and reaches for his slacks' zipper. I watch as he raises his hips and pushes the pants down. Notice, as he bicycles his legs to kick the pants off, he's wearing a pair of the new boxer-style underwear. I stare at their three-button opening. See the ridge of his sex pressing against the fly.

And all of a sudden it hits me anew what I've signed up for. I'm starting to panic when a log in the fireplace pops and a larger than usual flame shoots up, making the room momentarily brighter. And I see the scar on Booker's side.

"Oh, my God," I lean forward to run my fingers over the irregular oval pucker under his ribs. "What happened to you?"

He curls his fingers around my hand, lifting it off the scar. "It's nothing."

"It's *not* nothing! You were clearly badly hurt at one time or another."

"It's a bayonet wound. From the war." He shrugs. But my horror must show on my expression, because he adds softly. "Don't worry, it was a through and through."

"Whatever *that's* supposed to mean," I mutter.

"It means it went in here—" Booker reaches across to rub the scar "—and straight out the back here." Rolling slightly onto his other side, he points out a nearly identical scar on his back just around his side and maybe an inch lower than its mate. "Without hitting any vital organs."

"Good God, Booker." I anxiously pat my fingers around the scar. Raise my gaze to meet his. "That had to have been horrid. Weren't you scared to death?"

"It was no fun, I'll grant you. But it happened so fast I didn't have time to be afraid." He rolls onto his back again. "We were in the forest where the battle for Verdun had been fought in '16. That damn thing went on for three hundred days before the French finally claimed victory." Booker shakes his head. Brushes off the aside with a choppy sweep of his fingers. "Sarge was trying to map out a route through the woods without getting any of us caught up in the barbed wire or setting off one of the unexploded shells still littering the ground. And, out of nowhere, this lone German soldier suddenly pops up and runs me through. It burned like the fires of hell, lemme tell you. But it could have been a lot worse." He shoves up on his elbows suddenly. Pins me in his sights. "Bayonets are mounted on rifles, Lena. Kid could have shot me. I think he was taken as much by surprise as we were."

"What happened to him?"

Booker's eyes go flat. "He wasn't so lucky."

I have no idea how to address any of this. It's so far outside my experience, I can't even wrap my head around it. I hate the thought of all the death. But I hate the idea of Booker being wounded even more. So, I follow my impulse.

Leaning down, I kiss his old injury better.

32

Nothing but a flimsy pair of French knickers

BOOKER

Leaning forward, Lena puckers up and presses her kiss-ready lips to the scar on my abdomen. I sprawl back, half propped up on my elbows but frozen in place as I stare down at the back of her head and her long, bare back. Her beautiful unbound breasts press low on my abdomen, their lower curves momentarily encasing the head of my cock. As quickly as she folded herself in half, she straightens again. But that leaves her sitting there wearing nothing but a flimsy pair of French knickers and shooting me the world's sweetest smile. "All better," she murmurs. And, oh, God.

She slays me. Everything about her: her scent, her smile, her default reaction to my wound being the 'kiss it better' thing I told Will about not that long ago. Not to mention the fact the woman is the next best thing to nude.

Hell, every damn bit of it simply slays me. No ifs, ands or buts about it.

"C'mere." Snapping upright into a seated position, I reach to haul Lena up until I have her where I want her, straddling my lap. Crossing my ankles Indian fashion beneath her lush butt, I bury my face in the side of her throat. Then I press a kiss just beneath her jaw where it curves below her ear, a spot that used to get her every time.

If I wasn't trying so bloody hard to play it cool, I'd thrust up a fist in victory when my kiss earns me the once familiar moan in the back of her throat that I still sometimes hear in my dreams.

Lena, who as far as I've been able to tell has never been one to worry about the way others view her, shivers and wraps her arms around my neck. And suddenly I'm surrounded by her scent and heat as her breasts flatten against my chest and her smooth legs cross behind my butt. Leaving my hard on pressed flush against her sweet spot.

Reaching around her, I grip her ass to hold her in place as I rock my dick along the sweet damp furrow beneath her knickers. My teeth clench at the overwhelming sensations the action sets in motion. The sight of her eyes fluttering closed and of her slightly crooked incisor, which appears when her white teeth worry her lower lip, ratchets the heat from hot to incendiary.

It's not enough. Over the years, I've dreamed a whole host of things I wanted to do to this woman. Sweet things. Filthy things. But dry-humping her? That wasn't high on my list. Tightening my hold on her butt, I rise to my knees and shuffle us around to face the headboard. Carefully, I lay her down.

Lena blinks up at me, humming a non-word that is nonetheless an inquiry.

"I want to touch you, kiss you, lick you." My voice is a hoarse rasp, but it's not as if I have a damn bit of control over the thing. "And I want to be face-to-face to do them."

Pink sweeps up her pale skin, but she gives me a game little smile. "Okay."

Her arms are still entwined around my neck and I reach behind me to loosen her grip. Loosely encircling her wrists with my fingers, I press her bent arms against the bedspread next to her head. "I'd like you to stay just like this. Can you do that?"

She gives me a wry smile, the context of which seems to be: *don't hold your breath.* "I guess we'll see."

I laugh and kiss my way down her throat, over her collarbones, then lower still to where her breasts jut away from her chest. With Lena lying on her back, those proud beauties have shifted away from her breast bone, yet somehow flattened only slightly. I glance up to discover her watching my every move with shining eyes. "You've got the prettiest tits."

She makes a face. "Gotta say, I don't love that word."

"Then let me apologize and try again. You have the prettiest breasts it has ever been my pleasure to cast eyes upon." I kiss my way up the slope of her left breast.

"Booker, you don't have to say sweet things to me."

"Oh, that's where you are dead wrong, doll." I give her pretty pink nipple a quick lick then pull back to blow across it. Goosebumps flash down her arms and her nipples twist into tight little spikes. I glance back up into her eyes. "I really do need to say them, Lena. I can't think of anyone who deserves sweet nothings more than you." And keeping my gaze steady on hers, I pull her nipple into my mouth, curl my tongue around its underside and suck.

Lena's head kicks back into the pillow as a desperate little sound purls up out of her throat. Her hands fist next to her head, but for the moment, at least, she leaves them where I requested. Capturing her other nipple between my thumb and forefinger, I tug it in rhythm with the pull of my mouth on its mate.

Her thighs squeeze together, then shift apart, and I quickly abandon the breast I'm teasing with my fingers. There is another spot I've been dying to touch and I can't wait another second.

Trailing my knuckles downward, I lazily brush them along the smooth, hot landscape of Lena's skin until I reach the dramatic concave where the band of her French knickers provides a line of demarcation between the inward curve of her narrow waist and the sumptuous flare of her hips. Turning my hand over, I dip my fingers beneath the only scrap of fabric I left her wearing.

Lena grows still and seems to hold her breath the closer my forefinger inches toward its goal. I want nothing more than to slide her knickers down, so I can see everything there is to see of the sweet puss I'm about to stroke. But she may be nowhere near ready for this touch, let alone having to witness me watching myself diddle her. Last thing I want to do is scare her off.

Still. In for a penny, in for a pound, as the Brits like to say.

I slide my hand deeper into her knickers, my forefinger unerringly slipping into the soft furrow between plump lips. And— thank you, God—it's not only soft, it's *wet*.

I can feel Lena starting to tense, no doubt over that very thing. With a silent thank you to the French, whom I found to be so much more open and accepting of sex than we Puritanical Americans, I locate Lena's clitoris, a gift to the women possessing it and the men fortunate enough to have learned about it. Gently, I feather the slippery little bundle of nerves with my fingertip.

"Oh," Lena breathes, relaxing the thighs she just clenched against my marauding finger. "Oh, my goodness, gracious—ohhh!"

I move down the bed and tug her pretty knickers down over those sweet hips and ass and chuck the scrap of lingerie to the end of the bed. Then I shoulder my way between her thighs, which have been sprawling farther apart with every stroke of my finger. For a second I pause to simply admire the sight before me.

Her skin is smooth and pale and oh-so soft. Her legs are firm and shapely. And between her thighs is the prettiest little triangle of fine pale blond hair. Lowering my head, I inhale the heady, exotic scent of her. Then I thumb those plump lips apart to reveal the slick pink flesh and lower my head.

Only to find Lena's hands suddenly fisted in my hair as she half sits up. "Whoa, whoa, whoa there, cowboy!"

I look up the length of her body, enjoying the dips and curves of her along the way. She's pushed herself up onto her elbows and is staring back at me doubtfully. "You're not going to *kiss* me there, are you? I mean, do people actually *do* that?"

"Some do. I sure as hell plan to."

"Oh, but—"

"You're a modern woman, aren't you?"

"Yesss?"

I hide my grin at her less than certain response. Say gently, "And modern women try things before making unilateral decisions based strictly on their lack of knowledge, am I right?"

Lena has never been a pushover. I always loved that about her. "Beats me," she says coolly and shrugs, meeting my gaze squarely. "I'm not positive I know what uni-what-eral means."

"In this case, one-sided. As in, based on a single side of an equation. But I know you, Lena—you like learning new things. Hell, you told me that yourself. Which makes me think you're too modern to let that unilateral bushwa win the day." I'm slinging bull right and left here, but, God, I want to taste her. And I honestly do believe she'll love it, if I can just get her to give me the green light. Not above fighting dirty, I stealthily brush my thumb across her clit.

She sucks in a breath and her grip on my hair loosens. "I... suppose."

Okay, not ideal. But I can work with it. Lowering my head, I lap the flat of my tongue over her clitoris. Lena moans and I do it again. I tease her for a while, bringing her close, then backing away to kiss her stomach, tickle her belly button with the tip of my tongue, or lick the creases where her legs join her torso. When she cools down enough to relax a little once more, I return to her clitoris. And when she suddenly reaches out to hold my head in place, I slip a finger inside her and alternate again between her clit and everywhere except that sweet little hot button. She clamps down on my finger and once it appears she's grown accustomed to it, I slip in a second. Slowly I rock both in and out. Her breath catches, again and again and I give a plump lip a little nip of my teeth.

"Booker!" Her voice is breathy and I lean to grab one of the new latex rubbers out of the nightstand, which, thank you, Jesus, is right

next to me. I ease my fingers free and quickly sit up to kick off my
boxers and roll on the protection.

"Wait," she protests and blinks up at me. "You're stopping? Just
like that? You can't stop now!"

"We're not stopping," I assure her. "Just switching things up."

"Why would we wanna do that?" She digs her nails into my shoulders as I roll atop her body. "I liked what you were doing."

I line up my erection with her opening and slowly work the head
in. "But you didn't expect to, right? So, give this a fair shake, too. I'm
pretty sure you'll like it, as well."

"I'm pretty sure I won't," Lena mutters, but she doesn't tense up as
I begin to ease my way into her.

I'll take my good signs where I can get 'em.

I push further into her with small, gentle thrusts and with-
drawals, pushing in an inch or two, pulling back half as much.
Pushing in a little farther yet, retreating slightly. I get exactly zero
response at first and fear I am just not doing it for Lena. I, on the
other hand, am barely hanging on by a thread. But, I'm not reaching
her, dammit.

Then, as I finally sink in as far as a man can go, I realize I've been
ignoring everything else in my quest to fully penetrate Lena without
hurting her. Bending my head, I kiss her. I make love to her mouth
like I've got all the time in the world. And you know what? I do. Even
if I screw this up and lose control before I can coax a climax from
Lena, I'm pretty damn sure I've got more than one time in me. And if
not, I'll take care of her by any other means necessary.

But out of the blue, Lena moans, a low, carnal sound deep in her
throat that's music to my ears. And for the first time, she moves her
hips and tilts her pelvis up to meet my thrusts. I rip my mouth from
hers and look down at her swollen lips and flushed cheeks. At her
heavy-lidded eyes, gleaming in the firelight.

"Ah, God, Lena. You feel so good. It feels so damn good to be
inside of you." I kiss the warm skin below her ear.

Lena moans again and thrusts her hips up.

Hooking the backs of her knees with the inside of my elbows, I haul her very fine ass mostly off the bed when I plant my hands on the mattress near her shoulders. The move pushes her wide-splayed knees back toward her breasts.

I pull out almost entirely, only to promptly drive back in harder than before. I can tell by Lena's sudden heavy breathing, by the frantic way she starts imploring her Maker, I'm doing something right. I keep it up, repeating the slow withdrawal and hard, fast surge back in. I feel her hot, wet sheath gripping my cock and Lena's fingernails anchored in my back. My sac starts to draw up and I try to focus on something—*anything*—that might tamp down, or at least slow, this out of control fire raging inside of me.

Freezing rain.

Snow balls.

The glaciers on Mt. Rainier.

Lena grips my hair and tugs until I'm looking into her eyes. "Booker, please," she whispers. "Help me. I'm so...I don't know what to—" She abruptly tries to push me away. "I can't take any more!"

"Shhh, I've gotcha. This is the good part." Shaking her hands off, I bend my head to give her breast some attention. I got the impression Lena's nipples were crazy sensitive. Unfortunately, in this position I can't quite reach them. And since the position is clearly working for her, I'm not about to alter it.

"Baby, cup your hand under your ti—your breast." I stick my tongue out to demonstrate how close, yet at the same time, far away it is from making contact with her tits. No. Breasts. "Help me do this."

She does as I ask, sliding her hands beneath her breasts and offering them up. I suck a pink nipple between my lips, giving it the slightly rough treatment she seemed to like before.

Immediately Lena's breath hitches, her back arches and her arms wrap tightly around my back. I have no doubt her nails are pressing little crescents into my hide as I strive to push her over the cliff with each pull of my lips and tongue, with each thrust of my hips.

Then, suddenly, I do.

"Booker," she cries as the muscular sheath wrapped around my dick starts clamping down on it like a Chinese finger trap, gripping and only slightly releasing, gripping and slightly releasing, over and over and *over* again.

Until, I, too, toss back my head to groan Lena's name as I come in hot pulsations. It feels as if it goes on forever, but eventually both our bodies settle down, at damn near at the same time.

And abruptly wrung out and worn to the bone, I collapse like a felled tree on top of her.

33

Wearing our best pajamas and sipping gin martinis

LENA

Wh5at was that? Oh, my gosh, oh, my *God*—what in heaven's name *was* that? Never in my wildest imagination did I dream sex could feel like this. So astonishing, so downright miraculous, I'm just now realizing Booker's sudden weight is crushing the breath right out of me. "Can't...breathe," I wheeze.

He swears under his breath and pushes up on his palms, his biceps jumping into hard relief. Air rushes into my lungs even as I miss his weight pinning me down. I watch a very un-Bookerlike wash of color rise up his throat and onto his face.

"Sorry," he says. "That was just so damn incredible, it kicked the slats right out from under me."

"You, too?" That was comforting. But even as we speak, all the amazing feelings are fading, except for an occasional faint pulse deep between my legs.

Leaving me without the first idea of how to act around him.

What, what, what on earth was that thing he did with his *tongue*? I have worked in bars since reaching my majority at eighteen. So, while I may have only experienced sex one time before this morning—and *that* a world removed from what I just felt—I thought I'd at least heard most of what there was to know. People in bars talk. Heaven knows most of the women I've worked with over the years had a lot to say.

*No*body ever mentioned that tongue thing. I would have remembered that.

I clear my throat. "I have never in my life felt anything like this." Heck, I had no idea such sensations even existed. Then a sudden thought makes me freeze. "Oh, God, Booker. I could get *pregnant* from this!"

What the hell had I been thinking? I, more than most people, know what it's like to be the result of an unwanted pregnancy. I assume that's why my mother left me at the Blood of Christ, anyway. I always thought she had given being an unwed mom a try, found it just too difficult, and dumped me on the B of C's steps.

I *swore* I would never put another child through the same situation.

"No," Booker says firmly. "You can't and you won't. I used a rubber. I'm wearing it still. I can pull out, if you'd like to inspect it."

Even as my face flames, my new fear-fueled tension flows away. Whew. Yes. Okay. I do remember him rolling something down

down

down

the length of his sex. I blow out a huge sigh of relief.

I can feel myself blushing all over at the mere thought of inspecting the thing—although maybe I'm the tiniest bit tempted. "That's okay. I wasn't paying the strictest attention, I guess."

I wonder if Booker can read my mind, for the grin he gives me is truly wicked. Darned if his (clearly) dirty mind doesn't stir those crazy feelings once again. Suddenly overwhelmed, I shove at his shoulders, desperate to be somewhere—*any*where—else. "I should go."

Booker doesn't budge. "Go where, exactly? It's Sunday, Lena, everything is closed. Unless..." His dark brows scrunch briefly over his nose. "Do you need to talk to Clara or Dot about this?"

"God, no!" To my surprise, Booker's brows furrow deeper yet. Baffled, I peer up at him. I would have thought that would be the last thing he'd want—the rest of his employees knowing he and I were doing naked things together behind closed doors. "I don't imagine *you* want me to do that. Do you?"

"Hey, shout it from the rooftops, if you want to. Because, making love with you, Lena? Best thing that ever happened to me, far as I'm concerned."

His words steep me in a warm glow. Yet, I still feel an urgent need to push him away, to distance myself. Getting attached has never ended particularly well for me. And although a huge part of me wants nothing more than to stay wrapped up in Booker's arms, my smarter self is screaming to stick with making real *girl*friends this year and give the messy man/woman stuff a wide berth.

Before I can do or say anything further, however, Booker lowers his head to press a soft kiss into the curve of my neck where it turns into my shoulder. I feel him pulse inside me, growing a bit larger again. "You don't have to decide anything right this minute, Lena," he says in a husky voice that sends heat shooting down my spine. "Not today, and not tomorrow either, if you're still trying to come to terms with what you want from this relationship." He lifts his head. Pins me in a riveting blue-eyed gaze, which leaves me suddenly breathless.

"Why don't we just take things nice and slow," he continues softly. "You hear what I'm saying? Let's just enjoy each other for a while before we start slapping labels on whatever this thing between us is." One large, bare shoulder hunches nearly to his ear before quickly dropping back into its original position. "Let's see where it takes us."

Relief floods me. Seeing where it takes us is something I think I can do.

By Thursday, I'm not feeling nearly as dispassionate about this "seeing" business as I was last Sunday. I have a strong desire to keep this connection—whatever it is—strictly between me and Booker. At the same time, I so, *so* need to talk to someone who knows more about men and sex than I do. Which, frankly? Probably includes most of the population of Seattle.

I think of Will first, of course. But...no. Never in this lifetime. Will is the next best thing to a brother to me—I simply cannot talk about sex with him. Not when it's sex I'm participating in.

I make a rude noise. Who am I kidding? I'm pretty darn sure Will wouldn't be comfortable with any sex talk, either.

So, I seek out Dot and Clara, make some plans with them, then walk down to Booker's office. Seeing Leo industriously pouring over some kind of bookwork at the desk they seem to take turns sharing, I step inside.

Booker is nowhere to be seen.

"Hey," I say, and barely manage not to wince at the adolescent way my voice hits high C in the middle of the word. I clear my throat. "Have you seen the boss around?"

Leo glances up, then away while he combs through a stack of papers. "He's in the storeroom," he says in a distracted voice as he paws through the closest pile to him. "Counting liquor or something."

"All right. Thanks."

Leo hums a non-answer, barely glancing up as I withdraw. I make my way to the storeroom, where I find Booker, his jacket thrown atop a case of whiskey and his shirtsleeves rolled up his forearms.

I love seeing him like this; it reminds me of the young man I first knew. He dressed much more casually back then. And he looks so ...relaxed and easy, without so much as a hint of tension. I lean through the open doorway. "You got a minute?"

"Of course." Reaching for me, he draws me into the room. Into his arms. Bending his head, he kisses me, at first lightly, then more deeply. When he raises his head a moment later, I'm short of breath and my heart is pounding like Henry's percussion section in full swing. "This is a nice surprise," he says, brushing a couple of loose strands of hair back into the waves I'd had marceled. Then he smooths his hands down my back to cup my hips.

"I just wanted to let you know I'm going to spend the night with Dot and Clara tonight."

Booker stills, his grip suddenly a titch too tight. Yet when I glance up into his face, it's unnervingly expressionless.

Not being able to read him sends me into a hurried explanation. "I'm all at sixes and sevens over what you and I are doing, Booker. I really need some input from women who know more about these things than I do." I keep my insecure *Which is just about everyone* to myself.

He looks as though he wants to argue. But he merely gives me a brisk nod of his head and steps back, his hands falling to his sides.

"Have fun," he says calmly. Perhaps even a bit dismissively. Yet his eyes seem to be saying something entirely different.

I only catch glimpses of him throughout the rest of the night. He isn't at his normal table on the edge of the dance floor during my sets, and not once do I catch him watching me from the wings as I often do. But after my final act, as I turn the corners leading me back to my dressing room, I keep getting the oddest feeling. As if Booker turned the same one just before I came into view, or is approaching mere moments after I disappear around it.

It shouldn't bother me he is likely avoiding me; not when I feel such a strong need to do the same to him. Yet, somehow, it still does.

Less than an hour later, Clara, Dot and I are snuggled up in their living room, wearing our best pajamas and sipping gin martinis. I don't usually like drinking this late, as it can send me straight to sleep, only to find myself wide awake, tossing and turning an hour later. But I need a little liquid courage before I tell the Brasher girls what I've been up to.

Clara puts Marion Harris' *After You've Gone* on the gramophone and for a moment I forget to be nervous about the upcoming conversation.

"Lord, but I worship her voice." I sing a few bars along with the record, then, with an impatient shake of my head, stop. "Nope. Sounds better when it's just her."

Dot and Clara protest, but in this, at least, I know what I'm talking about. "I'm not being modest, or fishing for compliments; it truly does. Every now and then an artist sings a song that is simply perfection. Miss Harris has done that with this. I don't have a single urge to change it up and make it mine, and I can't tell you how rare that is. She *owns* this song. I honest-to-God doubt anyone could make it sound better."

The Brasher sisters, bless them, let me listen to it twice through, sitting quietly sipping their drinks while I steep myself in the glory of Marion Harris's voice. When the song fades the second time into the soft hiss and scritch of the gramophone needle caught in its final groove, however, Dot exchanges it for *Varsity Drag*. Clara and I hop up to join her in dancing the Black Bottom to its upbeat tune. I collapse back onto my chair a few minutes later and reach for my drink. After draining it, I set the empty glass on the little table next to me.

Slightly nervous, I draw in a deep breath, then softly expel it. "I have something I need to talk to you two about."

Clara and Dot exchange glances, making me sit a bit straighter on the chair facing them on the sofa. "What was that?" I demand.

"What was what?" Dot gives me an innocent look I have a tough time believing has ever found a proper home on her face.

"Don't pretend you're a dumb Dora. We all know that's a far reach from the truth. What was that *look* —" I wave two fingers from one sister's eyes to the other's "—all about?"

Clara grins at me. "Well, you're not exactly Sneaky Peeky, are you, missy. We've known something was up since the beginning of the week."

Dot blows a raspberry. "More like since Saturday night. "And let me tell ya, sister," she adds, "it's been killin' us to not demand you spill what the hell it is you've been hiding."

I draw a deep breath, then slowly ease it out. Straighten my shoulders. And confess, "I've been having—" I drop my voice to a bare whisper "—*sex* with Booker."

Dot and Clara squeal loud enough to wake up the dead—never mind the folks sharing a common wall in the apartments on either side of theirs. "Oh, my gawd, that is *much* more exciting than anything we thought of." Clara pats her left breast in the quick *tha-thump, tha-thump* rhythm of a racing heartbeat. Then, dropping her hand to join its counterpart in gripping the couch cushion on either side of her, she leans forward eagerly. "Tell us *everything.*"

I do. Well, not *every*thing-everything. But I explain how I was kicked out of the women's residence the morning of our big night out and the series of events that arose out of it. Much to Dot's disappointment, I don't go into detail about sex with Booker. I do, however, admit the way he makes me feel during it is bigger than anything I've experienced in my life. That it's better than ice cream. Better than Marion Harris' voice singing the perfect song, even. That it is simply...the most amazing experience *ever.*

Clara scratches her head, looking at me with one brow raised when I finally fall silent. "Soooo...I'm not seeing what the problem is here. If I was blessed with a lover with Mr. J's expertise and technique, I'd be making the most of it. What the hell is stopping you?"

"That would be my fundamentalist upbringing. Have you ever heard of the things a fella can do with his—" my voice drops "—*tongue?*"

The sisters look at each other. And grin. "As in using it right about —" Dot rubs a delicate circle over the spot between her legs where her satin pajama bottoms's seams intersect. "—here?"

"Exactly!"

"Nope. Never heard of it."

My jaw must have dropped because the Brasher girls laugh uproariously.

"I'm just kidding ya," Dot says. "Yes. We've indeed heard of it. And if one of us has been lucky enough to experience it—" casting her gaze modestly downward, she buffs her nails on her satiny breast "—well. I'd hang onto him."

"But surely anything that sinfully good will send me straight to hell."

"I doubt it," she replies drily. "If it worked that way, hell would be standing room only."

"Besides," Clara chimes in, "Booker may have plans for marrying you."

My heart gives a big, fat *thump* in my chest at the very idea of living as Booker's wife in that warm, welcoming Magnolia house for the rest of my years. Of being free to experience over and over again that overwhelming sense of rightness I had in Booker's arms—the almost out of body sensation, when the two of us merged into one, that this is where I belong.

But I shove it aside. I'm a realist. And realists understand darn good and well the odds of someone like Booker and someone like me ever being together long term.

They aren't good. Well, maybe once upon a time we had decent odds of making a relationship work, even though our respective positions in the social scheme of the world were miles and miles apart. Still are, as far as that goes. But these days, it's more about my own doubts. I try to ignore them, yet they're hard to shake. Unless I can find a way to work through them, I'm more to ball everything up.

And that's provided Booker's even interested in something like marriage in the first place.

I shrug with fake casualness. "I'm pretty sure, as far as the Blood of Christ is concerned, even wives aren't allowed to feel the way Booker makes me feel. I think we're probably supposed to close our eyes and recite scriptures until it's over." I grimace and confess, "Which was actually what I expected I'd have to do, until I learned better last Sunday morning."

I see Clara open her mouth to accept the detour I threw out and feel a moment of shame. Darn it, I came here with a very real desire for advice. Yet, here I sit, wasting everyone's time redirecting the conversation to avoid having to expose myself by chatting honestly. Looking at both my friends, I shoot up a hand to put off Clara's question.

"Okay, maybe I'm throwing up a road sign here to send you down a different avenue so I don't have to talk about this one."

Clara reaches out to pat my knee. "You don't have to talk about it at all, sweetie, if you don't want to."

The temptation is sugar sweet to grab the out she's offering. And yet—

"I think maybe I do. Because, we can joke about it, but one of the real problems is I *have* been indoctrinated in fundamentalist beliefs. And honestly? It's not that easy to just laugh them off as hilariously old-fashioned. I try, because my head actually believes they kind of are. At the same time, I hear Matron's voice screeching, 'Sinner. Sinner!' in the back of my mind way too often."

"And the other problems?" Dot asks gently.

"Is even if the fundamentalist upbringing wasn't an issue, there's still the fact—"

I hesitate, because this part is especially difficult for me to admit. No one likes feeling like a loser or, at best, simply not enough. I do want to hear what Clara and Dot have to say, though. And if I expect my friends to tell me anything useful, I owe them the truth. "Aside from Will, I have never had any luck with relationships lasting. People always leave."

With the uncanny silent communication thing they do, Clara and Dot rise as one to plop down on either side of me on the overstuffed arms of my chair. In an instant, I'm surrounded by their arms, their scent and their comforting warmth. I can literally feel my heartbeat slowing to a range closer to normal.

Then they release me and rise to their feet as one. "Okay, here's our advice," Dot says crisply as they plop back onto the sofa. "First of all, Clara and me have seen the way Mr. Jameson looks at you. More importantly, the way he *watches* you."

I open my mouth, but Dot makes a shushing gesture. "I know it sounds like the same thing—"

"But trust us, honey, that isn't the case here," Clara finishes.

"He *looks* at you when other people are around or you're talking to him or something," Dot says.

Is that supposed to be an explanation? If, so it's not getting the job done. I'm more confused than ever.

"And you can definitely tell that he admires you," Clara supplies. "At the same time, he sorta reins himself in."

Dot nods agreement.

I feel my eyebrows pleat above my nose. This is still not real clear to me. "So, what's the watch part?"

"Oh, honey." Dot gives me a knowing smile. "When you're not looking, he *watches* you like you're a filet mignon and he's starving for a steak dinner. And in those moments, doll? It's plain as that fine, manly nose on his face he thinks you're the sheba to end all shebas. The bee's knees, the elephant's eyebrows, the gnat's whistle."

Blowing a pithily rude sound through pursed lips, I call hooey.

They shrug as one. "You asked," Clara says.

"True tale," Dot agrees.

I did ask. And, oh, I would give a bundle to accept their version as gospel. But these are the girls who thought Will and I should be a couple. From whom I've resisted telling my news all week because I knew they'd weave impossible fantasies for me, regardless of the facts.

What the heck am I doing? Yes, this was my idea, and the Brasher sisters do know more about men than I will likely *ever* know. At the same time, the two of them see romance everywhere.

Maybe I should start thinking more seriously about moving on. My contract with Booker only has five more weeks on it, and my skill as a songbird is portable. I can go anywhere.

I can get through five weeks without doing something stupid.

Will often accuses me of being a runner. I prefer to view it as being the leaver instead of the left. And honestly? I've never under-stood why he has a problem with that. I learned a long time ago to read the signs. And I must say, once I realize something is simply never going to work, it's *not* as painful to make myself walk away as it is to be left watching yet another person's back waltzing out of my life.

Everything I have come to know about these friends of mine, however, warns me they won't agree—and they sure as heck won't let it go if I argue. I'm just not up for a dragged-out debate. I thought I wanted advice, but it turns out I only needed a bit of knowledge.

So, I flash them a big smile. "I'll think about what you said, but let's not talk about it anymore tonight." I pick up my drink to drain it, see I already have, then look over to Dot.

"Your martinis are the berries! Do you think we could have one more, then maybe teach me another dance?"

34

SUSAN ANDERSEN

Hey, Mistah Jaaame-es-son!

BOOKER

I've come home to a cold house in the dead hours of the morning more times than I can shake a stick at, and never have I given it a second thought. Depending on how my night has gone, I'll turn on the radiators and build myself a fire or just roll into bed.

Coming home without Lena this morning feels every shade of wrong. Which is kind of crazy, when I think about how she's only stayed in the house with me five days. Slept in bed beside me a mere four.

I toss my keys into the dish on the entryway table, then head for the dining room to pour myself a drink. I knock it back without even stepping away from the bar setup on the sideboard. Without missing a beat, I splash an additional finger into the glass to take with me upstairs.

What the hell made her decide to stay with the Brasher girls tonight? Lena and I have made love every night since last Sunday—some nights more than once. Hell, every night except Sunday more than once. I don't think I'm fooling myself to say she's been with me every step of the way.

I am so damn tempted to call Will to see if he has any insights into Lena he can share with me. Face it, he's been with her more than I have over the last eight years, so probably understands the way her mind works better. But it's three effing o'clock in the morning. How likely am I to get a straight answer—or, hell, any answer at all—if I wake him up for this?

I snort. Will thinks of Lena as a sister. If I tell him how my relationship with her has changed, I'm pretty damn sure he won't talk to me at all.

But I sure don't like this feeling I'm getting. Not when, at best, it feels too damn much as though Lena's pulling away from me. And at worst?

I heard her mention to Clara she needs a bigger suitcase. What if she's getting ready to hightail it out of town?

"**H**ey, Mistah Jaaame-es-son!"

It's been a long day. I've had to concentrate like hell to get anything done, and I sigh as I look over to see Sally bearing down on me. She's in full locomotion, her cigarette tray a stationary oasis between jiggling breasts and swinging hips as she weaves through the tables. It's pretty damn clear mine at the edge of the dance floor is her current destination.

Leo wasn't in the office when I arrived a short while ago. But he'd spread his usual shit all across the desk, so I just grabbed the high priority matters I want to make sure are taken care of and brought them out here. Thinking, of course, I'd get all kinds of privacy before the lounge opened for the night.

I swallow a sigh. Guess I was wrong.

Sally arrives at the table and I see that, while she's picked up her tray, she has yet to load its merchandise. "Leo had to run out for something," she says. "But he asked me to tell you that Ray Orland, the president of—I can't remember which bank he said—made reservations for this evening. Leo said Orland said he's bringing someone special you're sure to get a kick out of."

My first thought is he's bringing a girlfriend rather than his wife. But why would Orland believe I'd give a great big damn about his personal life one way or the other, let alone get a kick out of it? I ask Sally to put a reserved sign for the banker's party on one of our best stage-view tables. Then I get back to work. I have far too much to do to waste what little spare time I might scrape together wondering who the banker considers a special guest. Let alone one he thinks I might actually give two simoleans about.

After making a mental note to make an appearance at Orland's table, I put the matter aside and concentrate on finishing up the paperwork I've let slide a little too long. By the time the sound of arriving employees pulls me out of the roll I'm on, I've made serious inroads into my work backlog. Gathering up my papers, I put them back in the folder, then head to the office. I set it atop the file cabinet when I see that although Sarge has whittled down the mess on the desk, he still has a way to go before it's cleared. I head to the washroom to freshen up and change into my tux.

Not long after I've gotten myself ready, I hear Lena and the Brasher girls chatting and laughing as they sashay past my office. And damned if my heartbeat doesn't start thundering against the wall of my chest like so many winter storm waves crashing on the shore.

God, I've got it bad for this woman. Shoving my hand into my slacks pocket, I scoop up the small circlet of chain within, rubbing my thumb over its sturdy, yet dainty, links.

I give Lena a little time to settle in and prepare for her sets. Then I make my way to her dressing room. Outside her door, I smile at her bejeweled star, but hesitate to knock. Do I want to risk her telling me to go away? Or do I ambush her when she comes out? I'm usually not one to hold back when I have my eye on the prize. There is something to be said, however, about a guaranteed face to face meeting.

Resting my shoulders against the wall across from her door, I plant the sole of my right dress shoe flat against it as well, cross my arms over my chest and settle in to wait. I'm not letting her go, by God. Every feeling I ever had for Lena has rushed back these past several days—hell has *been* rushing back since the first night she performed here. And that's if my damn need for her completely went away in the first place.

I am going to get myself more time with her if it's the last thing I do.

Fortunately for my rapidly dwindling supply of patience, I don't have long to wait. The door across from me opens and I drop my foot to the floor.

Lena jolts when she sees me and I straighten away from the wall, thrusting my hands into my pants pockets. "Sorry," I say quietly. "Didn't mean to startle you. I missed you last night and just wanted to see you before things get busy."

I can't quite read Lena's expression. Part of her looks really happy to see me. At the same time, there's a reserve in her expression and a slight stiffness in her posture. "Did you have a good time with the girls last night?"

"Mostly."

Shit. What does that mean? I stroke the chain again, then pull it from my pocket. "I got you something." Shaking the little chain link bracelet down from my palm, I spread the clasped circlet open with my thumb and forefinger for her to see. "It's a charm bracelet. Or the beginning of one, anyhow." I turn it so she can see its only charm: a platinum treble clef.

"Oh, my gosh!" Lena's entire face lights up and she leans in to look at it more closely. "That is so nifty! But...is that a *diamond* in the bottom swoop?" Straightening, she takes a step back. "I can't accept something so expensive!"

"Yes. You can. It's a diamond *chip*. It would probably take two dozen of these to make the lowest fraction of a carat." And aren't I glad I resisted the one caret diamond I first considered? "C'mon, just try it on."

"I shouldn't," she says, but her body leans toward mine. And when I reach authoritatively for her wrist, she allows me to lift it so I can fasten the little open-link bracelet over it.

I arrange it until the single charm dangles, well, charmingly. "*Yes,*" I say. Seeing her wearing it gives me a massive surge of satisfaction. "It's you."

She turns her wrist this way and that, before looking up at me. "Thank you," she says with quiet sincerity. "Aside from the gowns and accessories you—that is to say, the *lounge*—bought me, I have never owned anything so beautiful in my life." Her fingers keep stroking the charm.

Even though I know I should let everything simply coast in the wake of this upbeat moment, I hear myself ask in a low voice, "Are you coming home tonight?"

"Oh." She loses some of her shine. "I, um, don't know. That is, I'm not sure."

I manage to resist issuing any ultimatums. But I can't stop myself from stepping forward, crowding her.

She takes a step back.

I step forward again and we repeat this little do-si-do across the hall until Lena's back hits the wall beside her dressing room door. Encircling her forearms with my fingers, I press them against the wall on either side of her head. The accelerated pulse in the fragile hollow of her throat catches my eye.

At least she's not unaffected. A slight smile tips up the corners of my mouth and I squat slightly to kiss the faint blue veins of her inner wrist just above the bracelet. After a moment spent lingering over the spot, I move to the fast pulse of her heartbeat in her throat and kiss her there as well. Not until I feel every bit of her tension flow from her muscles do I raise my head again. Reluctantly, I step back and release my loose hold on her forearms. I study her slightly unfocused expression, then trace the tip of my finger along the marcel wave curving from her temple to her jaw.

"Come home," I say gruffly.

Then I turn and walk away. I hate having no idea if she'll do as I bid. But I'm determined to hope for the best.

"Hey, Mistah J." Sally rushes up. "You told me to let you know when the Orland party arrived. They just took their seats. And it's the funniest thing. The man with Mr. Orland looks a lot li—"

"Miss? *Miss!*" an impatient voice interrupts. "Can we get a pack of fags over here?"

I look over, surprised someone would butt in while she's in a discussion with the club's owner. People just generally seem to assume if you own a speakeasy, you must be connected. The question is answered when I see the person hailing her is one of the many new customers we've been pulling in lately. He clearly has no idea I'm the owner.

I give Sally a nod and she bounces off to sell some cigarettes.

I rise to go pay my respects to Ray Orland and his mystery guest, fully intending to keep it brief. But when I walk up to the table and see who's sitting with him, I understand what Sally started to say before the impatient smoker interrupted her. "*Father?*"

What the hell is he doing here? I feel every muscle in my body tense. The old man has never made any bones about his opinion of the low-brow industry in which I elected to set up business.

"Hello, son." Clyde Jameson climbs to feet and thrusts out his hand. But to my utter surprise, when I reach out for a businesslike shake, he hauls me it for what would be a chest to chest bump if our right arms weren't bisecting our torsos. With a slap to my shoulder with his free hand, he turns me loose.

"Sit down, sit down," he insists, and leans into me the moment I comply. "This is a beautiful place you've got here!" His enthusiasm is unmistakable.

"I *told* you it was the best place in town," Ray interjects, making my dad grin.

"You did. And yet it's even more sophisticated than anything I could have envisioned." His wave of a hand seems to encompass the club's elegance in its entirety. He takes a sip of his drink and smiles appreciatively. "And did I mention you carry great booze? This is sure as hell no bathtub gin."

"We import the real deal from Canada." Import might be stretching the truth in the legal sense, but close enough.

"It isn't merely decent liquor, though," Father says and takes another appreciative sip. "This is top shelf gin. And I saw the label on the magnum of champagne delivered to the table next to us."

He goes on to praise the very things I'd insisted upon when putting my club together, and the way he talks to me, as if I'm every bit the great businessman he is, warms a cold part of me I never even realized I'd been carrying around. For the first time since I cannot remember when, he is the father I adored—right up until I reached puberty and got weighed down by his crushing load of expectations for the Jameson heir.

All the same, I brace myself when Lena strolls over after her final set. It's rare she even comes into the lounge, never mind putting herself in my father's path after the way he treated her the one and only time they met. He hadn't been kind to her and even my mother had made a snide comment about her knowing her place. Yet on a trajectory to our table she appears to be, and after half a dozen people stop her, she seems to remember the tip of focusing on her goal I gave her a while back.

Almost instantly, her admirers back off. It might be the *do your worst* gleam in her eyes. I can't help but think she's come out here specifically to make a point about the differences in our social status. I thought we'd long ago gotten past that, but maybe she feels the need to show my father that no one talks down to Lena Bjornstad these days.

It amazes me the girl has never figured out she's actually better than me. And if the old man utters one rude word to her, I will send him packing.

When I reintroduce her, however, Dad greets her cordially and speaks enthusiastically about her talent. He shares how Ray raved about her, telling Dad what a huge draw she has become to the Twilight Room.

I have long known that's true. The Twilight Room was popular before Lena started here and has always drawn a crowd. But since word of her talent got around, the place has literally been bursting at the seams.

Watching my father with Lena is like the cherry on top of this entire damn-near perfect sundae of an evening. So much so, it makes me question my long-held perception of him.

"We need a photo of this night!" Dad suddenly suggests and, catching Elsie's eye, I wave her over.

After she takes a photo of the four of us at Father's insistence, Dad grins at me across the table. "Thanks for asking your photographer to develop it right away, son. I can't wait to show it to your mother. Maybe then she'll see the Twilight Room is every bit as brag worthy as the restaurant she's been telling everyone you own."

"What?" I freeze. That can't be right. My mom has always been the supportive one.

"You know your mother." His father shrugs. "She's always very concerned about the way things may appear to others."

And just like that, everything I thought I knew about my parents flips upside down.

35

Whataya need that's so pressing it couldn't wait until morning?

LENA

Booker abruptly pushes back from the table and stands. "I'm sorry, Dad," he mutters, "but I'm going to have to cut this short."

"Are you okay, son?" his father inquires, looking concerned. "You're looking a little peaked."

No fooling. Booker's complexion generally leans more toward olive than fair skinned. Yet, all of a sudden, he looks downright pale. I move to check him out more carefully. "Yes, are you all right?"

"I'm feeling a little...off. Don't worry, though. I don't think it's anything contagious. I, uh, probably shouldn't have skipped dinner."

I blink, then blink again. Booker *never* skips meals, so that sounds like a big, fat lie. What on earth is going on with him?

"This was nice tonight, Dad." He looks over at Mr. Orland. "Thank you, Ray, for bringing him. It was a grand surprise." He promptly directs his attention back on his father. "Are you going to be in town for a while?"

"I'm attending a banking symposium all day tomorrow. I'll head home Wednesday in the early afternoon. If I don't get a chance to see you again before I go, I want you to know I'm real proud of you, son. Ray wasn't pulling my leg. You've built yourself one *helluva* fine business here."

Booker pulls a small gold card holder and a matching fountain pen out of his inside breast pocket. He flips the case open, pulls out a business card and scribbles something on its backside. He waves the card for a moment to dry the ink, then hands it to his father. "These are the phone numbers for the lounge and my house. Maybe we can get together and have lunch or dinner before you leave, if either fit into your schedule."

Booker's father takes the card and tucks it into his own breast pocket. "I'd like that." Reaching out, he hauls Booker in for a hug and murmurs something in his ear. Then he turns him loose. "You go get something to eat before you pass out."

Booker simply nods, grabs me by the hand and strides away, hauling me in his wake.

I trot a few steps to catch up, and neither of us say a word until we reach his office. The desk is neat and Leo isn't there, so I'm guessing he might have gone home after he finished his work.

Booker stops in the middle of the room and just stares down at his feet.

"What the devil is going on?" He doesn't answer and I touch his arm. "Booker?"

He blinks as if he'd forgotten he wasn't alone. He's looking right at me unblinkingly but I'm not convinced he actually *sees* me. Then his eyes focus.

"Can you call Will?" he asks. "Now, if possible—" He glances at his watch. "Shit. It's late. First thing tomorrow, then? Could you call him then? Or give me the number so I can? It's important I talk to him."

"You must not remember Will is a night owl," I say dryly. "The party he shares a line with might not be thrilled with a middle of the night call, but the heck with them. Will tells me they're constantly listening in on his calls. I'll get him for you."

"Thanks, doll," he whispers and collapses onto his desk chair. Elbows planted atop his desk, he buries his head in his hands.

Concerned, I perch a hip on the corner of Booker's desk and pull the tall phone over to me. Holding it by its candlestick, I lift the earpiece from the cradle and dial the operator. I give her Will's number and a moment later his line chimes. He picks up on the second ring.

"Will, it's me. Hang on a second." I lean over to jab Booker in the shoulder. He raises his head and I shove the phone at him.

He grabs it. "Will, it's Booker," he says urgently into the mouthpiece. "I know it's late, but can I come over? I need to talk to you. It's important. Yeah? Thank you." He slaps the earpiece back in its cradle and pushes to his feet, clearly energized where before he appeared exhausted. I half expect him to stride out the office door without so much as a goodbye. But my heart thumps eagerly when he rounds the desk to pull me to my feet and says, "Grab your coat. Will said we can come over."

Briskly, he makes arrangements with John the barman for closing out the till and locking down the club for the night, then ushers me out to his car. The instant both our doors are closed, he pulls away from the curb like he's in the race of his life and continues driving hell bent for leather through deserted downtown streets and up the steep hills to to Will's neighborhood.

In less than fifteen minutes from the moment Will first picked up my call, we screech to a halt in front of his apartment building.

He must have heard us coming up the stairs, for he's standing in the open doorway to his apartment, a dense shadow in the midst of light pouring out into the hallway. "Hey," he greets us quietly as we approach, then steps back to wave us in.

We enter, and Booker stops dead just inside the apartment. He draws in a deep breath. "God," he says quietly. "I'd forgotten the smell of oil paint and turpentine." He looks at Will's paint splattered smock and hands and grins—the first smile I've seen since before whatever it was that happened to make him look so downright ill at the lounge.

"That distinctive stink always reminds me of you. Of... good times with friends."

"Yep, some things never change." Will studies Booker through narrowed eyes. "Or do they?"

I have no doubt he's noticed Booker's complexion, which, while not as dead white as it appeared at the club, is still abnormally pale. Will exchanges a speaking glance with me. This strange and urgent meeting has him as concerned as I am.

He frowns at Booker. "Take a seat. Can I get the two of you something to drink?"

I decline, but Booker nods. "Thanks. I could stand something strong."

Will disappears into the little kitchen and comes back with three water glasses, two of which contain a couple fingers of what is surely whiskey. He hands one to Booker and hands me a glass of orange juice.

I raise my eyebrows at him and he says gruffly, "Drink it. You think I don't know you, girl? You've been singing in a smoky club all night. You need to keep your pipes lubed."

It's this very thoughtfulness that makes him such a darn fine friend. After thanking him softly, I take an appreciative sip of the cold juice.

He takes his own drink and sits on the chair facing the sofa where Booker and I made ourselves at home. "It's not the top-drawer stuff you serve," he says dryly to Booker, "but it ain't half bad."

We sip our drinks in silence for a moment. Then Will sets his glass on the table next to his chair with a quiet clink and looks at Booker.

"So," he says. "Whataya need that's so pressing it couldn't wait until morning?"

36

And my world caves in

BOOKER

I straighten on the couch. "The night you came over to my house, you told me you came into some money that enabled you and Lena to leave Walla Walla. Could you tell me who gave it to you?"

"Why, your mom," Will says as if it should have been obvious. Then his brows twitch together. "She didn't tell you?" He no sooner asks than he answers his own question. "Nah, of course she didn't. She's not one to brag, is she."

My stomach pitches and I glance over at Lena.

She's staring at Will in surprise and irritation. "You never told me that!"

"Huh. I thought I did." Will shrugs. "Life was hard and hungry for us then and we were so damn excited to get out of town, I must have forgotten."

He turns to me. "Both Lena and I put away every penny we could, but at the rate the two of us were going, we would have been in our dotage before we amassed enough. We were getting desperate, lemme tell ya, to put that goddamn narrow-minded town behind us. But you know how sweet your mom can be. She called me to your house one day. She said she'd always considered me a second son." Will's forehead wrinkled. "I gotta admit it surprised me. When we were kids, I always had the feeling she found me not quite good enough for you."

I begin to feel queasy, because Will's right. When he and I first became friends, my mother wasn't thrilled and gave me a lecture on class distinctions. With all the confidence of youth, I told her that was great, but the rules didn't apply to Will 'cause he was my friend. She eventually dropped the subject. But now I have to wonder if she truly had.

With a chop of one paint-smeared hand, however, Will continues, "Hey, clearly I misinterpreted things, because she said she knew I had ambitions beyond Walla Walla and knew I didn't have the resources you had, so she wanted to help. And she gave me some 'seed' money to get started."

Okay, I can almost see that. Will's grin further drags me from the dark hole beckoning me. I draw my first full breath in a while.

"Her generosity didn't end with me, either," he continues, happily. "She included an additional amount for Lena."

"*What?*" Lena squawks incredulously as I mutter, "Shit."

And my world caves in.

I don't know how long I sat there, bent over with my elbows planted on my knees and my forehead hard against the heels of my hands. Gradually, I became aware of Lena's warmth and the plush weight of her body. Until that moment I hadn't realized she'd scooted across the sofa to wrap me in her arms.

"Booker, you're scaring me," she says in a low, gentle voice. "If you don't tell Will and me what's bothering you, we can't help. You need to *talk* to us."

"Yes," Will agrees. "What the hell is going on?"

I rub at the headache brewing between my eyes and slowly

straighten, reaching for Lena's hand with my free one when her arms loosen and she straightens to sit up next to me. I immediately miss her warmth. But I take a deep breath, knock back the dregs of my whiskey—

And say, "You know how I figured all along it was my father who interfered with our letters and kept me and Lena apart?"

They nod.

"Well, it appears I was wrong. From something Dad said to me tonight and what you just told me, I am now pretty damn sure it was actually my dear, sainted mother."

37

I want to howl and smack that woman upside her head

LENA

"Your *mother* did this to us?" I stare at Booker, slack-jawed. "Stole our letters? Lied to *both* of us? I can't believe it."

But, oh. As if his words streamed light into a murky corner, I can see all the little instances that now make sense viewed through this new lens. All those times my heart broke just a little bit more with each overheard, seemingly private conversation Booker's mother held with others in my presence.

All planned out, apparently. I gape at her son.

Who looks literally sick to his stomach. "I can't prove it," Booker says dully. "But Mom has always—I don't know—been on my side. Supported the things I've done." He stares at me, and for a second I see devastation in his eyes. "Only to my face, it turns out. And here I thought I was *Dad's* biggest disappointment."

I suddenly remember the farewell hug Mr. Jameson gave him, when he'd whispered something to his son. "What did your father say to you when he hugged you goodbye?"

The aura of sorrow shrouding Booker seems to lift for an instant. "That he was sorry he'd gone about his interactions with me all wrong from my teen years onward. That all he ever really wanted for me was to succeed."

"So, that wasn't what made you look so ill." I give my head an impatient shake. "No, of course it wasn't. You suddenly looked sick to your stomach before then. What brought that on?"

"Like I said, while I felt like a constant disappointment to Dad, Mom was always my biggest cheerleader. Well, if cheerleaders were women." Booker waves off the qualifier. "All I've ever heard is how proud of me she is for building a business with nothing but my own initiative and money that I earned on my own."

Staring at me, he shoves his fingers through his hair. "Then, tonight, when Dad was raving on about the lounge, he said—and I quote—'I can't wait to show it to your mother. Maybe then she'll see the Twilight Room is every bit as brag worthy as the restaurant she's been telling everyone you own.'"

"Oh, Booker," I sigh in concert with Will's muttered, "Ah, shit."

I inch closer to lean against Booker's side, stretching my arm across his hard stomach to hug him close. "I am so sorry."

Will, seated in his chair across from us, suddenly angles his upper body in our direction. "Are you sure there isn't an explanation?"

Booker looks hollow-eyed. "I can't tell you how much I'd like to believe there is. I would love a good explanation, because I just can't wrap my head around the fact my *mother* did these things to me and Lena. And not accidentally, either, but with what I'm getting the impression was well-planned intent. So, what the hell could her rationalization be, Will? I honestly can't think of a thing that would explain this away. And when I responded to Dad's revelation with a less than brilliant, 'Huh?', he said, 'You know your mother. She's always very concerned about how things appear to others.'"

Booker gives Will a look. "He's not wrong. I've lost count of how many times she urged me to take some girl to a cotillion because she was from the "right" family and I had to "think of my future". Not to mention what you said about believing she never thought you were good enough to be my friend." He sighs. "She probably didn't."

Booker rubs his forehead. "It feels like a key puzzle piece has finally fallen into place. I goddamn hate the finished picture, but it fits too neatly to be anything else. It just...clicks." He turns to me. "I bet you know what I'm talking about."

Reluctantly, I nod. "I do—I all but heard the same click. So many little cuts that made me bleed and bleed happened when I overheard your mother talking to someone when we were in the same place at the same time." I, too, rub my forehead as entire memories all but swamp me. I don't mean to add fuel to the fire but words burst from my mouth. "I would bet my bottom dollar she worked hand in glove with Matron Henderson. That's the only way I can explain our missing letters.

"Come to think of it, the foundling home did have a few improvements during those years. Nothing huge, mind you. But a number of small but not minor things that made life a little easier. Our bellies a little fuller. *God*." I blow out a breath. "This is crazy."

"It is. Yet it feels right." The stricken expression on Booker's face breaks my heart. "No. It feels like *shit*. But so many things that never made a lick of sense—well, now do, in a bollixed kind of way." He scratches his chin, the rasp of his thumbnail over the stubble that's beginning to make an appearance the only sound in a room gone quiet. Until Booker adds softly, "Why then, though?"

Will and I must stare at him blankly because he gives his shoulders an impatient hitch. "I was gone for almost two years at that point. What made her offer you money at that that particular time?"

"I'd turned eighteen," I say hesitantly.

"And didn't you tell me," Will asks Booker, "that you wrote home a week or two before the war ended to find out what Lena was doing?"

Booker sits a little taller. "I did. Maybe Edna thought I was going to come home to find the answer for myself." Staring blindly down at his hands clenched on his knees, he breathes a dispirited, "Hell."

"What are you going to do?" Will asks.

Booker raises a long-fingered hand that spans his forehead as he massages his temples with his thumb and ring finger. "I have no fucking idea." Glancing at me, he grimaces. "Sorry, Lena." As he stiffly climbs to his feet, I get a glimpse of how he might look decades down the road.

Then he draws in a deep breath and straightens. "For now," he says to Will, "we'll get out of your hair. Thanks for letting me come over. This is all balled up, but I imagine it's better to know the truth than to always wonder how all our letters just vanished. I can't say I'm anywhere near the "better" part yet, but I'll get there eventually." His focus on our friend sharpens. "You grasped the unlikelihood of the missing letters far more quickly than either Lena or I did."

Will grimaces. "Not a swell accomplishment if it leaves you feeling this bad."

"Still." One of Booker's shoulders hitches.

"Still," Will agrees. "It's a helluva lot easier to see when you're not directly involved. I hate like hell this horseshit rained down on you two. Neither of you deserve it."

"Yeah...well." Booker shrugs fully this time. "Neither did you."

"Booker, she gave me money I needed," Will replies mildly. "It's hardly in the same category."

"I guess." Booker turns to me. "You ready to go?"

I nod and give Will a silent hug. Then I follow Booker out into the fast-approaching dawn.

———

Since learning of Mrs. Jameson's betrayal three nights ago, I have wanted to rant and rave and call her awful names. Every time I think about how she kept Booker and me apart for all those lonely years, I want to howl and smack that woman upside her head. But this is Booker's *mother* we're talking about. The sheer pain I hear in his voice when he speaks of her now, which he is trying to do as little as possible, paints a clear picture of how much the revelation is killing him.

So, I make it my job to be fair. I assure him one thing may have nothing to do with the other—that it's pure speculation at this point. I hold him and sometimes sing to him softly. But it both enrages me and tears me up inside to bear witness to the way the one person he counted on most to be on his side didn't think twice about breaking his heart.

And to *hell* with being fair and objective about that.

At the Twilight Room, Booker has been even more businesslike than usual. I've watched him shut down any hint of playfulness or even the garden variety friendliness I've occasionally seen him display with his employees before this hit the fan. I doubt anyone except Leo and I have noticed, but it saddens me. Here in his own home—maybe because it's the one place he's never had to put on a professional face—it's harder for him to hide his struggle.

Clearly, he doesn't want to believe Mrs. Jameson is capable of what we suspect. Heck, who can blame him? I don't know if it's a distraction to keep from having to *think* about the whole big, nasty mess for a short while, but he's been keeping me up in the waning dark hours after work. Making love to me with a fierce aggression that at once disturbs and excites me.

I would so like to talk to Dot and Clara about all this, but of course I can't. It isn't my story to tell. And the Booker I once knew has become an intensely private man. Could be war related, I suppose. Or not. His more guarded personality may simply be the newer, more mature model than the outgoing boy I knew back in our home town. I have no idea. Because, he won't talk to me.

Okay, fine. He talks to me.

But not about the thing that hurts him the most. I wish, wish, wish he would let me in. I want so badly to help him, but he's gone somewhere I can't follow.

Thursday morning—okay, actually one in the afternoon, but that *is* the night-owl worker's version of morning—Booker and I are in his living room. It's the lull before having to get ready for the rush of work and we're still lounging around, drinking our post-breakfast coffee and discussing a song I'm debating adding to my act, when the doorbell rings. See? We're talking.

Booker goes to answer it and I'm just rising to my feet to fetch the coffee pot from the kitchen to pour refills, when I hear a hysterical female voice in the foyer.

A second later, Booker's mother storms into the living room, Booker hot on her heels. When she catches sight of me, however, she stops as if she's run head on into an invisible wall. "You!"

It's not easy keeping a civil tongue in my head, but I manage a calm, "Hello, Mrs. Jameson."

"Don't you *Mrs. Jameson* me, you two-bit slut!" she screeches. "Not after you *ruined* my son's life and tarnished the Jameson name. How dare you talk him into running a speakeasy!"

I'm still struggling to close my sagging jaw when Booker comes over and slides a possessive arm around me, snugging me against his side. "I started the Twilight Room long before I hired Lena to sing in it," he says coldly. "And according to Dad, the fine folks of Walla Walla don't even know my Twilight Room is a speakeasy."

"They do now!" Mrs. J is all but spitting nails. "Your father is bragging about it all over town as if it's not an illegal blot on the family name. He's also talking about how *she*—" she thrusts an accusatory finger at me "—is growing the business with her so-called brilliant voice!"

Booker's eyes soften as he looks down at me, and he gives me a little smile. "Yeah, she is doing that," he agrees. Then he looks back at his mother and his expression turns arctic once again. "*You*, on the other hand, are a damn liar."

Mrs. J's hand slaps over her breast as if he's mortally wounded her. "I *beg* your pardon?"

"We know all about what you've done, Mother. We know how you and Matron Henderson kept our letters from us—how you literally tampered with the U.S. mail."

"Oh, the U.S. mail be damned," Booker's mother snaps. "I *saved* you from this floozy and I would do it again!"

"Is that a fact?" Making a deep-in-his-throat noise suspiciously close to a growl, Booker towers over the older woman. "Well, who's going to save you and the dragon of the Blood of Christ from spending the rest of your lives in the state penitentiary when I press charges against you? Stealing U.S. mail is a goddamn federal offense!" He leans into his mother's face. Says silkily, "Luckily for you, the penitentiary is located right in our home town. So, you don't have to worry about all your important friends not coming to call. They only have to travel a couple miles to visit you in The Hill."

Mrs. Jameson's face goes stark white although she must know The Hill, as the locals call the oldest operating prison in Washington State, is strictly for men.

I can tell the instant she remembers. Mrs. Jameson's chin shoots up. "Very funny," she says coldly. "Washington State penitentiary is a men's prison."

"It was," Booker agrees calmly. "Until they made an exception for that quack doctor, Linda Hazzard." He watches impassively as Mrs. J's face loses all color once again. "I'm sure they can make room for you, as well."

"That's enough, son."

From the way we all gape at Booker's father, I'm guessing none of us heard the door open again. Yet, there he is, standing in the opening between the foyer and the living room. I'd like to say the sight of him calms Booker down. No such luck—he is every bit as spitting-nails furious as his mother.

"No, Dad," he says flatly. "It isn't *nearly* enough. I'm just getting started." His face is leached of color, his lean jaw bunching and releasing as if he's grinding his back teeth down to stubs. "Did you two come together?"

"Yes. Your mama went a little crazy after I told her about our nice get-together at your club. So, when Smith told me she'd ordered him to drive her here, I thought it best to bring her myself. I really believed she had settled down during the long drive." Mr. Jameson looks at his wife. "I told you to wait for me while I parked the car, Edna."

"Oh, we all know how wonderful, wonderful *you* think this all is, Clyde Jameson," Booker's mother says bitterly. Then she pins me in her sights. "*And* her! Standing there gawking at me as if it doesn't stink when *she* passes wind! Why, she's just a little no-name, guttersnipe gold-digger who's been trying to get her claws into Booker since high school!"

"That's enough!" Clyde Jameson snaps at the same time Booker roars, "Get her the fuck out of here!" He shoots a glance at me. "Sorry, Lena."

Mouth agape, Edna Jameson stares at her son. "Well, I never! You apologize to your *whore* for using disgusting language? I would have thought her the most likely to have taught it to you!"

"No, mother, that would be the *war*. You remember the war, don't you? Where I spent day after day in muddy trenches, fighting to stay alive? Seeing men from my company get blown up or strafed around me—and wishing more than anything I would get a letter from Lena. Dying a little inside because I believed she'd forsaken me." His face goes stonier than those heads of the four presidents the papers are all saying will be carved into Mount Rushmore next year. "Oh. But that's right. She did write me—damn near every *day* Lena wrote me. But you and Matron Henderson know that better than anyone, don't you? Considering the two of you stole her letters to me and mine to her. Did you read them as well?"

Mr. Jameson stares at his wife as if he's never seen her before. "You interfered with their letters to each other, Edna?" he asks at the same time Mrs. Jameson says, "Don't be ridiculous," in response to her son's question.

She sniffs disdainfully. "As if I'm interested in the scribblings of an uneducated little nothing like her."

I've been biting my tongue, but now I snap upright. "*Excuse* me?" I all but dance with ire. "You certainly have a lot of opinions about someone you have never even had a beginning-to-end conversation with. I went to the same high school as Booker, Mrs. Jameson, and I graduated with straight B's except in science and math. Even in those I scored solid C's." Okay, so my math grade was a C minus.

Still a C.

Booker's mother gives me a tight-lipped, condescending smile. "Yes, I'm sure even trained monkeys can get it right sometimes."

"Shut. The hell. *Up*," Booker says in the grittiest, most glacial voice I have ever heard. He looks at his father. "Get her out of here," he says, "before I do something I might regret. I will always be happy to see you, Dad. I hope you'll stop by whenever you can." Then he looks at his mother. "You, on the other hand, are dead to me. I will never again step foot in the house I once considered my home."

As he stares at his mother, the saddest expression crosses his face. "I always thought you were the loveliest, most gracious woman in Walla Walla," he says slowly. "And I was so proud to be your son. But I was wrong, wasn't I? You're only lovely and gracious to those you deem worthy to be your equal, or, as in the case of Matron Henderson, when it directly benefits you. It turns out the real Edna Jameson is a self-absorbed, mean-spirited bitch, and I want nothing to do with her."

For the first time his mother looks concerned. Then she shakes her head. "Nonsense. You don't mean that. You'll get rid of this low-class bit of baggage and—"

"I mean precisely what I said," Booker interrupts firmly. "You just shattered everything I ever believed about you. Unless you change your attitude, I can't be around you." He looks at his father. "Dad, please escort Edna out of my house."

"No!" Edna tries to shake her husband's hand from her arm, but he retains his light, but firm, grip. "I have a great deal more to say!"

"It sounds as if you've said more than enough already, Edna," Clyde says wearily. "I don't think you comprehend just what you have destroyed here today." With a sad smile at me and a soft, "I'm sorry, Booker," to his only child, he hustles her from the house.

Leaving their son standing lost amidst the emotional wreckage, with only me to bear witness.

38

You haven't been *rough*-rough, exactly. But you're so *angry*.

BOOKER

Leo walks into the office while I'm staring off into space. I'd shrug, if I had the energy. It isn't the first time this week he's caught me at my new favorite activity.

Apparently, he's grown tired of it, however. Instead of leaving me to wallow in my misery as he has been doing, Leo makes a beeline straight for the partner's desk he and I have shared since we first started putting the Twilight Room together. Perching a hip on the corner nearest me, he crosses his arms atop his chest. Stares down at me. It's obvious Sarge's mood is dead serious. He's got that pinched together eyebrows thing happening above his nose.

"What the fiery, fucking hell is going on with you?"

My first instinct is to snarl back at him. But Leo is pretty much the man I look up to more than any other. I watched him put himself at risk over and over again for the men he led during the war. Watched him treat our company within the 1st Infantry like a disciplinary but benevolent father—or the closest facsimile any of us were ever likely to see, at any rate, given the harrowing circumstances. And this despite the fact he wasn't more than eight or nine years older than the youngest of our troop. God knows he shepherded *me* from boy to man during those long, *long,* damn terrifying, stress filled months we fought side by side.

He is definitely the man who listened with exceptional forbearance each and every time I cried in my beer over Lena never writing.

So, I quit acting like a petulant sixteen-year-old and tell him about my dad showing up. Then I admit to the painful stuff as well, filling him in on everything the woman who is no longer my mother has done.

Sarge absorbs it all in silence. Sits quietly on the corner of the desk for several heartbeats after I quit speaking. Then he shakes his head and climbs to his feet. Gazes down at me. "Damn, Booker," he says with quiet sincerity, "I'm sorry. That's rough and it's gotta hurt something awful."

I swivel my chair around to face him. "No fooling. Still," I continue thoughtfully, "I've been brooding over it nonstop since it happened." A fact I was too self-absorbed to realize until this instant. "I need to get my shit together."

I shift uncomfortably, thinking of the sex I've instigated with Lena ever since the morning Mothe—*Edna*—showed up at my door. It's been more hard, furious fucking than the love making Lena deserves. My fury isn't directed at her, of course, but Lena has borne the brunt of my rage at my...with Edna.

God love her though, for being in the moment with me every time. I know I haven't hurt her and I'm pretty sure my aggression has even kind of excited her. Well, for the most part. I admit I have seen her wide-eyed more than once when I've pushed up on my hands, my face no doubt fierce as I pound in and out of her with hard, deep, forceful strokes.

As if she's maybe wondering if this can possibly be considered normal.

If anything could make me smile this week, that thought would damn near do the trick. Lena left the foundling home at eighteen, and has since worked in a number of bars—some of them real dives from what I understand. Yet she's surprisingly easy to shock at times.

She's sure as hell not shy. But she is a woman who likes to know what she's doing. Hell, who wants to be in charge of anything she finds herself involved in. Add that to having grown up in the B of C, and yeah. Sex is outside her area of expertise.

If I were a good man, I would cut her loose. Lena is going places and she doesn't need to wade through my family shit with me. Not that I have the first *desire* to let her go. Still, it would probably be better for her.

"I have a feeling it's going to get worse before it gets better," I tell Leo. This is the first time I've said as much aloud, but it's a gut feeling I have that's been keeping me on edge. "Edna is acting crazy. And I don't mean slightly off normal. I'm talking committed to a state institution insane."

Okay, that's an exaggeration. But the rational mother I thought I knew has definitely gone off the rails.

"Jesus, Sarge." I rub at the headache that staked a permanent claim on my temples from the moment Dad unwittingly dropped the bomb mom's been lying to my face for *years*. "I always thought Edna Jameson was the gold standard for gracious womanhood. Not in a million years would I have dreamt she could be so vicious." The bark of laughter exploding from my throat is miles shy of actual humor. "It never occurred to me she even *knew* such offensive language, and I certainly never would have believed she could turn downright ugly-mean."

I scowl at my friend. "She called Lena a guttersnipe gold-digger, a floozy, a slut and a whore, for cri'sake. Then she insulted her education, which Lena pointed out was exactly the same as mine."

"Your mother has clearly never taken the time to have an actual conversation with Lena," Leo says.

"Yeah, she was too busy working on her agenda to drive the two of us apart," I agree. "Hell, if she were a man, I would have flattened her."

"Damn, Booker," Sarge says. "I wish I had some words of wisdom to give you. Unfortunately, never having encountered anything like this myself, I don't. All I can say is continue living your life on your terms."

Leaning down, he grips my shoulders in strong, work and battle hardened hands. His thumbs and fingers dig at the tension there as he locks me in the cross-hairs of his steady gaze. "I'm sorry I don't have something more concrete to offer. Just...take it a day at a time. And like I said, live your life on your own damn terms. Never anyone else's."

I remember Sarge's words as Lena and I are letting ourselves into the house several hours later. And since it's three am, and therefore a literal new day, I decide now is the perfect time to take his advice. I follow Lena up the stairs to the bedroom, coming up behind her as she's removing her earrings by the dresser. I kiss the side of her neck gently.

A groan of remorse promptly escapes me when she stiffens slightly, and I abandon every thought I had of cutting her loose.

"Ah, no," I croon regretfully, straightening up and turning Lena to face me. "Don't be afraid of me. I'm sorry I've been an ass this week. I've been rough with you."

"You haven't been *rough*-rough, exactly. Not like hurt me rough." She stares at me unblinkingly. "But, Booker, you're so *angry*."

"And making you feel like you're taking the brunt of it? I am so sorry, baby. I have been beside-myself furious. But not with *you*, Lena. Never with you. Hand to God." I slap my left over my heart and lift the right to the unseen heavens above. "You are the only thing keeping me sane." Seeing the tension leave her body, I bend my head to kiss her softly on the lips.

Then I carefully pick her up and carry her to bed.

Showing him exactly what a girl can do when she's put in charge

LENA

The Booker I've grown accustomed to is back. Unlike the past several days, during which his lovemaking was bossy and underlined with anger and unquestionable hurt over his mother's betrayal, he now is tender. Where his kisses were hard, hot and deep, they now are soft and—

Okay, the hot and deep part hasn't actually changed. But his mouth now entreats where the past few nights it was very much *I'm in charge*.

When it comes right down to it, I love his kisses any which way I can get them. Oh, but *this*—

Booker is propped up on one forearm, casting a shadow down half my body. He's flung a heavy thigh over mine, and his wide-palmed, capable hands imprison my wrists against his beautiful bedspread. All the while, his amazing lips—oh, *my*—feel somehow softer and fuller than usual as they delicately press and tug with devastating effect at my own.

They slide away before I'm ready. I can't gather the wits to tell him as much, however, because Booker's mouth is already pressed to the curve of my jaw below my ear. It's a spot that has drawn greedy moans from me since the first time he kissed me there back in high school. Then he slowly drags kisses, with an occasional hint of teeth, lightly down my throat.

He licks the delicate hollow at its base. "You have too many clothes on," he murmurs and removes them from me as if he has more hands than an octopus has tentacles.

The way I, apparently, possess an equal number of needy, highly sensitized zones. Zones that have me moving to the beat of a pulsating need when he takes sweet his time pinching, tugging, stroking and penetrating with his fingers, his lips, his tongue.

Without warning, Booker pushes away from me. He tears off his own clothing, then grabs me up again and rolls onto his back. I find myself sitting with my knees on either side of his hips, blinking like a demented rabbit at the abrupt change of positions. He grins up at me.

"You're in charge. You know what to do?"

I shuffle my shins against the luxurious spread on either side of his thighs, glance down at his sex, which is pointing somewhere between the ceiling and his chin, then quickly look back at Booker's face. "Sort of."

"I trust you to figure it out. Unless—" His brows scrunch together. "Would you rather I be in charge?"

That puts a poker up my spine. "*Again*? No, sir! You're right. It's my turn." I can feel my face flaming, but I sit a little straighter. Shift forward a bit and strop my girl parts against the rigid length of his cock. And, oh, boy, that feels so good I find myself wriggling for more.

I manage not to let my eyes roll back in my head, though—I'm darn proud of that. Instead, I look at him through lowered lashes past my snootily raised nose and demand, "How hard can it be?"

"Real damn." He raises his hips to nudge me with something extremely hard indeed.

I cut loose a laugh that ends in a loud, inelegant snort and slap my hands down on his chest. "Give me one of those rubber thingies."

He looks pained. "Please. They're rubbers. Not thingies. Never thingies, okay?"

I blow a disdainful breath out the side of my mouth.

Booker laughs, a sound I'm thrilled to hear again, then twists slightly to reach into the bedside table drawer. I ride the movement like a one of those Barnum and Bailey bareback horsewomen.

He rolls back and hands me the rubber. I carefully rip the packaging, then study its contents a moment. Reaching out, I slide my hand around his man part (Okay, okay, so I still have a little trouble with the language options he gave me) and balance the rubber atop it. It tips slightly, looking like a jaunty little cap, and I blow out an exasperated breath. Then I meet Booker's gaze.

"Fine," I say. "I don't exactly know how to get this from here—" I tap the little disk atop his tip "to down to here." I squeeze the base of his sex in my fist.

"You're killing me, here." Booker contracts his hips, dragging a portion of his length a short way through my grip, before thrusting up to push it back where it was. The rubber falls off and he slaps blindly at the spread until he finds it again. He shows me how to put it on and I smile inwardly to see him sweating by the time the job is done.

He watches me suspiciously. "With all the readying, you're probably out of the mood. I should get you back up to speed." He reaches as if to grab my waist and lift me off him.

I slap his hands away. "Don't you worry about me, I'm rarin' to go!" And I am. It's emboldening knowing I'm wanted this much, and I raise up onto my knees and align my entrance to the upright column in my hand. Carefully, I lower myself.

And go about showing him exactly what a girl can do when she's put in charge.

It's been several hours since I got to be boss, yet I'm having one heck of a hard time wiping the smile from my face. I can't help myself, I just feel on top of the world. Because, you know what? Maybe this time I am *not* going to default to the runner behavior Will accuses me of. I feel as if I'm where I'm supposed to be when I'm with Booker. And danged if he doesn't seem equally happy to be with me.

I've just finished my final song and am making my way toward Booker's table where I last saw him from the stage. I've gotten better at not being sidetracked by fans, courtesy of the aiming-for-my-goal trick he taught me. But a silver-haired, barrel-chested gentleman, smelling of Brilliantine and expensive cigars, suddenly rises from his table to block my way.

"Miss Baker," he says in a mild, refined voice. "I apologize for intercepting you out of the blue, but I'm Chester Moss. I own The Black Door in Los Angeles."

Struck speechless, I simply gaze up at him. Everyone in this business knows about The Black Door. It's the biggest legit lounge on the West Coast.

"If you can spare me a few minutes," he says, when I continue to stand there in silence, "I would love to discuss a business opportunity with you."

His words scramble in my mind for an instant before I get a grasp on them. "Okay." I shrug and take a seat in the chair he pulls out for me.

Ten minutes later, I walk away in a daze. Booker is no longer at his table and I make my way backstage, desperate to talk to him.

When I hit the deserted hallway to his office, I laugh out loud, do a little dance and hug myself. Chester Moss just offered up my long-time fantasy on a sterling silver platter, all tied up with a big red ribbon. So, isn't it funny how I find myself with zero interest in accepting his proposal? He urged me to think it over and I'm clutching the business card he thrust into my hand. In addition to The Black Door's professionally printed contact information is a handwritten phone number of the Olympic Hotel where he's currently lodging.

I grin to myself as I approach Booker's office. I can hardly wait to tell him about this. Maybe I'll let him wiggle on the line a little before I let him talk me out of it.

I poke my head in his office and see him sitting at his desk staring into space.

"Hey," I say, stepping inside. "You'll never guess what—"

Booker looks up at me, and his dull, dead-eyed look stops me in my tracks. I rush across the room. "What is it? More problems with your mother?"

"What? No." He sits up, and in next moment it's as if that look never existed. He's once again Booker Jameson, suave owner of the Twilight Room. He flashes me a strained smile. "Sorry. I...might have been thinking about her. I was definitely woolgathering."

He's saying everything right, but something feels off. Before I can pin down what, precisely, Booker says, "So—" An expression I can't identify flashes across his face. "Were you saying something when you came in?"

"Omigod, yes!" I laugh like a loon. "You are never going to believe what just happened?"

"I'm not, huh?"

"Not in a million years!" I'm laughing myself silly again and, knowing I must sound like a crazy person, I try to get a grip. Still, Booker will just have to excuse me, because I have never received and refused an offer quite like this one before.

Booker's still sitting at his desk, so I round it to his side and hop up to sit atop its solid corner. Leaning back on my hands, I cross my legs and twirl my uppermost foot, pretending to be the sophisticate whom, even if I live to a ripe old age, I likely will never be. "I was coming to your table after my set when this man stopped me. He introduced himself at Chester Moss of the Black Door in L.A." I look at him expectantly, but he merely stares at me with no expression at all.

What on earth? I falter, but then gather myself. "He offered me a gig there and, Booker, the terms are *crAzy*." I wiggle my eyebrows at him, waiting for the negotiations to begin.

Pushing back from the desk, he rises to his feet. "So, are you leaving right away?"

"W-what?" I seem to be having a tough time processing this conversation.

"You should," he says in a voice so cool we might as well be strangers. "I have found once an employee decides to leave, they don't work for shit. So, you might as well go pack up your stuff."

Employee? That's all he has to say? He sees me as an *employee* who is going to shirk my job until I can go to my new and improved one? Suddenly cold to the core, I wiggle off the desk. "Then that's what I'll do," I say through frozen lips. But I walk extra slowly as I leave his office, waiting for him to call me back. To say, "Gotcha."

Something.

Apparently, however, he has said everything he plans to say.

Back in my dressing room, I find myself turning in slow circles, trying to figure out what to do next. I was downright visionary earlier this week when I told Clara I need a bigger suitcase. Of course, at the time, I was talking about sometime far, far down the line. I have added greatly to what I owned when I arrived, though.

I walk over to the closet and look at the clothing within, both old and new, but shut the door again rather than start pulling them from their hangers. I wander over to my dressing table and fiddle with my makeup brushes, then pick up the wire cage holding the champagne cork from the standard Henry gave me. I turn it over and over in my hands, before carefully setting the thing back down again. I glance over my shoulder at the bejeweled star attached to the outside of the still open door. This doesn't make a lick of sense.

I freeze. *It doesn't make sense.* Shoving aside my hurt, I consider the reasons why.

Booker punched Will because he thought his one-time best friend might be my lover. After I spent the night at Clara and Dot's— before I basically moved in during this mess with his mother—he asked me if I was coming home. Not coming to *his* house; *home,* he said. And every time after that, as if it's mine as well as his. So, what is this *don't let the door hit you in the butt* beeswax?

The knot in my belly slowly unwinds and I quit feeling so dang cold. Booker thinks he's giving me my shot at fame and glory—I *know* he is. As if my *career* is what I want more than anything else in the world.

Well, the devil with that. I storm from the room, not bothering to close the door behind me. If someone wants to rob me blind, let 'em. It's only stuff. Well, if they take my door star or champagne cork, I will eventually go gunning for them. But I can't be bothered over anything else.

When I arrive at Booker's office and see he is right where I left him, I stop in the doorway to look him over. But smooth Booker is nowhere to be seen. Instead of busily tearing into tasks with his usual single minded industry, his always squared shoulders are slumped, his elbows are on his desk, with no regard for the papers they've knocked out of place, and his hair is standing on end as if he's been plowing his fingers through it. I can't see his face because it's buried in his hands.

Praying to the heavens I'm not fooling myself—that what I think is true isn't merely an illusion I badly want to be the truth, I step silently into the room.

But I don't take any particular effort to close the door behind me quietly.

Yeaaah, I'm thinking maybe I'd better not hold my breath

BOOKER

"Not now, Sarge," I mutter without bothering to look up. "I want to be alone."

"Too bad," says the voice I was just thinking I'd be hearing in my dreams for the rest of my days, and my head snaps up.

Ah, Jesus, Lena's standing just this side of the closed door. And she's so damn beautiful. But I stiffen my spine because I don't think I can dispatch her twice in one night. "What are you doing back here?"

"I have a question you need to answer, then I'll get out of your hair."

Yeah, fat lot of good that offer is, when she's so deep under my skin I'll never get her out. I don't have a lick of energy to push myself up in my chair, so I prop my chin on my hands and soak in everything about her while I can. "Shoot."

"You're not even going to make me a darn counter offer," she demands indignantly, "just tell me to pack my bags and go?"

That jerks me upright, infused with new energy. And hope.

"What did you have in mind?" I ask coolly. *Name it. I'll give you anything.*

"A raise to match Call-me-Chester Moss's offer. And I want a bigger dressing room than that closet you have me in."

"Done. What else?"

"Top billing. No matter what new acts you get."

"It's yours. And...?"

"Another two gowns for my act." She actually looks guilty about that one, making me want to throw back my head and laugh out loud.

"I'll give you three. Is that it?"

Lena hesitates, then lifts her chin. "No. I want your heart."

Her words are an arrow lodging in said heart, and I can barely breathe through the relief of realizing she apparently feels as deeply for me as I do for her. "Don't you know that's already yours, Lena?"

"It is?"

"Hell, yes. It's always been yours."

Her faces simply lights up. She crosses the office in a couple ground eating strides, leans forward...and punches me on the arm.

"Hey!" I rub the slight sting. "What the hell was that for?"

"For being such a poop. Why didn't you tell me that in the first place, instead of showing me the door?"

"Because I'm an idiot."

She studies her nails in silence for a moment, then looks up. Widens those baby blues at me. "Oh, is this the part where you're waiting for me to protest you truly aren't?"

"Yeaaah, I'm thinking maybe I'd better not hold my breath waiting for that to happen."

"You booted me out of the best job I've ever had, out of your *life*, without blinking. I wanna know why."

"I saw Moss stop you. Watched while you sat at his table." I scrub my knuckles atop my left pectoral muscle as the heart beneath hurts all over again in remembered pain. "I recognized him and knew he had the means to give you everything you ever dreamed of."

"Professionally speaking, he does." Lena licks her lips. "And it was the berries learning my voice could take me to heights I never truly imagined." She watches her slender finger outline the corner of my desk. Then she looks up at me. "My dreams have changed, though, Booker. I have loved you since I was seventeen years old. I've been mad at you longer than I've loved you, but even then? My feelings for you never truly went away. *This* love is...different than it was when I was a teenager. But that only makes it deeper, richer."

For one horrified minute, I fear I might actually break down and cry like a girl. I clear my throat of the ball of emotion lodged there. "God, I love you so much, Lena. I thought I was losing you, and I was sick to my soul." I perk up. "You want me to go with you when you tell Moss you aren't taking the gig?"

"Oh, I told him already when he made me the offer."

"What? And you didn't *lead* with that?"

She gives me that *don't be an idiot* look. "Of course, not. I was looking forward to hearing your negotiations before I let you know you already had me." She scowls at me. "I didn't expect to be kicked to the curb."

I tug her around the desk and pull her down onto my lap. Trace my finger over the little divot between her brows. "I'm sorry, doll. I might have panicked a little—" or, okay, flat-out "—and I didn't deal with it well. On the bright side, though, I didn't punch him."

Her lips curl up despite the way she's pressing them together to keep me from seeing her amusement. Then in true Lena fashion, she gives up the fight and laughs out loud. "That is an improvement." She gives me a prim little lopsided smile. "And they say men aren't trainable."

"Hell, yeah, we are, and I can prove it. Stick with me, kid. And in forty, fifty years or so, who knows? I'm liable to be downright housebroke."

Lena kisses me, then pulls back and presses her forehead to mine. My heart damn near explodes when her breath feathers across my lips as she sighs happily. And murmurs, "You have got yourself a deal, Mister."

EPILOGUE: 7 YEARS LATER, PART 1

SUSAN ANDERSEN

I finally understand what family means

LENA

Sunday, March 5, 1933

"God, I love this town."

I glance at Booker across the end table separating our favorite side by side overstuffed chairs. We've been enjoying reading in front of the living room fire, Booker with his paper and me with Alice B Toklas's autobiography. The big pot of stew simmering on the stove scents the house, and flames dance through the logs in the grate. A piece of fir suddenly pops, throwing up a small shower of sparks as Booker grins at me over the folded down top corner of the Seattle Post-Intelligencer. A stack of newspapers in addition to the P-I rests next to his chair.

"I wuv it, too, Papa," three-year-old Lucy declares from the floor where she's playing with her Flossie Flirt doll not far from Booker's feet. Her blonde brows meet briefly over her little button nose. "Why we wuv it, 'gain?"

"Because Seattle is our home, Baby Girl," he gently informs his daughter. "And it's chock-full of good people." Lucy clearly loses interest before he finishes his explanation and Booker shoots me a wry smile.

I raise my eyebrows at him. "Why do we love it in particular today?"

"I'm just proud to live in a town where businesses help their employees—especially during this bank holiday experiment. Which, incidentally, the papers are all calling a smart move."

Unlike many states, Washington has had darn few bank closures. But due to the huge number of loan defaults, it struggles with the same diminished cash flow banks are facing nationwide. Governor Martin ordered a state wide, three-day bank closure in solidarity with several other states hell bent on forging ahead without awaiting the new president's approval. Our old president's waffling, which made the banking situation even more dire, is still fresh on everyone's mind.

"The papers have done a good job explaining what the closure really means and are urging patience rather than hysteria. They're reminding their readers that Seattle banks, especially, have kept themselves in strong condition and have the highest degree of liquidity in the country." He gives me a cheeky grin. "God knows having a cash business has helped our liquidity situation."

"Ow licka-diddy saysun," Lucy whispers to her doll and Booker and I exchange mutually besotted smiles.

We have been so fortunate. Seattle speakeasies are surviving this depression extremely well. Washington has always been a wet state, and in Seattle, jazz is a hot commodity that's going strong—especially down on Jackson Street. So, the police and city officials for the most part continue to look the other way.

Not for free, of course. But I'm pretty sure the men down in the immense Hooverville encampment would call that a rich man's problem.

"A lot of businesses are stepping up while their employees can't access their money," Booker continues. "Many are paying them in cash, and Boeing Aircraft—"

The doorbell rings and our oldest, five-year-old Jack, thunders down the stairs hollering, "I'll get it!"

I snag him as he rushes past, swinging him around until I can mold my palms over his skinny little shoulders. "Jack Joseph," I say sternly, "what have we told you about running and yelling at the top of your voice in the house?"

"Don't do it," he says, then flashes me his father's charming get-out-of-jail-free smile. "Sorry, Mama."

I tug him in for a quick hug and a kiss, then hold him at arm's length. "I don't want to hear your sorries, young man," I admonish as I set him loose. "I want you to quit doing what we have told you over and over again not to." I shake my head as he promptly dashes for the door. Give his daddy a look. "That lack of manners didn't come from my side of the family."

Booker laughs and surges up from his chair to haul me out of mine, pulling me into a bear hug that lifts me off my feet. "I'll talk to him again, baby. But I don't think either of us should hold our breath waiting for my lecture to find fertile ground." He sets me back on solid footing. "He's a wild little Indian."

That's putting it mildly. Being pregnant with Jack was like hosting one of those Olympic gymnasts we heard so much about last year on the radio and in theater newsreels. And I swear that child hit the ground running the moment I gave birth to him. Unlike Lucy, who's our snuggle-bug and loves to be read to, Jack is constantly on the move and has no patience for lap cuddles.

"I'm an In-ee-an, too, Papa," Lucy says, jumping up to tug on his trouser leg.

"Nah." Booker scoops her up and blows a raspberry on her cheek, closing his eyes briefly when her chubby little arms wrap around his neck. "You're Papa's princess."

"Look, Mama, Papa!" Jack charges back into the living room. "It's Uncle Will!"

Will strides in on our son's heels, making Jack laugh uproariously. "Something sure smells good in here," he says cheerfully and crosses the room to kiss my cheek and shake Booker's hand. Lucy hops to her feet, demanding "Unca We-o's" attention and Will bends down to scoop her up. In between talking nonsense to her, he nods at the pile of Sunday papers next to Booker's chair. "You as impressed as I was when I read Boeing bought three thousand streetcar tokens and arranged credit for gasoline and groceries for their workers? I heard more than sixteen-hundred employees were unable to cash yesterday's pay checks."

"I was just telling Lena how much I love this town. Fisher Flour and the local Ford Motor branch cashed their employees checks. Fisher also offered car tokens and credit at certain stores."

Will nods. "I read that, too. And about the utilities advancing their worker's enough cash for necessities." Then he sobers. "I hope to hell the new President can get the men in Hooverville working again."

"Roosevelt's New Deal seems geared to putting people to work. That right there is a huge improvement over Hoover's inactivity. So, here's hoping. There are too damn many people out of work."

The doorbell rings again and before I can get up, Jack thunders through the living room once more to answer it. Most of the time I not so secretly enjoy the racket my kids make. Booker and I got married in February of '27, and I felt then I finally understood what family—real family—meant. But with the birth of our kids...?

The two of them multiplied the family aspect a thousand-fold for us. So, I let Jack's inability to walk when he can run or talk quietly when he can yell, slide.

"It's Auntie Clara," he shouts, trotting back into the room, hauling Clara behind him with his grip on her wrist. "And she made brownies!"

I will be working on his manners again tomorrow, however.

"Jack, unhand your auntie." I rise and relieve Clara of the plate she's balancing with her free hand as Jack's full-speed-ahead locomotion has her almost doubling the length of her stride to keep up.

Booker quirks both eyebrows at Clara. "The ball and chain still out parking the car?"

Clara relinquishes the dish to me, pries her hand free from Jack's clutches and grimaces at Booker. "Unfortunately, no. He's at home icing his shoulder and sipping whiskey to manage the pain of the muscle he pulled trying to put something up in the garage rafters."

"Trying?" Booker rises to his feet. "You need us to put it up for him?"

"Oh, Booker, would you?" Clara beams at him. "You know how he is—he's not going to rest until the damn thing is put away. And that means more whiskey, which probably isn't a great idea."

Booker transfers his attention to me. "We have time before dinner?"

"Sure." I shrug. "There's nothing that can't be kept hot or refrigerated. If you're too long, I'll feed the kids."

"No," Jack yells, "I wanna go with papa and Uncle Will."

"Me go, too!" Lucy dances in place.

"Help your sister with her coat," Booker says and heads for the foyer to collect his keys. After a noisy couple of minutes, the door slams behind the group of four.

"Ah, silence," I say contentedly to Clara as the kids' chatter fades away. "Come on into the kitchen," I invite. "I'll get you a drink and you can keep me company while I make a salad and cut the bread. What do you hear from Dot?"

Clara had to reinvent herself as a solo act a couple of years ago after a Canadian businessman dropped by the lounge for a quick drink and ended up sweeping her sister off her feet. Dot now lives up in British Columbia.

"You know what?" I fetch a couple goblets from the cupboard. "Forget the salad and bread for now. It's a clear day and the city looks magical when the sun goes down. Grab that bottle of wine over there," I direct, pointing to it. "Let's take this out into the backyard and enjoy the view. You can catch me up on all the news from north of the border while we still have the house to ourselves."

We make ourselves comfortable on the patio, with its view of the city, the Olympics and part of Puget Sound. I pour us each a glass a wine and pass Clara hers. "Here's to us." I raise my glass. "Did you ever think our lives would turn out the way they have?"

"I really didn't. I wasn't looking to fall in love at all, but I must say —" She shoots me a sly smile "—Dot and I could see the writing on the wall when it came to you and Booker."

"I feel so lucky, Clara. I have everything I ever dreamed of, and more. Booker. The hooligans. And good friends like you and Dot and Will. How the heck did I get so lucky?"

"Oh, it's not luck, kiddo—you get what you give. And you're not just a good wife, mother and friend, you're the *best* at all those things." Clara reaches to give my free hand a squeeze. "So, like I said, sweetie. You get whatcha give."

EPILOGUE: 7 YEARS LATER, PART 2

SUSAN ANDERSEN

What a lucky bastard I am

BOOKER

I make my before-bed rounds to ensure the house is buttoned up. After locking the front door and turning off the porch light, I kill the lights in the living room and check to make sure the dying fire is properly banked. Then I head upstairs. This is one of my favorite parts of the day, when the kids are tucked in their rooms and it's just Lena and me for a while.

It was a great day and as I wash up and brush my teeth in the bathroom, I can't help but think what a lucky bastard I am. I have a profitable business that allows me to make payments on our home during a time when far too many men are out of work or have had their wages cut back to poverty levels. More importantly, I have the loves of my life and a small, but golden, group of friends. My dad and I have a good relationship—which reminds me, I need to call him tomorrow to see how his bank is doing. Walla Walla county banks opted not to participate in the banking holiday the rest of the state is currently in the midst of. I want to know how that's working for them.

Lena and I even have a guarded relationship with my mother these days. I will never again feel the same about her as I once did. But shortly after Jack was born, Edna accompanied Dad out of the blue on one of his trips to see us. She apologized with what appeared to be genuine sincerity for betraying our trust, as well as for her inexcusable behavior the last time she was in our home. And she asked to be allowed a relationship with her new grandson.

Lena was the one to point out Edna and Dad are the only grandparents Jack and any future children would ever know. So, after much discussion between Lena and me, and not until Mother accepted the ground rules we made damn sure she understood were nonnegotiable, did we give our permission. She knows one negative word about their mother to our kids and it will be the last time Grandma Edna sees either one of them. There will be no third chances.

Like I said, a guarded relationship.

I let myself into our bedroom a moment later and suck in a breath as I watch Lena with her arms in the air, dropping a nightie over her head to slither down her nude body. I will never tire of seeing this woman unclothed. No, her beautiful breasts aren't quite as high as they once were. Neither is her waist as narrow as it was when I bought her those first five gowns back in '26, and her stomach now possesses some pale silvery stretch marks. But those changes? They're courtesy of the incredible kids she bore us. There's not a flawless-bodied female in the world who could tempt me from my wife's side. Being loved by Lena is the best thing that ever happened to me.

"Hey, beautiful," I murmur, crossing the room.

She flashes me a dazzling smile. "Hey, yourself, handsome."

Reaching her, I bend my head to kiss the lips she puckers up at me. We linger over the kiss a while before finally pulling back. I brush a tendril of hair out of her eyes. "Let's go to bed."

"Oh, good plan. I'd rather be laying down when I tell you I need to cut back to Fridays and Saturdays at the club."

"Can't work with the lack of sleep any longer?"

"Not three days in a row," she agrees. "I'd like to shoot for two, though."

"You ever regret turning down the Black Door offer, Lena?"

"No."

"You sure? I have no doubt you'd be a huge star now."

"Maybe. But here's the thing." She climbs into bed and flops back, reaching to bunch the pillow under her head. "I want a loving family so much more than a successful career. My biggest wish was *always* for someone to love me. And when it looked like that wasn't in the cards, I just wanted to be good at something. Now here I am, with my biggest wish fulfilled. As for my backup plan, right now that's being a good mom and wife." She tilts her chin to look up at me. "And a good singer. You know I love making music, Booker. But I didn't know what it was to have a mom growing up and I want to be around for our babies. They're still at an age where they're asleep before we leave and only rarely have they woken up to find Mrs. Tilley instead of us." Lena waves an impatient hand. "Sorry, you know all this."

"I do." I'm kicking off my trousers but pin her in my sights to let her know I take her issues seriously. "I also know Jack and Lucy get up ungodly early and you and I get home late. I could kind of see this coming. You're good about letting me sleep in weekdays. I haven't been great about doing the same for you on the weekends or noticing you've been burning your candle at both ends. I should have—it's not like I don't know damn well how hard you work taking care of the kids and the house and running the choir you started at Seattle Children's."

I get in bed and roll onto my side to face her. "You want to quit entirely?"

"No! Oh, honey, no, I don't. I *love* all those things and I don't want to give up the club until the kids start to realize one or both of us aren't here most evenings. I can honestly say I don't feel a single pang about dropping a night from my schedule, though." She laughs her infectious whole-hearted laugh. "You gotta admit, sleep is so darn *seductive*." Turning over, she spoons her butt against me.

Wrapping an arm around her, I rearrange her until we're both in our sweet zone. I've actually been thinking I might want to switch to a business with more regular hours, myself, when the kids are a little older. I haven't determined as yet what that business might be, but I've never lacked imagination. The perfect idea will occur to me sooner or later.

But for now? "What do you say we change up the schedule so you sleep in Saturday and Sunday mornings?"

Lena sighs contentedly. "Oh, have you got yourself a deal." She turns in my arms, kisses me from my jaw to my Adam's Apple, then slips her hand down my chest on an ever-southbound journey. "Interested in sealing that deal, Big Boy?"

Oh, yeah. Always.

ABOUT THE AUTHOR

Susan Andersen writes sexy, edgy romance often containing touches of suspense and humor to keep things interesting. Her books have spent many weeks on the NYT, Publisher's weekly and USAToday bestseller lists, and were twice included in RWA's Top Ten Favorite Books of the Year.

Susan is the proud mother of a grown son and a native of the Pacific Northwest, where she lives with her husband and two cats. She has written twenty-five books.

For more information, visit Susan at
www.susanandersen.com
susan@susanandersen.com

ALSO BY SUSAN ANDERSEN

Notorious

Please check my webpage for more titles and excerpts

www.susanandersen.com

Made in the USA
Lexington, KY
27 November 2017